TIME TO HUNT

* * * * *

A NOAH WOLF THRILLER

CHAPTER ONE

"I spent all night online with Molly," Neil said at breakfast, with his computer on the table beside his plate. "She's got Wally's people studying the problem now, and we all know there's no better research facility in the world when it comes to things like this. They'll come up with something, some way to get that thing out of you without setting it off."

Noah and Sarah both nodded. "If anybody can," Sarah said, "they can." She gave him a sad smile. "Don't get me wrong, I know you're a genius, but you don't spend every day coming up with new ways to kill people. They do, so if anyone can figure out a way to disarm this thing or get it out, my money's on them."

"Oh, I've got some ideas that I shared with Molly, but it's that pressure thing I'm worried about. If it was just a matter of blocking a signal, I could build a Faraday cage and put you inside it while we have some doctor cut it out, but I can't figure out how to keep the pressure steady. If losing the pressure of your muscle and tissue around it is enough to set it off, I just don't know how we could keep pressure on it."

"What about pulling it into a tube of some sort?" Noah asked. "I mean, if we had a way to get hold of one end of it with something run through a tube of the right diameter, maybe we could pull it in and let that tube keep the pressure on."

Neil shook his head. "That runs into the problem of not reducing pressure on the end of it that you grab, and then we have to make sure the tube is stretchy enough, but then it might collapse as we're pulling this thing out. If it does, pressure drops and it goes bang."

"There's got to be a way," Sarah said. "There just has to be."

"Give them time to work on the problem," Noah said. "What about Monique?"

Neil sighed. "I gave Molly all the information we have," he said, "and she spoke with Allison and Mr. Jefferson, but neither of them have any idea who she can be. Allison suggested she might not be CIA after all, at least not herself. They're thinking that she might actually just have CIA people under her control, just the way she had some of ours. Unfortunately, that means we can't trust anybody at the CIA to ask about someone fitting her description, so we're kind of on our own."

Sarah blinked, then turned her eyes toward Noah. "Okay, look," she said. "We have to keep up our act, so I'm just gonna pretend these problems don't exist for now." She smiled sweetly. "What's on your agenda today, Rex, honey?"

"Ralph is going to be working with Sneed all day," Noah replied, "working out the details of taking over the drug operation. I'll probably sit in on some of it, but I'm going to get Forney to start introducing me to some of the other lieutenants, start building an idea of who needs to be taken out when the time comes."

"Cool," Neil said. "Anything you want me to do?"

"Yeah, there is. Wally had an interesting idea about coming up with something like jewelry that the entire organization would want to wear. If we can get all of the top people wearing some sort of necklace made of our explosives, then making the hit all at once could be pretty easy. Think about that and see what you can come up with, okay?"

Neil narrowed his eyes in thought. "Jewelry? I don't know, that sounds kind of far-fetched to me. I mean, what are the odds that we'd come up with something everybody would like and want to wear?" He chewed the inside of his cheek for a couple of seconds, then nodded. "The idea might have merit, though. Not necessarily jewelry, but something everybody would want to have with them all the time.

Maybe some sort of a communication device? Like a pager, or walkie-talkie? A way for Morgan to be able to reach any of them or all of them instantly."

Sarah scowled. "They use cell phones for that," she said.

"Yeah, but then they have the problem of cell phones being on open frequencies. You can buy scanners that let you listen to cell phone conversations, and Morgan ought to be aware that any feds who might be looking at him would be doing their best to monitor every call he makes, him or his people." He looked thoughtful for a moment. "What if you could sell him on an encrypted communication system that worked through cell towers, so it would be just like a normal cell phone, but no one could listen in?"

Noah had begun nodding as he spoke. "That could be exactly what we need," he said. "The only question is where do we get them?"

Neil grinned. "All you need are cell phones with scramblers built in. They take what you say and encrypt it, and then the receiving phone decrypts it so that the other person can hear exactly what you said. Anybody in the middle, however, is only going to hear screeching and beeping that means nothing. It's exactly the system E & E uses, and all we'd have to do is put them in a case made of our explosive material. If you can get me a count on how many you need, Wally could probably get started on them today."

Sarah's eyes were wide. "That really is an awesome idea," she said. "And if Morgan hasn't already thought of it, it could be a big feather in your cap with him. That could get you in tighter, so you learn more about who's important in the whole organization."

"And not a bit hard to sell," Noah added. "I've already told Forney a couple times that he needs to be careful what he says over the phone. This kind of system would let Morgan and his people talk about anything openly, without worrying about who might overhear. Would it require a special phone company, carrier, or whatever?"

"Nope. It will work with any carrier. Artel is most common around here, and that'll work just fine."

Noah nodded. "This might be exactly what I'm looking for. How long would it take to get some examples made up and shipped in? I'd like to be able to show this to him as soon as possible."

The tall, skinny kid shrugged his shoulders. "I'd bet Wally has a pretty fair inventory of them. If you can give me an idea of how many you might want, he could probably get some cases made and send a few of them out today. We could have them by tomorrow."

"I think tomorrow would be too quick," Noah said. "I need to plant a few seeds about this first, so let's try to have a few of them in a couple of days. I actually like this idea better than any of Wally's. This is something that Morgan would want everybody to have, and if it's got the explosive built in, then it's actually very likely they'll each have one on them when we set them off."

"And here's another benefit," Neil said. "I can have a server set up that can send a text message to each and every one of these phones at the same time, or conference them all into a single call. I know you worry about collateral damage, so we could use this when the time comes to make sure each person is alone, or even get them all gathered up in one place."

Noah looked at him. "Getting them all into one place would reduce the possibility that one of them might be with an innocent family member or in the middle of a crowd. As far as getting them all on conference call, that could also help. They'd naturally want to get away from everybody else while they were on a call like that." He chewed the inside of his cheek for a couple of seconds. "Of course, it's going to cause quite a stir when thirty or forty local mobsters all get blown up at the same time. We'll be starting a whole new class of conspiracy theories."

Neil laughed. "No doubt," he said. "People around here will be saying everything from 'the government did it,' to 'it was aliens, dude!' Most of them will probably just be glad these people are gone."

"That's true," Noah said. "I think we should go ahead with this idea, or at least have it as an option."

"Neil," Sarah said, "this is brilliant. Tell Molly I said you are every bit as smart as she is, and maybe even smarter."

Neil grinned. "Actually, I'm not. I've seen her paperwork; she's got me by twenty points on the IQ scales. She just hasn't gotten used to thinking about ways to kill people, yet, but hanging around Noah all the time must be rubbing off on me."

"Well, it's working," Sarah said with a chuckle.

Noah looked at her, and the thought crossed his mind that she was forcing herself to forget the microbomb in his armpit. He leaned over and kissed her, reinforcing her desire to put that thought out of her mind.

"I'd better get going," he said. He got out of his chair, and Sarah stood, then reached up and put her arms around his neck and pulled him down for another kiss.

"Mmm," she said, "I could almost get used to this. I know we're on a mission, but this is kind of like you just going off to a regular job. Any idea what time you'll be home?"

"Probably around four," he replied. "I'm gonna look for opportunities to complain about cell phone use, and then I'll bring up the idea of encrypted phones to Jimmy the first chance I get. With any luck, he'll ask me to go ahead and get some samples. If not, I'll just try to pass it off as me taking the initiative when they come in, and hope he sees it as a good idea that he needs to put to work throughout the organization."

"All right," Neil said. "I'll ask Wally to get a half-dozen of them out to us ASAP. Try to give me an idea of how many you might need altogether, though. The sooner he can get started on them, the sooner we can deliver. Bear in mind, these phones wouldn't be cheap on the open market. Probably around fifteen hundred apiece, maybe more."

"And the sooner we can get out of here," Sarah said.

"What do you mean?" Noah asked.

"Well, isn't it obvious? Morgan is going to want all of his top people to have one of these phones, right? Once they get delivered and everybody has one, you could complete the mission. When all of the top people are dead, we can go home."

Noah looked from her to Neil. "In theory, that's correct," he said. "It would also give me the chance to show Monique that I don't waste time." He hugged Sarah, who was still holding on to him. "Of course, it's kind of nice to just go to work every day and come home to you. Even with the mission, this is probably as close to a normal life as we're ever going to know."

Sarah looked up at him for a moment, then slowly nodded. "And I'm going to enjoy it for as long as we have it," she said.

Noah kissed her again, then turned and walked out the door. She stood where she was until she heard the Charger start up and start down the driveway, then sat back down in her chair and looked at Neil. Suddenly the tears overflowed, and she didn't even try to stop them.

"That was a brilliant idea," she said slowly. "Now, turn that brain of yours on to the real problem. You find a way to save his life, Neil."

The skinny kid looked at her across the table, his own eyes moist. "We will," he said. "I swear we will."

NOAH CALLED FORNEY while he was still on the highway. "It's Rex," he said. "You got the kid?"

"Yep," Forney replied. "We're headed for Sneed's office. Ralphie wants to start working on the liquid pot today..."

"Cut that off," Noah said suddenly. "Don't you know that anybody could be listening in on these calls? These are cell phones—you can buy scanners that make it possible to hear everything people say on a cell phone. All it takes is for one of the feds to hear you talking about stuff like that and we end up with a case that doesn't magically go away."

Forney laughed. "Rex, relax," he said. "We got it all covered. Feds don't mess with us—they know better."

"Yeah, that's what my guys thought, back in the day. Trust me, they may move slowly, but they're moving. Sooner or later, somebody is going to try to make a case stick against the boss, and I wouldn't want to be the guy whose loose lips gave them the ammunition they need. Would you?"

Forney was quiet for a few seconds, and then he chuckled again. "Okay, I see your point," he said. "I'll be careful from now on. Thing is, even the boss doesn't worry about it. Who's to say it wouldn't be his loose lips?"

"Geez, are you serious?" Noah asked. This was exactly the kind of opening he was hoping to find, but he needed to be careful how he played it. "Enough recordings of things like that and it'd be hard to make the charges disappear."

"Yeah, well, what are you gonna do? He's been at this so long he feels like he's invincible, I guess."

"Nobody's invincible," Noah said. "I learned that the hard way. There's ways to minimize the risk, though. You think you could get him to sit down and talk to me about some ideas?"

Suddenly interested, Forney said, "I think I could. What have you got in mind?"

Noah chuckled. "One of those things we shouldn't talk about on the phone. I'll see you at Sneed's place. We can talk about it then." He ended the call and put the phone into his pocket as he came into town.

It took him another ten minutes to get to the old car lot that housed the headquarters of the Morgan Mafia drug operation, and he saw that Forney and the others had arrived already. The two security men were standing near the front door when he parked the car. This time, he got out of the car and walked into the building.

Ralph was in the small inner office with Ronnie Sneed, and Noah could see through the french doors that they were arguing a bit. Forney was sitting on a couch in the foyer. He looked up and smiled when Noah walked in.

"Hey, Boss Man," Forney said. "They're butting heads in there a bit, so I decided to wait out here. So what's this idea you got?"

Noah glanced around, as if to make sure no one could overhear them, then turned back to him. "I've got a buddy out in Colorado," he said, "who can get just about anything you might want. Last time I talked to him, just before I came out here, he was telling me about these new superencrypted cell phones. You can literally talk about anything on them, and as long as whoever you're talking to has one of the same phones, they can understand you perfectly. Anybody who tries to listen in on a scanner, though, won't hear anything but noise. I'm thinking it might be a good idea if we can talk Jimmy into investing in some of them."

Forney nodded, a grin on his face. "Probably be easier than convincing all these idiots to be careful what they say," he said. "I had a feeling it was going to be something good, so I already called and set it up. Jimmy wants you to come on out to the house."

Noah's eyebrows went up. "What, now?"

"I just called and said you had an idea you thought might avoid problems with the feds," he said, "and he said to tell you to come on out and fill him in. If it was me, I would think that means now."

Noah stared at him for a moment, then rolled his eyes. "Oh, great," he said. "I wasn't really ready to go into it this morning, sorta wanted to think it through a little better, you know?"

Still grinning, Forney said, "Hey, sounds to me like you got it figured out. You sold me on it already; I want one no matter what he does. Just go see him, you'll be fine."

Noah glanced through the french doors again and saw that Ralph was grinning as Sneed apparently gave in to one of his demands, then shook his head and turned around to walk out of the building again. The men outside said nothing as he walked past them and got into the Charger, but a glance in his rearview mirror as he was leaving told him they were questioning his sudden departure.

He headed west out of town and followed the path that took him to the Morgan house. He had already figured out that Jimmy didn't like to leave the house early, but that suited him fine. There were at least a couple of hours every morning when he knew exactly where the criminal boss would be, and that could come in handy.

He got to the house and parked in the driveway, then walked up and knocked on the door. One of Jimmy's security men nodded to him from a chair on the front porch, and then Marlene opened the door.

"Come on in, Rex," the woman said. "Jimmy's in his office. He said to tell you to just go on in when you got here."

"Thanks, love," he said with a wink. The older woman blushed a little bit and smiled, then hurried back into the kitchen as Noah made his way to the office. The door was closed, so he tapped gently on it and heard Morgan call out, "Come on in."

Noah turned the knob and opened the door, then stepped into the office. Jimmy was alone, sitting behind his desk, and looked up with a smile.

"Rex," Morgan said, rising enough to reach across and shake hands. "Scott tells me you're shaking things up a little bit."

Noah put on a nervous grin. "Well, sir, I've been noticing some things," he said. "I'm not trying to tell you how to run things, don't get me wrong, but I've noticed that a lot of the guys don't seem to think about who might be listening when they talk. That's kinda what I wanted to talk to you about."

Morgan sat down again and pointed at another chair for Noah, then leaned back and folded his hands over his belly. "Okay," he said. "What do you mean?"

"Well, I've sorta jumped on Scott today for talking too much over the phone," Noah said. "I understand that the cops around here won't bother you, and I've even heard stories about feds being run off, but anybody can buy a scanner that can listen in on cell phone calls. That's one of the ways the feds jammed me and my people up back in Ohio, by catching some of the guys talking about drug deals over cell phones."

Morgan pursed his lips and cocked his head, then nodded for Noah to go on.

"Maybe I'm overreacting," Noah continued, "but I've always tried to live on the principle of avoiding problems rather than trying to solve them after they start. I've got a friend who hustles all kinds of stuff—I mean, he can get anything you might want and save you a bunch of money while he's at it—and he's got these special cell phones that nobody can listen in on. They got some kind of scrambler in them, so if one of them calls another phone like it, it scrambles the signal all up so a scanner can't pick up what you're saying. I was sort of thinking that if we all had one of those phones..."

"Then we never have to worry about what anybody overheard, right?" Morgan asked with a grin. "That sounds like it might be a pretty good idea. How much these phones cost?"

Noah grinned and tried to look a little more confident. "Well, that's the thing," he said. "If you wanted to buy one most places, they'd cost you about fifteen hundred a pop, but I can get them for seven hundred apiece. I, um, I already ordered a few of them myself. I was going to give them to all my guys so nobody could use a scanner to find out where Ralphie was going to be."

Morgan narrowed his eyes. "You were buying them out of your own pocket? Hell, just give me the bill, I'll pay it. That's some good thinking, Rex, but let me ask you this: what happens if you use one of those phones to call some regular, old-style phone?"

"Well, then it turns off the scrambler so the call can go through," Noah said, "but then anyone listening on a scanner can understand whatever you say. We'd just need to make sure everybody knows to be careful what they say if they, like, call the old lady or something."

Morgan sat there and looked at him for a long moment without saying anything, then suddenly sat forward. "What about the service plan? Is it something special?"

"No, sir, they work on any carrier. They'll do just fine on Artel, around here."

"I don't think we have to worry about what they might say to the wives and girlfriends," Morgan said. "Most of them keep the old ladies in the dark, anyway. As far as our own people, we've been pretty lucky when it comes to feds, but that doesn't mean I want to be stupid. And you're right, the last thing we need is somebody getting a recording that can hold up in court against us."

Noah tried to put an expression of relief on his face. "Thank you, sir," he said. "I wasn't sure about bringing this up, but the last thing I want is to go back to Beaumont. My PO seems to be pretty cool, but that doesn't mean he wouldn't burn me if the FBI started pushing him."

Morgan nodded. "Let me figure out how many of these things we need," he said, "and I'll give you a number this afternoon. That work?"

"Yes, sir," Noah said. "I'll get back with Ralph and..."

"Hold on, hold on," Morgan said. "Scott tells me you've got Ralphie pretty well set up, now, and just now you came up with something to help cover all our asses. Rex, I like a man who can think. Let me ask you a question. Just where would you like to end up in this organization?"

Noah made us show of swallowing hard, then wiped the grin off his face. "Honestly? Sir, a long time ago I learned to find out who the boss is and do what I'm told, but I also learned that there's always a benefit to being as close to the top of the heap as I can get. I guess I'd like to go as high as I possibly can."

Morgan had a shrewd grin on his face. "You see, I like an honest answer, and that's what you just gave me. Rex, I realize we just met a few days ago, but you've impressed me. I'm thinking that we need to improve the bloodline up near the top a bit, and I think you might fit right in. Don't get me wrong, what I'm talking about is going to mean a lot of work, and nobody goes to the top overnight—I'm sure you know that. If you're willing, though, I want to keep you with me for a while, see how this thing goes. What would you think about letting Scott handle Ralphie's security detail?"

Noah relaxed his posture a bit. "Scott's a pretty good man," he said, "and I think he'll learn quickly. I'd say he can probably handle it, especially if it's all dumped on him at once. Nothing teaches a man like the old sink or swim, right?"

"That's correct." Morgan reached over and picked up his own cell phone and thumbed a number into it. "Scott? It's Jimmy. Listen, I wanted to say thank you for sending Rex out to me this morning, and then I want to congratulate you on your promotion." He suddenly burst out laughing. "Yes, I said promotion. I'm gonna keep Rex with me for a few days, and he and I both agree that you can take over Ralphie's detail. You can handle it, can't you? Yeah, I think so, too. Tell anybody who has a problem with it to check with me. And Scott? Don't let anything happen to my boy."

Morgan ended the call and dropped the phone back on the desk. "Okay, it's official," he said to Noah. "You're going to be with me for the next few days. We'll go out in a bit and figure out how many of these phones were going to need."

Noah smiled at him. "Yes, sir," he said.

CHAPTER TWO

"Ho-o-ly cow!" Jimmy Morgan said, as they stepped out the front door of the house an hour later. "I heard about that car of yours, but this is the first time I've gotten a good look at it. What is that, a '69?"

Noah smiled. "Yes, sir," he said. "Five-hundred-forty-cubic-inch Hemi putting out over nine hundred horsepower. It was custom built from the frame up to be lighter and stronger than the original, and I can assure you it's the fastest thing I've ever driven."

Morgan shook his head in admiration. "Well, hell," he said, "you don't mind being my chauffeur for a while today, do you?"

"Not a bit," Noah replied. "I love showing this thing off." He went quickly down the steps and used his remote to unlock the car, then slid in behind the wheel as Morgan got into the passenger seat. He noticed the appreciative look in Morgan's eyes when the big engine fired up. "Buckle up," he said.

Noah drove sedately out the driveway but then gave the car its head when he got onto the main road back into town. Morgan laughed when the acceleration pressed him back into his seat.

"I do love a fast car," he said through his laughter. "You ever want to sell this, you better come to me first."

"Sorry, boss," Noah said with a big smile. "I don't think that's ever going to happen."

Morgan directed him to the junkyard, where he kept his own offices. Noah drove through its gates slowly, because the lot was rutted from truck tires and had a number of potholes. He parked the car in what he considered to be the safest possible place, close to the building, and the two men got out.

Noah followed Morgan into the building, where more than two dozen people were sitting around. He was introduced to all of them, and told which section of the criminal business each of them ran or worked in. Several of them were women, and Noah was intrigued to find that two of them ran the prostitution and liquor-theft wings of the enterprise.

"Liquor theft?" Noah asked, and Leanne Davidson smiled at him.

"Oh, yes," she said. "We've got people all over the Midwest who acquire a few cases here, a few there, sometimes even a whole truck-load—it's amazing what truck drivers will do for money—and bring it to us. We buy it for about thirty cents on the dollar from its wholesale price and sell it to all of the bars and clubs within a couple hundred miles."

Noah grinned and shrugged. "Sounds like a winner, then," he said. He chatted with several of the other "lieutenants" of the organization, filing their names away in his memory so that he could give them to Neil when he got home.

"Well," Morgan said as they left the office for lunch, "looks like we need about forty-seven of those phones. How soon do you think we can get them and get them turned on?"

Noah shrugged. "I can call my buddy tonight and find out," he said. "I'm gonna guess probably a week, maybe less."

"All right, do it. I want them as soon as possible. Just bring me the bill; I'll take care of it."

"Yes, sir," Noah said.

At Morgan's direction, Noah drove the car toward the KFC franchise, and the two of them went inside to take advantage of the buffet. A number of people greeted Morgan while they ate, and Noah was introduced to several of them.

"This is Rex," Morgan said more than once, "my new right hand."

And more than once, Noah heard, "Well, I'll be sure not to make you mad. Hate to see this guy coming after me." There was always a chuckle, but the look in the eyes of the speakers told Noah that they were quite serious.

He grinned at each of them but kept his eyes cold. "That's good," he said. "I got enough to do, already." He wasn't surprised when they shivered, even behind their own smiles.

The rest of the day turned out to be more of the same. Noah met seven more lieutenants, including two other women. These were involved in other aspects of the business, and Noah was only slightly surprised to learn that Morgan actually had an online operation. It was mostly concerned with selling some of the high-dollar auto parts, but it seemed that he had a few people who were capable of milking a credit card. Milking a credit card, he was told, meant running it through bogus websites that were based in other countries, so that the charges were impossible to reverse.

"That makes me about eight or ten million a year," Morgan said with a grin. "People never know what the charge is for, and you'd be absolutely surprised how many of them never even question it. We know when they do, but it's almost never."

"Sweet," Noah said. "I always wondered how that worked."

At three o'clock, Morgan said he was ready to go home, so he and Noah walked out and got back into the Charger. Noah fired it up and put the car in gear, backing out of his space and turning around slowly so as not to bounce the car too much in the ruts and potholes. Once they got onto the paved road outside the junkyard, Morgan turned to him.

"Couple times today," he began, "it looked like you might've had something to say. Why did you hold back?"

Noah shrugged. "It wasn't that I really had anything to say," he said. "I'm the kind of guy who's always thinking, always having ideas.

There were a few things I heard today that made my imagination explore some possibilities, that's all."

Morgan grinned. "Okay, like what?"

Noah was quiet for a moment, then glanced over at Morgan. "Well, when I was talking to the lady about the liquor thing," he said, "it occurred to me that there might be some possibilities you haven't explored. I'm thinking of some guys I know back east; if I made a few phone calls, I might be able to get even more product shipped your way, but I didn't want to bring it up because I don't know how big your market is."

"The market is as big as I want it to be," Morgan said. "There are probably five hundred liquor stores and bars within a two-hundred-mile radius, and I'm only selling to a third of them, right now. I've actually thought about setting up a liquor warehouse before so I could run all the hot stuff through it and make it look clean. Only reason I haven't done it is because I haven't had enough coming in to justify the expense. What kind of volume you think your people can do?"

"Well, I'm thinking of a guy named Matt," Noah said. "Matt owns a trucking company, but he's got a number of drivers that sort of specialize in trailers that aren't necessarily their own. They work in teams and can back in and hook on to a trailer and be gone in a matter of seconds, then stop somewhere dark and quiet and change the markings and plates so that it looks like one of Matt's own."

Morgan's eyebrows went up. "How do they change the markings on a trailer? Aren't they all painted up with their owners' logo?"

Noah grinned as he nodded. "Most of them are, yeah," he said, "but Matt came up with this system. Each of the teams carries this big roll that sticks to the side of the trailer, and it's painted with Matt's own markings. He's got a few dozen trailers that are ghosts, old trailers he scrapped but kept the paperwork for. Slap this banner on the side of any trailer and it suddenly looks like one of his, and if the tags come back to his company..."

"Then DOT doesn't bother with it," Morgan finished for him. "That's pretty slick. How do you know this guy?"

"We were cellmates back during my first year in the Fed," Noah said. "We got to be friends because he's from a town that's close to where I grew up. He did two years for dealing pot, but his father was already in this racket back then. The old man died a couple years ago, and he took it all over. My stinking PO back in Ohio wouldn't let me get a CDL, or I'd have been driving a truck for him right after I got out."

Morgan laughed. "Sounds like his loss is my gain. You think he could get a reasonable number of trailers to us every month?"

"No doubt in my mind," Noah said. "Of course, we have to make the trailers disappear. They drop it where it's going, take the banner off the side and the tags off the back, and they're gone. It all happens so fast nobody really notices anything, and that's why he never gets caught."

Morgan chuckled. "I got a cutting operation down by Huntsville," he said, "a place where we cut up big farm tractors and equipment. We sell the engines and major parts, and the rest gets run through a crusher and hauled to a scrapyard up in Missouri. Those boys could cut up a semitrailer in less than an hour, so that wouldn't be a problem. And there ain't no cops around here that would bother to pull us over, even if they noticed the trailer was stolen."

"Then it could work," Noah said. "As long as you got a way to get rid of the trailers, there shouldn't be any problem all."

"That's what I'm thinking. How long you think it would take you to get it set up?"

Noah shrugged. "I'm not sure," he said. "I have to get hold of Matt—that isn't always easy, because he drives one of the trucks himself. I don't have his number with me, but I got it at home. I can call him tonight, and if I don't get hold of him, he'll call me back when he gets the message."

Morgan nodded and then reached over and patted Noah on the shoulder. "Rex," he said, "I think I'm gonna be very glad to have you around. Did you have anything else you want to suggest?"

Noah twisted his face as if trying to remember. "Seems like I thought of something, but I can't remember right now what it was. I'm sure it'll hit me again at some point."

"Well, when it does, you speak up. Have you got my phone number?"

"No," Noah said. He took his phone out of his pocket and passed it to Morgan. "You want to put it in there?"

Morgan pressed a button to activate the phone, then went into the contacts and added his own name and phone number before passing it back. "Give me a call now," he said, "so I can save your number, too."

Noah thumbed the contact and Morgan's phone began to ring. He didn't bother to answer but then saved the number to his own contacts.

"Good," he said. "That way I can reach you if I need to." He turned his face toward Noah again. "I'm thinking you might be my new enforcer," he said. "You okay with that?"

Noah gave him his shark-tooth smile. "Just call," he said.

A few minutes later, Noah dropped Morgan off at his house and then headed for home. His GPS showed him a shortcut that shaved off several miles, so he was home only ten minutes after leaving Morgan's place.

Kate's car was sitting in the driveway, so Noah parked beside it and walked into the house. Kate, Sarah, and Neil were all sitting at the kitchen table.

"Hey, babe," Sarah said, jumping up to put her arms around him. She gave him a quick kiss and then let go, holding on to his hand and pulling him into the kitchen. "Kate called a while ago and I invited her out for dinner."

"Hi, bro," Kate said. "How was your day?"

A quick glance at Neil, who gave him a silent thumbs-up, told Noah that it was safe to talk openly. "I now know the names of all of Morgan's lieutenants," he said. He looked at Neil again. "How did it go on the phones?"

"I'll have ten of them day after tomorrow," Neil said. "I take it you got somewhere with that idea?"

"Yeah. I need forty-seven of them, as soon as we can get them. I got promoted today to enforcer, and I got the chance to talk to Morgan directly about the possibility of feds using cell phone talk to build a case. When I told him I knew where to get phones that could keep that from happening, he was all for it and wants me to get them as soon as possible."

Kate's eyes were bouncing back and forth between the two of them. "This sounds like something I don't even want to know about," she said. She turned to Sarah. "Angie, is there anything I can do to help with dinner?"

Sarah grinned at her. "Are you kidding? We're having pizza. I'm still recovering from the trip to get here; I don't feel like doing a lot of cooking tonight." She got up and opened the freezer, then pulled out four of the frozen pizzas that were inside. "I've got three supremes and one pepperoni. That cover everybody?"

"Works for me," Neil said, and Kate echoed him. Sarah set the twin built-in ovens to preheat and started opening boxes. "Rex, I made iced tea. It's in the fridge."

Noah got up and grabbed her for a quick kiss, then searched through the cabinets until he found a glass. He turned around and looked at Kate before he opened the refrigerator. "Sis? Want some tea?"

She held up a glass that was sitting in front of her and rattled the ice cubes in it. "Already had some," she said, "but I could use a refill."

Noah got the pitcher out of the refrigerator and poured for her, then refilled Sarah's glass, as well. Neil had a bottle of beer in front of him, so Noah poured himself a glass of tea before sitting back down at the table.

"So," Neil said, "you said you know who all the lieutenants are?"

Noah nodded, then looked at him and started reciting the list of names. Neil had opened a notepad and typed them in as he rattled them off.

Kate's eyebrows rose on a couple of the names. "Geez," she said, "I never would have guessed they were involved with Morgan. This thing is even bigger than I imagined." Her face took on a pained expression. "And do you—are you going to have to kill them all?"

Noah nodded. "I'm afraid those are my orders," he said. "I can't leave any of the lieutenants to try to rebuild the organization."

Kate shook her head. "That's a pity," she said. "Leanne and Heather—they've got kids. If I wasn't so sure you know exactly what you're doing, I don't think I could believe they were part of this mess. I've known both of them for, well, pretty much as long as I've been here. Heather recruited me to help run a benefit for a couple of local kids who were hurt in a car accident last fall. Until tonight, I would've said she was just your average housewife."

"Average housewives can get sucked into something that makes a lot of money, too," Sarah said. "I—I used to know this girl. She and her father were professional car thieves, but they were both pretty nice people as far as anybody else knew. You just never can tell, you know?"

"There have been pretty nice people," Neil said solemnly, "who have murdered their friends because somebody found out what kind of weird stuff they were really into. Think about how many serial killers have been arrested, and the neighbors all say they can't believe it, he was such a nice guy, all that crap."

Noah nodded. "Unfortunately, they're right. If your friend Heather knew who you were, she'd probably be one of the first to tell Morgan, and she'd be fully aware that she was signing your death warrant when she did it. These people will kill, or arrange for someone else to kill, in order to protect the secret of what they do, no matter how nice you might think they are in their public lives. That's precisely why DOJ decided it was time to call us in. Too many people have already died so Jimmy Morgan can keep his secrets and his money, and far too many others have been threatened. Once I'm done here, I suspect you'll see an awful lot of cops and prosecutors being rounded up."

"Of course," Kate said. "They won't have Morgan to protect them anymore. And as much as I might not like seeing those kids become motherless, I completely understand why you have to do what you have to do." She looked at her glass for a moment, then looked up at Noah again. "Can I ask how you'll do it?"

"No. I'm afraid that goes higher than your clearance allows."

Kate nodded, then took a big drink from her glass of tea. "No problem. Not sure I really want to know, anyway."

They sat around the table and talked until the pizza was done, and then Sarah suggested they carry it into the living room and find a movie. Noah traded his glass for a bottle of beer on the way, and Sarah handed him the remote. He scrolled through the satellite channel selections and settled on an old Schwarzenegger film called *Raw Deal*.

The movie was about a small-town sheriff who was recruited by the government to infiltrate a Mafia organization in Chicago, where he had to pose as a hit man. Kate laughed when she figured out what was going on in the film and told Noah she thought it was rather appropriate.

"It's one of my old favorites," he replied. "I just never thought I'd have to play the part in real life."

"Yeah," Kate said, "I suppose not."

They ate as they sat through the movie, and then Kate said she had to go home and get some sleep. Noah, Sarah, and Neil walked out onto the porch with her and then waved as she drove away.

"I got a message while the movie was playing," Neil said. "Molly talked to Wally, and the phones will be ready in about four days, all of them. They'll come in a big box, all at once, overnight shipment."

Noah nodded. "That'll be good. This thing is going a lot faster than I expected, but with everything going on with Monique, I think that might be a good thing. Did you relay up the list of names?"

"Yeah," Neil said as they went back into the living room. "My only question is how big a mess it's going to make if you blow them all up at once. It's like you said, there's enough conspiracy theories floating around as it is—do our bosses honestly think a couple dozen criminals can all die from an exploding cell phone without people wondering if the government wasn't behind it?"

Noah thought for a moment, then looked at Neil. "Any idea what brand these phones are? I hate to ruin some phone company, and I know some of them have had issues with batteries blowing up and such in the past."

Neil chuckled. "They were actually made in China, or at least the electronics are. Once they blow up, there's not going to be enough left to identify, anyway, so it's not likely anybody will realize they were all the same kind."

"Some people will," Noah said. "Some of these people have wives, girlfriends, husbands. They'll know, but as long as there isn't a particular brand on them, it shouldn't make a lot of difference."

"That's a good point," Neil said. "Let me send a message right now, suggesting that they have some phony brand marked on them." He sat down and picked up his computer. A few minutes later, he looked up and grinned. "No worries," he said. "It turns out, according to Wally, there won't be enough left of anything to be able to determine where the explosion originated. Any leftover cell phone parts will be mixed up with pieces of guts and bone."

Sarah rolled her eyes. "Geez, what a lovely thought."

"As long as they get the job done," Noah said.

Noah and Sarah sat down on the couch, with Noah keeping Sarah on his right side. She snuggled close and then looked around him at Neil.

"We're all clear, now," he said. "Tell him the other thing."

Noah turned and looked at the skinny kid. "The other thing?"

"Yeah," Neil said. "We may have a little solution to the problem of that nasty device in your armpit. Molly went out and talked to Wally about it directly, today, and he called in some of his evil geniuses for a brainstorming session. They came to the conclusion that the pressure sensor on that thing must have been activated after it was put in place. That means it read the pressure your tissues put on it at that moment, so as long as the pressure on it doesn't go any lower, you'd be safe. Higher doesn't matter—blood pressure, exertion, lots of things can make the pressure go higher—but only removing it from where it's at could take it lower."

Noah nodded. "Okay, that makes sense," he said. "And they have a way to get it out?"

"Well, they're pretty sure it would work," Neil said. "What they have in mind is to put you inside one of those things they use to keep deep-sea divers under pressure when they come out of the water. They crank up the pressure, then take out the device and put it into a high-pressure canister filled with water. Since the pressure will be higher than what your tissues could normally put on it, it most likely won't explode. They can keep it in the pressurized canister until they are ready to let it go off, but you come out of the chamber perfectly safe a few hours later."

Noah sat there and looked at him for a moment, then nodded. "Sounds like it would work," he said. "Did they give you the odds of success?"

Neil grimaced. "Well, they said it should work, and they're giving it an eighty percent chance. That's not perfect, but it beats the hell out of a one hundred percent chance you'll die any other way they could think of."

"Eighty percent," Noah repeated. "You're right, that's not bad odds. Maybe once this mission is over, we can get it done."

Neil's grimace got bigger. "Yeah, well, that's the other thing. Wally went ballistic and said he wants you back there right now so they can take care of this."

Noah's eyebrows went up. "I can't go right now," he said. "The mission has to come first—Wally knows that."

"You know that, and I know that, but Wally went screaming to the Dragon Lady. Her response was that you will get your ass back to Kirtland at the first possible moment and report to R&D. Now, she didn't say tomorrow, so I'm assuming she's going to let you interpret when the first possible moment might be, but me and sis, here, we're both on Wally's side. We think you should go right now."

Noah shook his head. "I can't," he said. "Ducking out right now, for any reason, could blow the inroads I've made with Morgan. I don't see how I can ask for any time off..."

His eyes suddenly went wide, and the flicker of a grin started to form on his face before vanishing. "Unless," he said slowly, "Morgan were to tell me to go. Hang on just a moment." He took out his phone and glanced at the time. It was almost seven, and he quickly tapped the contact for Jimmy Morgan and put the phone to his ear. He listened for a moment, then smiled into the phone.

"Boss? It's Rex. Listen, I'm sorry to bother you tonight... Okay, yes, sir, I understand. The reason I was calling was that I got hold of my buddy Wally, the guy with the phones. He says I can have as many as I want, but he wants cash and he wants me to come pick them up. He's in Colorado, not too far from Denver." He paused and listened for several seconds, then began nodding into the phone. "Yes, sir," he said a moment later. "Like I said, they normally go for about fifteen hundred each, but I can get them for seven a pop, with cash." He listened again, then nodded once more. "Yes, sir, I'll be there first thing in the morning."

He cut off the call and smiled at Sarah and Neil, his genuine smile that had only recently begun appearing on his face. "It worked," he said. "Morgan wants these phones as soon as possible, so I made it sound like the only way we could get them quick was if I go pick them up. He wants me to come get the money in the morning and get on the road."

"Yes!" Neil said, pumping his fist up and down. "Road trip!"

Noah held up a hand. "Hold on," he said. "You guys are staying here. One of the things we haven't considered was whether this thing might have a GPS chip in it. If I had designed such a thing, I'd probably want to include one so that I knew where it was at all times. If Monique and her people thought of that, it's always possible that seeing me headed back toward Kirtland would be enough to make her think I was canceling our deal, so she'd set it off. I'm not going to take a risk of either of you getting hurt if that happens."

Sarah and Neil tried to talk over one another, but Neil was smart enough to give up the floor. "There is no way," Sarah said, "that you are going to take that trip without me. I don't care how stubborn you get, I don't care how illogical it may seem to you, I'm going with you. You might as well just get that through your head, right now."

"Sarah..." Noah began, but Neil cut him off.

"Hey, remember me? I got a suggestion!"

Noah and Sarah both turned to him. "What is it?" Noah asked.

"Try calling that last number you had for Monique. I'll bet she has it set up like before so it lets her know you're trying to get hold of her. Then all you have to do is tell her you have to make a fast trip back to Neverland, part of the current mission. Hell, you can even tell her what it's about. She'll probably get a laugh out of it."

Sarah started laughing. "See? You really are smarter than Molly." She turned to Noah. "I bet he's right, and I'll bet it will work. Then we can go with you, and we don't have to worry about her deciding to blow you up on the way."

Noah looked at her for another moment, took out his phone and scrolled through it until the found the last number that Monique had used to call him, then tapped it twice. The dialer appeared, and the line began to ring. A moment later he heard a recording telling him that the number was no longer in service, and hung up.

CHAPTER THREE

It was only thirty seconds later when his phone rang. He answered it on the second ring. "Hello?"

"You tried to reach me?" Monique asked. Her voice was clear this time, without the distortion software she had used previously.

"Yes. I've got a situation, and I didn't want to take a chance that it might be misinterpreted. You're aware of my current mission, right?"

"I am," she said with an odd chuckle. "What's the situation?"

"In this mission, I've got to take out a number of targets all at once. I devised a way to do that, by using explosive cell phones. To make that possible, I convinced the head guy here that we need some special phones with signal-scrambling capability, and I'm having them made with explosive cases back at Neverland. The problem is that the boss guy here wants me to go get them as soon as possible, so I need to make a quick trip back there. I didn't want to take the chance you might think I was trying to weasel out of our deal."

There was silence on the line for a few seconds, but then she came back. "I take it the phones are being produced at your R&D facility?"

"Yes, ma'am."

"Well, if anybody could do it, Wally can. All right, go get them. Just bear in mind that I have a lot of people in that organization. If you start talking, I'll know it."

"Hell, there's no chance of that," Noah said. "I want the deal you offered me. This is our only chance to get out of that life, and I want it for all of us."

"Then we have no problem," Monique said. "Don't let me down, Camelot." The line went dead, and Noah put the phone back into his pocket.

"Okay," he said. "Let's go pack for an overnight trip."

Sarah jumped up with a smile and hurried to the bedroom, while Neil headed for his own. Noah got up and followed Sarah, entering the room in time to find her throwing an overnight bag she had just unpacked onto the bed.

"If it's just for overnight," she said, "we don't need much. We can stay at the house when we get there, so we don't need to take clothes. I'll pack your shaving gear—anything else?"

Noah simply looked at her for a moment, then walked over to her closet and took out one of the negligees she had worn on their honeymoon. "Pack this," he said. "You won't be needing it tonight."

THE CHARGER ROLLED up to Morgan's house at a few minutes after seven the following morning, and Noah told Sarah and Neil to simply wait in the car. Neil was in the back seat, his lanky frame stretched across so that he could be comfortable.

The security guys out front gave him a wave as he walked past them, and he tapped gently on the door. Marlene opened it just a moment later and smiled, then stood aside and let him in. "They're at the table," she said and led the way.

It took only a moment for Morgan to get up and go to his office, where he already had fifty thousand dollars in cash packed into a briefcase. "I threw in enough to cover the trip," he said with a grin, "and a little bonus for you. Just don't be gone too long; I'm starting to like having you around."

"It's a fairly long drive," Noah said, "so if I don't make it back by tomorrow night, I'll be back the next day. I'll give you a call when I know for sure."

Morgan slapped him on the shoulder. "No problem," he said. "Take a couple extra days if you need to. We lasted this long without those phones." He lowered his voice. "On the other hand, I understand why you think they're necessary, and I agree. Some of these guys don't know how to be careful what they say."

"That's exactly why I thought of it," Noah said. He shook Morgan's hand and was back in the car only a moment later.

The GPS suggested that he could save time by going up into Missouri and taking Highway 65 up to Interstate 44, so he turned north when he got out to the highway. The road crossed into Missouri a few minutes later, and then the GPS told him to turn right onto Highway 86.

"Noah," Sarah said sweetly, "you do realize that if you don't let me drive this thing, I'm going to make your life miserable for a week, right?"

Noah glanced over at her, then turned his eyes back to the road. A moment later, he came to a gas station and pulled into its lot. "Fine by me," he said. "You're a better driver than I am, anyway."

Sarah let out a squeal of delight as she opened her door and ran around the car. Noah got out and grabbed her for a kiss, then walked around himself and got into the passenger seat. Sarah took a minute to get the seat adjusted properly for her smaller build, fastened her seat belt, and grabbed the floor shifter.

She drove out of the lot sedately, then eased into the throttle. The road had a lot of curves and hills, but the car seemed to hold on to it as if by magic. "Oh, my gosh," Sarah said, her eyes gleaming. "I don't think I've ever driven anything as perfect as this car."

This route took them through some scenic areas and then cut across Table Rock Lake. The rickety old iron bridge was narrow, but the mountains and the water made it an enjoyable ride. As early as it was, there was very little traffic on the road. Sarah shot across the bridge at over a hundred and twenty miles per hour, and the tires squealed as she rocketed through the S-curve that was waiting off the east end of the bridge.

It was only ten minutes later when they finally turned north onto 65, and Sarah followed the speed limit. They were rolling through the countryside and passing through part of the tourist town of Branson, where dozens of country music singers had opened theaters over the last three decades. Sarah pointed out several billboards about shows she would love to see, and Noah filed them away in his memory. He didn't know whether they'd have a chance during the mission, but he planned to take her to see some of them whenever he got some free time. E & E didn't forbid their agents from taking vacations, after all.

They stopped for lunch just after passing through Kansas City; then Sarah let Noah take the wheel again as they got back onto the road. The entire drive would take about nine hours under normal circumstances, but Noah decided to push the big Charger just a bit. Its cruise control was keeping the speedometer at just over eighty-five miles per hour, and he managed to shave almost an hour off the trip. They rolled into Kirtland at a little after three, local time, having gained an hour as they moved into Mountain Time.

Since Monique knew about the trip, and knew exactly where he lived in Kirtland, Noah couldn't see any point in getting a hotel room. He rolled through town and headed straight to R&D, stopping at each checkpoint to show their IDs. The guards ignored the names on the IDs and simply scanned them with a small device that read the encrypted RFID chip inside each one. This was another of Wally's innovations, so that no matter what mission ID they might be using, it was still fully functional for the secure areas at Neverland. They arrived at R&D just over a half hour after they got into town.

The guard in the lobby checked their IDs once more, then picked up a phone and pushed a button. "Camelot is here," he said, and then he replaced the handset in its cradle. A minute later, Wally came running down the hall once again.

"Holy jumping Jiminy," he yelled when he saw Noah. "Come on, hurry!" He grabbed Noah by the hand and started dragging him down the hallway with the others following. When he'd gotten far enough away from the security guard, he stopped and turned to face them.

"This is the highest-security operation we've ever had," he said softly. "Only a handful of people are aware of what's about to happen, and all of them have volunteered to go into lockdown until the mole is silenced. Allison isn't taking any chances that she'll find out what we're doing, today. Now, come on, we've got to get you in right now. I've got the doctors..."

"Wally, hold on," Noah said. "Did you get the message about the phones?"

Wally nodded his head vigorously. "Yes, yes, they'll be ready before morning. Now, come on, I've got the doctors waiting at the hyperbaric chamber—it just got here an hour ago. They're ready to get you in there and get that damn thing out, but we need an X-ray of it first."

Noah nodded. "All right, then," he said. The three of them followed Wally down the hall, and he led them to R&D's medical clinic, where an X-ray machine and its technician were waiting. Wally, Sarah, and Neil waited outside while the operator did his job.

Noah was told to remove his shirt and stand against a box on the wall, where an X-ray plate was waiting. The operator had him lift his arm and extend it outward, and then stepped behind a leaden shield. There was a loud clank and a buzz, and the operator returned to remove the plate. He took it into another room, and a couple of minutes later he came back with the printed image.

"Okay," he said, "it's clearly visible in this picture. Show that to the doctors so they know what they're dealing with."

Noah thanked him and took the picture, then stepped out of the room. Wally took out a key card and swiped it, locking the technician inside the room, then grabbed the picture from Noah and glanced at it. He led them all through a doorway and into an outdoor lot where a semitrailer awaited them with a large steel box inside it. Numerous cables and hoses had been run to the box from the building, and there were a set of steps that led up into the open back doors of the trailer.

Two men stood at the base of the steps, both of them wearing anticontamination suits. Wally grabbed Noah by the arm and hurried him up to meet them.

"Dr. Slocum, Dr. Reed, this is Camelot," he said. He turned to Noah. "Camelot, this is Drs. Slocum and Reed. When we told them what was going on, they both volunteered to perform the operation. Once it's complete, they'll also be locked in here at R&D until this is all over."

Noah shook hands with both of them and Wally handed over the X-ray image. Both of the doctors began looking it over, but then Noah looked up at the hyperbaric chamber inside the trailer. "I appreciate this," he said, "but do you both actually need to be in there? If this thing goes off, there's not much chance anybody inside there is going to survive it."

"We know," Slocum said. "Dr. Reed is going to perform the procedure, while I handle anesthesia and vitals. You'll be awake throughout the procedure, but I want to make sure you feel as little pain as possible."

Noah looked at the man and nodded. "Okay," he said. "What do we do first?"

"This chamber was designed as a positive-pressure emergency operating room," Dr. Reed said. "It's normally used when deep-sea divers require surgery before they can be fully decompressed. It was flown in on a C-130 this morning from the naval base in San Diego, then loaded into the trailer to bring it here. There is a decontamination room just inside the door, where we'll scrub you down and get you prepped for surgery; then we'll go into the main room and get this done as quickly as possible. The pressure inside should be greater than the pressure your muscle tissue is applying to the device, so we're confident we won't run into any problems—like getting ourselves blown to bits."

"And then," Dr. Slocum said, "we'll put the little bastard into a canister that can keep the pressure constant, but contain the explosion if it does go off. That way it can be held safe for as long as necessary, then detonated whenever it needs to be."

Noah turned to Wally. "Before we do anything else," he said, "I need to know if this thing is putting out any kind of signal. If there's a GPS signal, for instance, the person who put it here might be able to monitor its location. I don't think it would be a good idea for me to show up somewhere else when it says I'm supposed to be here."

Wally looked at him for a moment, then pulled out a walkie-talkie and spoke rapidly into it. A moment later, two men bearing several types of electronic equipment came rushing out the door. They surrounded Noah on the asphalt and started scanning him with the various devices, and then one of them nodded toward Wally.

"It's emitting a signal, but it's weak. It's nothing that could possibly be detected from more than a few feet away."

Wally furrowed his brow. "Damn, we should've thought of that," he said. "It's a close-proximity transmitter, and you can bet that little bitch carries something that can detect its signal. If she gets close to you and it isn't there, there's a whole new kind of problem called *you're dead*."

Sarah's eyes were wide. "But, there's got to be some way to beat this," she said. "Come on, Wally, you're the genius."

"Oh, I've already got it figured out," Wally said. "It just means we have to not only take out the device that's there, we have to put another one back that will emit the same signal." He turned to the man who had spoken to him. "Have you got it?"

"Yes, sir," the man said. "It's just a simple repeating numerical sequence. As low as the signal strength is, the transmitter can't be sophisticated enough to do anything else, but it could run for fifty years just on the natural electricity present in his body. Give me a couple of hours and I can make up one that will give off the exact same signal at the same strength."

Wally nodded. "Then get on it," he said. He snatched the X-ray from the doctors and handed it to them, and both men hurried back inside. He turned back to Noah and the rest. "Okay, sorry about this, but we'll have to do this a little later. We can't take the chance that you run into this little monster again and she can't detect that signal. Tom and Bob, there, they'll have one ready in pretty short order, and we can get on with this, and then they get locked in, too."

The doctors were standing there looking at each other, then at Wally and then at Noah. Everyone seemed upset, so Noah took charge.

"Okay, then this has to wait," he said. "Let's go look at the phones."

Wally hesitated for only a moment, then nodded and led them all back into the building. The doctors did not follow but simply sat down in a pair of folding chairs to wait.

In one of the many shops within the building, Wally showed Noah the assembly line that had been set up. Several of the phones had already been completed, their electronic innards taken out of the original cases and inserted into the new ones that had come out of the printer. Nearby, two women were taking more phones apart, while two others were putting them back together. Noah picked up one of the finished ones and compared it to one of the originals. Except for an embossed label on the new cases that said "Delphine," they were identical.

"Delphine?" Noah asked, looking at Wally.

"Delphine was an electronics company in Louisiana," Wally said. "They went out of business about three years ago, and they were owned by some other, now-defunct company in India, so we decided to put their logo on these. If anybody asks, you can always say that your supplier bought out the last of their inventory. We even put some crap on the internet about how they used to make these kind of phones."

Noah raised one eyebrow and nodded. "Good thinking," he said. "I'll be sure to use that. What about the explosive force? Is it going to be enough to make sure nobody can survive it?"

Wally burst out laughing. "Are you kidding? There's enough of our best explosive in one of these cases to blow up a Volkswagen. Anybody who has one in a pocket is going to disappear in a big greasy cloud."

Noah looked at the phone in his hand. "That only leaves a stronger possibility of collateral damage," he said. He turned to look at Neil. "I hope we can get everybody away from their families when we set these off."

"Yeah," Neil said.

Noah put the phone back and turned to Wally. "Okay, well, it looks like we've got time for dinner. Care to join us?"

Wally's big smile was answer enough. "Sure, yeah," he said. "Where you want to go? I'm buying!"

They went back out to the car and climbed inside, with Wally tucked in behind Noah. It cramped Neil a bit, but Sarah pulled her seat as far forward as she could to give him a little more legroom. He thanked her, and they decided to stay in the restricted area and visit the Assassin's Club. Neil had never been there, and Noah had only been there once with Gary Mitchell, but he knew they had a full kitchen.

They saw several people they knew and said hello, and then Neil almost jumped out of his skin when a pair of small hands suddenly wrapped themselves over his eyes.

"Guess who?" The voice was obviously feminine, and Neil's face broke into a big grin. He yanked the hands away and spun in his seat to find Jenny grinning at him.

"Hey," he said. "I didn't know you were back."

"We got in yesterday," she said, "and I was really pissed that you were gone, but that's the way it goes. I knew you were supposed to be coming in sometime today, though, because the boss lady told me this morning, so I bribed Renée to let me know when you showed up. She called me a few minutes ago to tell me you guys were headed here, so I snuck out to join you. You mind?"

"Of course not," Neil said, and then he snagged another chair from a nearby table and put it between his own and Sarah's. Jenny slid into it and leaned over to give Sarah a quick hug.

"Allison briefed me on what's going on," she whispered into Sarah's ear. "You doing okay?"

"I'll be better once they get that damn thing out of his arm," Sarah whispered back. "They had to make something to put in its place so nobody will know it's gone. It's supposed be ready in a couple of hours, but I'm nervous. If anything goes wrong..."

"If anything goes wrong," Jenny said, "I'll be right there with you." The two girls exchanged a little smile, and Jenny turned back to Neil.

The conversation around the table was simple, sticking to things that could be overheard in such a place. The only subjects that were not acceptable, they all knew, was any mention of Monique, or any talk about the explosive device in Noah's arm that anyone else might overhear.

Several people stopped by to say hello and shake Noah's hand, and a few even congratulated them on their wedding. These were people who had been out of the country when it took place and were not able to attend. Sarah smiled a lot as she showed off her wedding rings, and more than one of the girls who spoke to her told her they were jealous.

"So," Jenny said when all the extra attention died down, "how's the mission going? I heard you're going to be there for quite a while."

Noah shrugged. "Maybe not," he said. "We're here to pick up a load of special cell phones, designed so that I can make the cases explode all at once. Each of the top people in the organization will get one when I get back, and I may be able to bring this to a conclusion a lot sooner than we thought. It seems I'm just exactly the kind of person the head guy wants for his right-hand man, so I've been introduced to all of his most trusted people. Unless something comes up that I'm not expecting, those are exactly the people I'm supposed to eliminate."

Jenny's eyes went wide. "Seriously? Like, how soon?"

"I'm going to give it a few days after I get back," Noah said. "I need to be sure I'm getting everyone who could possibly resurrect the organization, because this thing needs to come to an end. This guy Morgan is bad news for everybody around him, and that is the truth. I never knew a lot about organized crime before this, but I bet he's worse than any of the big mob bosses. Capone probably could have learned things about running a criminal operation from Jimmy Morgan."

Jenny frowned. "Damn," she said, "I wish I was in on this one with you. He sounds like the kind of guy I love to take out."

Neil looked at Noah. "Hey, boss, how about that? Think she could come on down for a while? I mean, we could tell everybody my girlfriend was visiting, right?"

"No," Noah said. "I don't have the authority to okay that, and I'm already in place. We got Marco coming in a few days from now; it might look funny if too many new people start showing up."

Sarah patted Neil's arm. "Don't worry, baby brother," she said, "this mission should be over pretty soon, and you can get back to your cuddle bunny." She giggled when she saw Jenny blush slightly. "Oh, my gosh, does he actually call you that?"

Jenny shrugged but didn't say anything. Neil glared at Sarah for a moment, then leaned over and put an arm around Jenny and whispered to her. Whatever he said made the girl smile, and she turned around to give him a kiss.

"Hey, Noah," Wally said as they were waiting for their orders to appear, "we got a few new gadgets you might like. Are you gonna have time to take a look at some of them tomorrow morning, before you leave?"

"Possibly," Noah said. "What kind of gadgets?"

Wally grinned, and Sarah thought once more that he really did look a bit like a mad scientist. "I had this wild idea a few weeks ago," he said, "and I turned it over to a couple of new kids we hired, and they handed me a working prototype day before yesterday. I call it a smart gun. It looks like a brick on a small tripod, but it has a three-hundred-and-sixty-degree camera mounted on top. You use a cell phone or a computer to feed it a photo of the target and then just set it someplace where you expect the target will pass by. When it sees the target, it will lock on and track until it gets the perfect shot, and then it will fire. You can actually give it several dozen targets, and it will look for each and every one and shoot them. Well, until it runs out of bullets, anyway. The base model only holds fifteen rounds."

Noah's left eyebrow went up a notch. "Like having a sniper in your pocket," he said. "I can think of times it would've come in handy."

"I can't wait to demonstrate it for you," Wally said, and then he leaned close to whisper into Noah's ear. "Another thing you might like is super classified—a pair of sunglasses that can tell you when someone is lying to you. It has a super-micro-computer built into it, along with a camera so small you can't even see it, and it reads microexpressions. It can tell you instantly if someone is being deceptive by flashing a little display that only the wearer can see."

"Now, that could be interesting," Noah said. "How accurate would you say it is?"

"We've tested the technology, before we used it in the glasses, on over four hundred subjects, including a hundred who were specifically told to lie, and none of them have been able to fool it. So far, it's running a hundred percent accuracy. The only drawback is that it can't necessarily tell you exactly which part of what the subject says is untrue, but it can definitely tell you if the subject is trying to conceal something. In testing, however, we've been able to spot the actual lie about ninety-eight percent of the time."

Noah looked at him for a moment, then nodded. "I want one," he said, still in a whisper. "Do you have one I can take back with me tomorrow?"

Wally's smile got even bigger. "We've got several sets made," he said. "I'll make sure to have one ready for you in the morning."

The food arrived a few moments later, and they all dug in. They chatted a bit as they ate, but Noah, Sarah, and Neil were quite hungry, so they tended to listen more than speak. Jenny told them about her latest mission, which had involved the assassination of a Colombian drug lord, and Neil was careful to express shock, horror, and admiration in the right places. He'd already figured out that Jenny often second-guessed herself and needed some kind of approval for the way she handled her assignments in order to avoid self-doubt. The more he gave her, the happier she seemed to be in their burgeoning relationship.

When they finished dinner, Wally convinced them to stay a bit longer for a couple of drinks. Noah decided to forgo any alcohol, since he knew he would be going into surgery before long, but didn't object when Sarah decided to have a wine cooler. Considering that there was still a chance the explosive in his arm would kill him before the evening was over, he figured the small bit of alcohol in the bottle might help ease her nerves slightly.

Wally's phone chirped about half an hour later, and he glanced at it. He smiled and then looked up at Noah. "They're ready," he said.

The five of them, including Jenny, headed for the door. Wally took care of the tab, and then Neil decided to ride back to R&D with Jenny. That let Wally sit behind Sarah and stretch his legs out a bit more comfortably. It took them only a short time to get back, and the security guards did not even challenge them as they entered with Wally.

Wally led them straight back to where the hyperbaric chamber still sat in its trailer, and they were met by Tom and Bob, the electronics technicians, who had already given the doctors their handiwork.

Dr. Slocum was looking at it closely, comparing it to the image on the X-ray. "Looks almost identical," he said. "Certainly seems to be the same size and shape. We shouldn't have any problem at all sliding this right in where the other comes out." He looked up at Noah. "What we're going to do is use a cylindrical extractor. It's sharp, like a hypodermic, and will pierce the skin the same way it was done when this was put into you, and we've got a tiny mechanical grapple that we can slip through it. That will grab on to the device and let us pull it out, and then we'll drop it into the containment canister and use the same system to put the new device into place. The whole procedure won't take more than twenty minutes, but we need to completely deaden the area first. I don't even want to put a needle into you there until we're inside the chamber and under pressure."

"And then, of course," Dr. Reed said, "once the explosive is in the containment canister, we have to decompress. Now, the pressure won't be a lot higher than it is out here, but decompression will still take about a half hour. We're probably looking at an hour, hour and ten minutes, from the moment we go in until we come out."

Wally grinned and rubbed his hands together. "Which is why I'm going to take Neil and these lovely young ladies back to my office, where I have a rare and expensive bottle of wine I intend to share with them. By the time you come out, Noah, we're all going to have a pretty good buzz going on."

Sarah started to protest, but Jenny took her by the arm and pulled gently. Noah leaned down and kissed her, then gave her a little push in Wally's direction. "Go ahead," he said. "I'll be there in an hour or so."

Sarah stood there and stared at him for a moment, tears starting to flow down her cheeks. "You better be," she said, and then she let Jenny lead her away.

Neil stood there beside Noah for another moment, then just held out a hand. The two of them shook, and Neil followed Jenny and Sarah.

CHAPTER FOUR

"Let's get you inside and prepped," Slocum said, and Noah walked up the stairs onto the trailer. Dr. Reed opened the first thick steel door, and the three of them stepped inside. The door closed behind them and was secured with a large wheel that slid a number of bolts into place.

"This is sort of an airlock," Dr. Reed said. "Go ahead and strip down, and we're going to spray you with an antiseptic mixture. It'll probably be pretty cold, but there isn't a way to warm it up, I'm afraid."

Noah shrugged. "I've taken some pretty cold showers," he said. "I doubt it can be much worse than that." He stripped out of his clothes and stood where he was told as the doctors sprayed him down, and then he was handed a thick paper towel.

"Wipe yourself off with that," Slocum said. "That solution will kill any germs that might have been on you, so that we won't be risking any infection once our extractor punctures your skin. Once this is done, we'll be using surgical superglue to close the puncture back up, so a simple stick-on bandage will be enough to protect it after that."

He pushed a button on the wall and Noah heard a hissing sound.

"That's the pressure valve," Dr. Reed said. "It's letting pressurized sterile air into this room so that we can open the door into the next one."

The two doctors removed their anticontamination suits, and Noah saw they were wearing scrubs underneath. Slocum picked up a hypodermic that was lying on a shelf and turned to Noah.

"Would you lift your arm, please? I want to go ahead and deaden the area." Noah did as he was told, and the doctor injected the area

44

around where the device had gone in four different times. "That'll take a couple of minutes to work, but it should stop you from feeling any pain once we begin."

There was a loud beep, and Reed spun the wheel on the inner door, then pulled it open. "In we go," he said with a smile. Noah stepped into the actual operating room and saw that it was very much like any other he had ever seen, although a bit smaller. The lights were very bright, and there were many different kinds of surgical instruments lying on trays near the operating table. "Jump on up there," Slocum said, and Noah did so, lying on his back. Dr. Slocum picked up a blanket and laid it over his lower half, concealing his nudity.

Dr. Reed took hold of Noah's arm and positioned it on a shelf that extended out from the table, twisting and turning it a bit to get it right where he wanted. "Hold it right there," he said, and then he nodded to Slocum, who went to the other side of the table and affixed a blood pressure cuff to Noah's right arm, then began sticking sensors to his chest.

"This is just a precaution," he said. "I'll be monitoring your vital signs while Dr. Reed performs the procedure. It's probably not necessary, but we don't want to take any chances. If your blood pressure drops drastically or your heart rate slows or speeds up, we want to be certain we are aware of it and can take whatever action is necessary."

"Okay," Noah said. He felt a strange sensation on his left arm and glanced over to see Dr. Reed poking at it with a sharp implement.

"Can you feel that?" Reed asked.

"I can feel pressure," Noah said, "but I can't feel the point of that thing. Kind of feels like you're just pressing on it with a finger."

Reed nodded. "We're ready, then," he said. He turned around and picked up another implement, a long tube with a large hypodermic needle–type point on one end. Without saying anything else, he leaned close to Noah's arm and quickly pushed the sharp end into his skin.

Noah could feel the point moving around inside his arm, but there was no pain. It seemed to be searching, and he realized the doctor was trying to find the implanted device with the point. There was a slight thumping sensation a moment later, and Dr. Reed smiled.

"There it is," he said. He picked up another device, something that looked like a miniature broom made of wire, and slid it into the center of the extraction tube. He pushed it farther in, and Noah felt a slight sensation as it came into contact with the implanted microbomb. Reed seemed to concentrate hard for a moment, and then he grinned. "I've got it," he said. "Now, what I've got to do is push the extraction tube farther in around it. If I tried to pull it, I might lose it, so I'm just going to hold it in place while the tube frees it from the surrounding tissues."

Noah felt a few odd sensations, and then Reed smiled again. "Okay, here comes the tricky part. Dr. Slocum, are you ready?"

Noah glanced at the other doctor and saw that he was holding the containment canister, a round metal container with walls that seemed to be a couple of inches thick. It was about the size of a coffee can and filled with water. There was actually very little space inside, and the lid was on a hinge and looked like a miniature vault door. There were several thick rods that would lock it into place once it was closed. Slocum was holding it over Noah's chest and leaning forward to get it as close to his left armpit as possible. "I'm ready," he said.

In a very quick motion, Dr. Reed withdrew the flexible grapple and dropped the microbomb into the containment canister. Slocum slammed the lid and turned the center of it once, and Noah could hear the rods lock into place.

Both of the doctors suddenly wore expressions of great relief, and Noah realized instantly just how terrified they had been. If the device had blown, none of the three of them would have survived it.

"Okay, the hard part's over," Reed said. "From here on out, it's all downhill." He picked up the little transmitter Tom and Bob had made and fitted it into the extraction tube, then used the flexible grapple to push it down and into the same spot where the bomb had rested only a minute earlier. As soon as he was satisfied that it was in place, he withdrew the grapple and pulled out the extraction tube, then applied the superglue to the slightly gaping hole.

"We are all done," he said with a smile. "How are you feeling?"

Noah looked up at him. "Haven't really felt anything," he said. "I imagine I'll be a little sore tomorrow, but it already was, so I might not notice."

Slocum chuckled. "Your vitals are all perfect," he said. "I'm going to start the decompression sequence, so we should be able to leave here about half an hour from now."

There was a vibration that began, and Slocum told Noah that it was the decompression valve. It would slowly reduce the pressure by opening and closing rapidly, letting only a tiny bit of pressure out at a time.

"Is decompression actually necessary?" Noah asked. "I didn't think we were actually under enough pressure to require it, were we?"

"Probably not, to be honest," Dr. Slocum said, "but we decided to err on the side of caution because, as minor as it was, you did just undergo a surgical procedure. It's entirely possible that some of that pressurized air got inside your body. If we let the pressure off too quickly, there's always the risk of an embolism, and you're just too valuable for that risk. Another half hour isn't going to kill you, but rushing actually could."

Noah nodded. "Okay, I can see the logic in that."

"Yes," Dr. Reed said with a smile, "I thought you might."

Noah looked over at the canister. "What's going to happen with that?"

"I understand Wally wants to examine it," Slocum said. "Something about finding out how much power it actually contains. He seems to think it might involve some kind of technology that was stolen from us, but I'm not sure whether he means the explosive or the controller. Until then, the canister can maintain the pressure so that it won't go off on its own."

"I've seen what his explosive can do," Noah replied. "I can't say I like the thought that thing might have been made of the same stuff he came up with a while back. If it is, it would've taken off more than my arm."

Slocum gave him a wry grin. "Yeah, there probably wouldn't have been anything left of you."

"Or anyone within twenty feet," Reed added. "I got to see what that explosive can do a while back, myself. That's some powerful stuff."

Noah sat up on the table, and the three men chatted while they waited for the decompression to complete. When the machinery finally beeped to say it was safe to leave the chamber, Slocum opened the door into the airlock, and Noah picked up his clothing.

"I smell like iodine," he said. "Is there a shower around here I can use?"

"How about this?" Slocum asked. He held out a jar and several of the thick paper towels. "This is a cleanser we use on our hands," he said. "Just scoop some out and spread it over yourself, then it will wipe right off and not leave a residue. Sorta smells like cheap aftershave, but that's better than smelling like iodine."

Noah thanked him and used the cleanser and towels as directed, then agreed that he smelled better as he got dressed. When he was finished, Dr. Reed opened the outer door and they stepped out into the late-afternoon sun. The air was slightly cool, but Noah paid no attention to it as he skipped down the steps and led the way back into the building.

A moment later, he tapped on the door to Wally's office-slash-workshop and then turned the knob. Sarah leapt out of her chair when she saw him and threw both arms around his neck.

"Oh, God, I was so scared," she said, trembling as he wrapped his arms around her. "Are you okay? Did everything go all right?"

"I'm fine," he said, "and it's gone. It's okay, babe."

Neil, Jenny, and Wally were standing around them, each of them patting his shoulder or congratulating him on the successful removal of the device. Noah thanked each of them, especially Wally, and then suggested they go home. "We'll be back in the morning," he said to Wally, "to pick up the phones. They should all be done by then, right?"

"Oh, yes, yes," Wally said. "They'll actually be done within a couple of hours, but I'm sure you want to get home and get some rest. I'll be here at seven, so you can pick them up anytime you want to after that." He patted Noah's right shoulder one more time, then leaned close. "I think you better take this girl home and just let her hold on to you for the night," he said softly.

Noah nodded and turned to go out the door with Sarah clinging to him. Neil and Jenny, holding hands, followed them out to the parking lot, then climbed into Jenny's car, and they made a small convoy back to the house.

They'd all had a late lunch and weren't terribly hungry, even though it was a little after six thirty by the time they got there, so Sarah broke out some bags of chips and soft drinks to snack on. The four of them went into the living room and found a movie, but Neil and Jenny couldn't seem to concentrate on it. About halfway through, they excused themselves and headed over to Neil's trailer.

Sarah looked at Noah. "They seem to be getting pretty serious," she said. "Think there's anything we need to worry about?"

Noah shook his head as he looked into her eyes. "They're both adults," he said. "I'll grant you that it sometimes feels like Neil is part of the family, but we're not his parents. I don't think Jenny will hurt him, so we might as well just let it play out."

"I'm actually a little more worried about him hurting her," Sarah said softly. "While we were waiting in Wally's office, Jenny told me she's happier with him than she's ever been. I guess he's the kind of guy she's been looking for, the kind who doesn't mind taking charge in the relationship. I just hope he doesn't get tired of it."

"He won't," Noah said, "not anytime soon. Neil has a lot of alpha traits, but between his height and his brains, he's always been picked on. He's finally developing the confidence he's needed, and it's showing in his personality. That's why he and Lacey broke up, because he couldn't handle her trying to run things. I think Jenny gives him what he needs, and he does the same for her."

Sarah giggled. "I'm sorry, I just still have problems trying to understand how Jenny, with the way she loves to be violent and murderous out on the job, can be so—I don't know, I guess submissive is the right word, with Neil. It just seems like such a contradiction."

"I see what you mean," Noah said with a shrug, "but it really isn't. On a mission, she has to be the team leader and in control, and the violence is just something inside her that lets her do the job. When she's off duty, though, she can let that part go and just be herself. Her idea of a proper romantic relationship seems to include a man who takes care of her, and the only way she can have that is to let him be in control when they're together. As long as it works for the two of them, that's all that matters."

She popped a potato chip into her mouth and crunched it, then smiled up at Noah. "I know what works for us," she said. "And it isn't this movie." She kissed his cheek and got up, heading toward the bedroom. Noah waited a full minute before following, then stripped down and joined her in the shower.

The sexy negligee he had told her to pack was completely forgotten.

NOAH WOKE UP JUST BEFORE six in the morning, then took another quick shower while Sarah slowly came to life. She entered the bathroom as he was about to get out, told him to leave the water on, and pushed past him to get one of her own. She was out by the time he had finished shaving, and they were both dressed and ready to go a half hour later.

Noah started to walk across to Neil's trailer and wake him, but Neil and Jenny came out the trailer door at that moment. They waved as they crossed the yard, and Sarah came out a moment later.

"I need breakfast," Neil said. "Charlie's?"

"That'll do," Noah said. He and Sarah got into the Charger as Neil and Jenny climbed into her Jaguar. Noah pulled out first, with Jenny following closely.

It was already seven o'clock by the time they got to Charlie's, so Noah called Wally to let him know that they would be late.

"Hey, no problem at all," Wally said. "I'm actually running a little late myself, not there yet. I'll see you after breakfast."

They were sitting at their table, their orders already in, when Noah heard his name. He glanced around to see Marco coming through the door and headed in his direction. The burly man grabbed a chair and turned it around backward, straddling it and crossing his arms on the back. Since their table was off to one side, Noah wasn't worried about being overheard as long as they kept their voices low.

"Hey," he said, "I heard you were coming into town. Renée told me what went on yesterday. Everything okay?"

"Oh, yeah, just minor surgery," Noah said. "All taken care of. How's it going for you?"

"Gary says I'm ready," Marco replied. "I gar-on-tee, I be ready to go do some work wit you, *mon ami.*"

Jenny's eyebrows went up. "Nice accent," she said.

"I growed up wit dat accent," Marco said with a grin. "Ain't hard to go back to it. I talk like dis all de time when I need to."

Jenny giggled at him. "And you do it very well," she said.

"I do, yes." Marco grinned, then turned to Noah. "So, you decide when you want me to come in yet?"

"I'll be back in Arkansas tomorrow," Noah said, "and I want you to give me a call there in the morning. If you call around nine o'clock, I should be with Morgan, so he'll be able to hear my side of the conversation. Tell me about getting out of prison and tracking me down, and I can pitch him on letting me bring you in. He's basically turned me into his new right-hand man, so I'm pretty sure I can get away with it."

Marco's eyes widened and his smile got bigger. "Awesome," he said. "Don't waste any time, do you?"

Noah shrugged. "It's all happened a lot faster than any of us expected," he said. "My first night in town, I happened to be in the right place at the right time to keep some drug addict from killing Morgan's son, and it got me his attention. He hired me to run the boy's security team at first, then decided I was smart enough to be in his inner circle. You know about the phone thing?"

Marco nodded. "Yeah, Renée told me. Smart idea."

"Well, I pitched Morgan on using these encrypted phones to avoid letting the wrong people listen in on conversations, and he liked the idea. I shot him another idea, something that would make him a lot of money if it were real, and that's when he decided to take me off security and keep me close."

"Hey, if anybody can fit in, you can. You think he'll be okay with you bringing in someone of your own?"

"I think he'll at least hear me out. Since we did time together, he should think you might be his kind of people."

"Cool," Marco said. "You know my backstory, right? Aubrey did nine years for accessory to murder, helped his girlfriend get her hands on some kind of poison to kill her husband with."

"Yes, I know," Noah replied. "And that seems to be the kind of people Morgan likes having around, someone who isn't afraid to kill." He lowered his voice a little bit more. "First thing I had to do was kill that drug addict," he said.

"No problem there," Marco said. "I be a loaded gun, I gar-on-tee! You point me, you pull my trigger, I go bang!"

Jenny snickered again.

Marco joined them for breakfast, and they dropped into simple small talk. Sarah told Marco and Jenny about the house in Arkansas and how much she loved all the antique furniture, and Marco let slip the comment that he and Renée were thinking about making their relationship more permanent. Sarah and Jenny gave each other a high five and began coming up with ideas for a wedding, but Marco's eyes went wide.

"Hey, slow down," he said without the accent. "I didn't mean we were getting married—we've just been talking about moving in to-gether. That's all."

Neil rolled his eyes. "Yeah, that's what you think," he said. "Just wait till these two get a chance to talk to Renée alone. I hear bells in your future."

Marco stammered a bit, but Sarah and Jenny promised to behave themselves and he relaxed. He carefully avoided any further mention of Renée as they finished breakfast.

Since he had nothing better to do, Marco decided to follow them out to R&D. Sarah told Noah she thought he was just trying to make sure she and Jenny didn't corner Renée, but she was chuckling as she said it. They made a three-car convoy with the Charger in the lead, but they got separated a bit when they reached the first security gate.

Noah and Sarah waited for the rest of them when they got to the R&D building, and then they all went in together. The security officer carefully checked their IDs, then notified Wally. He came up front again but didn't run this time.

"Okay, we got everything ready," he said. "Noah, I've got something special for you, if you'll come with me." He led Noah into a small room and closed the door behind them, then reached into his pocket and pulled out a pair of stylish sunglasses. "These are the ones I was telling you about," he said with a grin. "Put them on and ask me a question."

Noah accepted the sunglasses and put them on, then looked at Wally. On the inside of the lenses, he saw numerous tiny orange dots appear over various points on Wally's face, at the corners of his eyes, different points on his lips, on his eyebrows and around his nose. "Is your name George?"

"Yes," Wally said with an excited grin, "yes, it is."

Several of the dots blinked, turning from orange to red. A text box that read "Deception detected" opened up in the upper right corner of both lenses. A second later, the dots turned orange once more and the text box disappeared.

"This is pretty cool," Noah said. "How did you come up with this?"

"Oh, it came to me in a dream," Wally said, and the dots blinked red once more as the text box appeared again. "Actually, there is an existing software that's used in deception-detection training to assist students in learning to recognize microexpressions. We just took it a few steps further, added in a facial-recognition algorithm and then some AI functions that let it make its own determinations." He leaned close to Noah, as if he had something to say that no one else could hear, but didn't lower his voice. "Allison's been using a pair to check for other people the mole might have gotten to, and she's already cleared a lot of them. Anybody who shows any sign of being deceptive is put under direct surveillance, but so far there's only been a few of them."

"I can see that," Noah said. "All she'd have to do is tell people not to let anyone outside the organization know about something the mole might be interested in. Anyone who was under Monique's thumb would automatically show signs of deception because they'd know they had to relay the information on, but of course whatever it is would be false, anyway."

"Exactly," Wally said. "I don't know exactly what it is she's using, but she's confident that it's working." He reached up and took the glasses off Noah's face, then pointed at a small red decoration on each of the temples. "Right button turns it on, left button turns it off. When it's on, if you grab the left temple and adjust it on your face, it waits two seconds and then snaps a photograph of whatever you're looking at. Hold the left button for five seconds and it turns on Bluetooth, so you can download the pictures to your phone or something." He handed Noah an eyeglasses case and pointed to a small slot on the bottom. "A normal phone charger plugs in here, and you just put the glasses inside to charge the batteries. Full charge lasts about sixty hours, but it's best to charge it every night."

"This is perfect," Noah said. "Is there any possibility that knowledge of this technology has gotten out of your department?"

"Not counting you," Wally said, "only eight other people know these exist. That's the two people who developed and made them, me, Allison, Donnie Jefferson and his daughter, your girl Molly, and Dr. Parker. Allie said she didn't want anyone else knowing about it just yet, so we're keeping it quiet."

Noah thanked him and put the glasses into his pocket, and they stepped back into the foyer. Wally motioned for them all to follow him and started down the hallway. "Come on, let's go get your phones."

All of the phones were completed and packed into boxes like any other new phones. Wally opened one and held it out. "These are Android phones, and they are as good as just about any smartphone on the market today. The only real difference is that they have our case on them, all but this one. I mean, it has our case, but it doesn't have a detonator. This one would be yours, and it's got this special app that sends out the detonation code." He turned the phone on and opened its apps screen, then pointed at the icon for a war game. "All of these phones have this game on them, and if someone got hold of your phone and tried to play the game, it would work. The only difference is that yours would allow you to input a special password that will open the actual detonation screen. The password is 'absolution,' and all you need to do is tap the screen twice, wait two seconds, then tap it six more times to get to where you put it in. Once you do, you'll see every detonator that's been programmed for you—these phones are already programmed in, by the way—and they'll be in a list format with check boxes, and if you've got a contact name assigned to the phone, it will show that, too. Just select the ones you want to set off and then tap the button marked 'GO.' As soon as you do, it will send the detonation code to all of the ones you selected, whether it's a single detonator or a number of them at once. Wherever they are when that code comes through, they're going to explode."

He showed his evil grin. "And if you happen to get them all together at the same place when you set them off," he said, "make sure you're at least a mile away before you send the code. I'd hate to think what would happen if all of these phones went off when they were close together."

"I don't think I want to know, either," Noah said. "Can we go ahead and switch my number over to that phone? I don't want to take a chance on it getting mixed up with any of the others."

Wally signaled one of the technicians in the room, and she came over to take the new phone from him. She punched a couple of buttons on its face and then used the touch screen to enter some information before handing it back. "There you go," she said. "It's got your number and all of your contacts already programmed in."

Noah handed Wally his iPhone and slipped the new one into his pocket. "Thanks, Wally," he said. "Incidentally, Morgan gave me a satchel full of cash to pay for these. Any idea what I should do with it?"

Wally shrugged, chuckling. "Buy something nice? I'm pretty sure we don't need the money; my budget here is almost a billion a year, and it comes through some kind of black ops funding arrangement, so nobody on Capitol Hill even knows about it."

Noah blinked but didn't say anything. Marco picked up the box, and they all followed Noah back out to the Charger, where he put it in the trunk.

"Okay, now one more thing," Wally said. "All of you, follow me. You're gonna freaking love this!"

They followed Wally back into the building and through the hallways, until they ended up in a large, warehouse-sized room that seemed to have been set up as some sort of mock battlefield. A couple of technicians were walking around the room, and Noah saw that they were setting up a couple of small tripod-mounted contraptions.

"Ladies and gentlemen," Wally said with a flourish, "let me present the smart gun. We've got four of them set up at different points around the room, and they've been programmed to spot and kill some manikins. We mounted the manikins on remote-controlled movable platforms so that they simulate living targets walking past. Watch this." He waved at one of the technicians, who gave him a thumbs-up before taking a box out of his pocket and pushing a button on it.

"Okay, he just armed the guns. Now, watch what happens when our manikins go roaming around."

A door opened on one side of the room, and five manikins on wheels came rolling out. Each of them turned and went a different direction, maneuvering around the big trees and other obstacles. They made slow progress, but then suddenly one of the smart guns moved, aiming at the nearest manikin. It wobbled for a second as it centered its targeting system; then they all heard a loud *puff.* The head of the manikin exploded.

A second gun aimed and fired, and then a third. The first one got another manikin, and then the fourth gun fired last. All five manikins were completely decapitated.

Noah nodded appreciatively. "How do you program the targets in?"

"Each of the guns has its own cell number," Wally said. "All you have to do is take a picture of the target and send it to the gun. It uses enhanced facial recognition, so even a profile photo is good enough."

"What's its margin for error?" Neil asked.

"Less than one percent," Wally replied. "In two hundred targets, we only had one mistaken hit and two misses." He shrugged. "It's brand-new technology—it's going to have a few bugs to work out, but one misidentified target out of two hundred is pretty impressive."

Noah nodded. "Are they available yet?"

Wally grinned and rubbed his hands together. "I can give you six of them right now, if you want them. They fire 9 mm rounds, and the magazine holds fifteen."

"Okay," Noah said. "I want them."

Wally called out to the technician, who put six boxes onto a wheeled cart and brought them over. Marco took over pushing it as they went back out to the car, then loaded them into the trunk with the phones.

Noah shook Wally's and Marco's hands while Neil was saying goodbye to Jenny. He was planning to get on the road immediately so that they could get back to Arkansas before dark. The three of them climbed into the car and waved at Marco and Jenny as Noah started it up and backed out of the parking space. Wally, in catlike manner, simply turned around and walked back into the building.

CHAPTER FIVE

They were almost out of the restricted area when Noah's phone rang, and he glanced at it to see that it was Allison calling.

"Camelot," he said.

"What, you thought you were going to sneak out without seeing me?" Allison asked.

"I was actually avoiding you," Noah said. "I didn't want Monique to hear that I'd been to see you. Was I supposed to come by?"

"No, I'm just yanking your chain. I just figured I'd give you a call on your new phone, since it's completely secure, now. Of course, your old one was, too, but since she had you unconscious when she implanted that device, we couldn't be absolutely certain that it hadn't been physically compromised."

"I agree," Noah said. "You've been apprised of the entire situation with Monique?"

"Everything Neil sent, so I'm sure the answer is yes. How's the mission going?"

"Better than we ever expected. With these phones, I may be able to complete it within the next few days, unless you want me to hold off."

"Goodness, no," Allison said. "If you are certain you have everyone who should be targeted, you take them down as soon as you can. It might not hurt for you to let Monique think you hurried it up a bit, like you wanted to get it out of the way so it won't interfere when she comes up with her plan to pull you out."

"All right," Noah said. "Any leads on who she might be yet?"

"None," Allison said. "She's got power of some kind, and she has to be tied to the CIA somewhere, because even they think the mole is one of theirs. There aren't many people I trust over there, but I'll be visiting one of them tomorrow. I want to know everything they know about her, though I'm afraid we might be ahead of them on that score. If I'm right, this all may still be resting on your shoulders."

"I'm okay with that," Noah said. "Especially now that we got her little booby trap out of me. If she was telling the truth, killing her is going to automatically kill everyone she's actually allowed to get close to her. I doubt I'm the only one who ever got one of those implanted in an armpit."

"And you are undoubtedly right. What that means for us, though, is something good. Since we found out the device puts out a close-proximity signal and we were able to copy it, we're putting together a way to detect them. If we can find anyone else who's got one of those gadgets implanted in them, it may give us a lead on identifying her."

"What surprises me," Noah said, "is that she's so difficult to track down. How many women her size could there be connected to the CIA?"

"More than two dozen," Allison said, "but none of them fit the description you gave us. There are a few in the right age range, but none of them would ever be considered attractive. Noah, we've even looked at wives of Company men, and we can't find her anywhere. Whoever she is, she's very well insulated."

"That's an extremely sobering thought," Noah replied. "I suppose the only thing to do is ride this out. At some point, I should find some kind of information that will allow us to track her down. I'll just keep you apprised of every development."

"That's all we can do. Complete your mission, but stay safe." The line went dead.

Noah put the phone back in his pocket and stared straight ahead through the windshield. "They can't seem to find Monique," he said.

"No one connected to the CIA fits her description at all, but she's got to have some sort of tie to it."

Neil, in the back seat, shook his head. "I wish you could've gotten a picture of her," he said. "I'd love to run it through facial recognition, starting with the Russian databases. If she's connected to CIA in any way, they'd have something on her."

"I'll bear that in mind. Maybe I'll get the chance, someday."

THEY MADE THREE STOPS for gas on the way back, taking time for lunch at one of them, and rolled back into Berryville at just before five o'clock. Noah called Morgan to let him know that he was back, but the big man told him to get some rest and they would meet the following morning.

"That's a long drive," Sarah said as they headed out toward the house. "I hope you don't want anything complicated for dinner, because I'm tired."

"I can fix that," Noah said. He turned in at the farm supply store and went inside, returning ten minutes later with a big bucket of chicken and side dishes. He passed them to Sarah and then drove them on home.

When they got to the house and went inside, Sarah set the food on the table and dug out plates and silverware, then told the men they could dish up their own. She made a plate for herself and carried it into the living room, plopping herself on the couch.

Neil grinned at Noah and made himself a plate, and Noah followed suit. They followed Sarah into the living room, but Neil set down his plate and went back into the kitchen to bring them each a bottle of root beer. "Root beer is the only soda pop that goes with chicken," he said. "Nothing else tastes right, not to me."

"You won't get any argument from me," Sarah said, twisting off the top and taking a swallow. She leaned herself gently against Noah, who had sat down beside her.

Noah picked up the remote and turned on the television, and quickly found a movie that appealed to them all. They watched it as they ate, and then found another one when it was over. For that evening, the mission and everything else were forgotten as they simply relaxed together.

Noah got up quietly the next morning, intending to let Sarah stay in bed and get some sleep. She woke, however, while he was in the shower and was sitting up when he came out.

"Do you have any idea," she began, "just how hot you are when you walk out of the shower like that?"

Noah looked down at himself, then back up her. "In a towel?" he asked.

She nodded, grinning. "Yep," she said. "In a towel." She suddenly jumped up off the bed and snatched at the towel, stealing it away and leaving him standing naked in the bedroom. "Of course, that's something of an improvement," she said, the grin turning into a smile.

Noah took her face in his hands and kissed her, then turned and started getting dressed. "I need to go see Morgan," he said, "but I promise to make it up to you later. Would you mind to go make some coffee, since you're already up?"

She snapped him with the towel and ran out of the bedroom, her tongue between her teeth as she laughed. Noah stared after her for a moment, then continued dressing. By the time he got out to the kitchen a few minutes later, she already had a cup poured for him and Neil was sitting at the table with one of his own.

"New development," Neil said. "I woke up this morning to a message from Molly. She says Wally's people dismantled that little bomb in a high-pressure chamber yesterday, and it turns out the explosive in it wasn't a whole lot more powerful than a firecracker. It still would've probably killed you, because it was right next to a major artery, but it wasn't anything special as far as explosives go."

"I guess that's something," Noah said.

"Yeah, but that wasn't all. Remember how Monique told you that it had some kind of receiver built in, something she could send a code to, in order to set it off?"

"Sure," Noah said. "What about it?"

"It was one of ours. The same detonator chip we're using in the phone cases. She could send a signal through any cell tower, anywhere, and it would've gone off."

Noah looked at him for a moment. "Ours were developed recently by Wally's people," Noah said. "That means she's almost certainly got somebody inside R&D."

Neil nodded sadly. "That's how it looks," he said. "And we have absolutely no idea who it could be. She may already know that it's been removed from your arm."

"In which case, she's going to know I'm working against her and will want me dead."

"Oh, geez," Sarah said. "Can't we ever get a break?"

"Don't get upset yet," Noah said. "We don't know for sure that she knows anything."

"She knew we were going back to Neverland," Neil said. "She knew you were going out to R&D to pick up the phones. Do you really think there's much chance she didn't have somebody there watching what was going on with you?"

"Probably not, I grant you," Noah replied. "I just don't see any sense in anticipating a problem until we are certain that it really does exist. I'll keep an eye out for anything that seems amiss, but all we can do at this point is hope for the best and wait to see what happens."

Sarah looked up at him. "I'll be glad when Marco gets here," she said. "He can help watch your back, if nothing else."

Noah nodded. "He's supposed to call me this morning, and I'm going to pitch Morgan on letting me bring him in. If I can, I'll try to keep him with me all the time." He took a drink of his coffee. "While I'm gone, get your own guns out. I don't want anybody coming through that door that you don't know. If somebody tries, shoot first and then call me. I'll handle it."

Neil got up and went to his bedroom, returning a moment later with his own machine pistol and Sarah's Beretta. He handed her the pistol, and she quickly checked its magazine and then chambered a round.

"Trust me," she said. "Nobody is getting in who shouldn't."

They talked for a few more minutes, and then Noah headed toward the door. Sarah grabbed the chance for another kiss, and then Noah returned to the car, fired it up, and was out the driveway only a minute later.

When he pulled up at Morgan's house, he popped open the trunk and motioned for one of the security guys to come over. "Grab that box," he said, "and follow me." The man nodded and did as he was told, and Noah led him up the stairs and onto the porch. He knocked on the door and smiled when Marlene opened it for him.

She returned the smile. "Oh, my goodness, it's about time you got back," she said. "I swear, Jimmy seems to think you're one of the best things ever happened to him." She glanced at the man holding the box. "If that's the stuff you went to get, he says to just take it into his office and he'll be there in a minute."

"Sure thing," Noah said, and he motioned for the man to follow him through the hallways. The office door was standing open, so he told the guy to set the box down on the floor and then go back to what he was doing.

Morgan came in a moment later and clapped Noah on the shoulder. "Good to see you, Rex," he said. He pointed at the box. "That them?"

Noah bent down and opened the flaps, took out one of the new phones, and handed it to Morgan, then pulled his own out of his pocket. "I went ahead and set one up for me. I hope that's okay. They work just like any other smartphone, so everybody should be able to handle them."

Morgan was grinning from ear to ear as he took the new phone out of its box and began looking it over. "This is actually pretty nice," he said. "Delphine? Is that a new brand?"

"Not really," Noah said. "Wally said they went out of business a few years ago, and his company bought the last of their inventory of encrypted phones. These weren't actually available to the general public—they were for government and police, that sort of thing—but he was able to buy them when they shut down. That's why I could get them so cheap."

Morgan nodded. "How do we get them turned on?"

"They're already set up for Artel, so all we have to do is take them to any Artel store. It only takes a few minutes to turn them on and copy the phone number from your old phone, and it even keeps all your contacts and such."

"Then let's get busy," Morgan said. "I'll start calling everybody to come and get their new phone, and they can run by the store out by Walmart and get it activated. The sooner we have this security, the sooner I'm gonna like it."

The big man sat down behind his desk and took out his current phone, then started making calls. Forney and his daytime security team were already present at the house, so they came to get theirs only a few minutes later. Noah explained how to take them to the Artel store and have the technicians there activate them.

"Looks a lot like the one I've got now," Forney said.

"There's a lot of similarities," Noah said. "I think the Delphine company may have copied one like yours. I can tell you they work great, though. I already got mine turned on."

"And once we've got them all working," Morgan said, "nobody can listen in on the calls we make to each other. Just make sure your boys know to be careful what they say when they call home or talk to anybody that doesn't have one of these. We don't need any feds getting any recordings of stuff they shouldn't know, know what I mean?"

"Don't worry, Jimmy," Forney said with a grin, hooking a thumb at Noah. "Rex already read me the riot act about that, and I've been doing the same thing to my guys ever since. We'll make sure nobody screws it up, won't we, Rex?"

"Damn straight," Noah said.

Forney took an extra phone for Ralph and then gathered up his men and the boy to go and get them activated. A couple of other men had shown up by then, and Noah went through the explanation again, and then again a few minutes later when the next group, with some of the women, arrived. As he handed over each phone, Noah adjusted his sunglasses and photographed each person.

It was almost eight thirty by the time all of the phones were passed out, with the exception of the ones that would go to the evening and night-security men. Morgan said he would have someone see to those later.

The two of them were talking about Noah's idea for enhancing the liquor business when his phone rang. He took it out and looked at it. He recognized Marco's number but deliberately put a slightly confused expression on his face as he answered.

"Hello?"

Marco's voice boomed through the speaker loud enough for Morgan to hear it across the desk. "That be Rex over dere? Hey, man, it be Aubrey! Aubrey LeBlanc, you remember me?"

Noah let a smile spread across his face, as Morgan cast him a quizzical look. Marco's Cajun accent was enough to make anybody curious.

"Aubrey," Noah said. "Yeah, it's Rex. How you been, man?"

"I've been out dat bad place goin' tree weeks now," Marco said loudly. "I call de man whose number you gave me, and he tell me this be your phone number. What you doing, now? You stay out of trouble, no?"

Noah chuckled. "Yeah, for the most part," he said. "I live in Arkansas, now. Where are you?"

"Ah, I be in Baton Rouge. I come see my sister, it do been a long time. I spend a few days, den I call dat man, I say tell me where is Rex, and he give me dis number. I will come see you, yes?"

"Aubrey, hold on a minute," Noah said. He muted the phone and looked at Morgan. "Jimmy, I know I'm new here and all that, but do you think you might have a place for a good friend of mine? We were in Beaumont together, and I got to know him when I was in the hole. He's our kind of people, as long as you don't mind a Cajun."

Morgan looked at Noah for a long moment, then nodded his head. "Tell him to come on," he said. "If you vouch for him, that's good enough for me. Where would you suggest we put him?"

Noah turned his grin into a vicious one. "You said something about making me an enforcer," he said. "Aubrey LeBlanc is the kind of man I'd want watching my back. He saved my ass a couple of times when we were out for rec, when some of the gangbangers tried to jump on me. Between the two of us, we took down seven of them. Even the COs were impressed."

Morgan gave him a single nod. "You realize I'll be holding you responsible for him, right? Okay, then, he's all yours. Tell him two grand a week, but make sure he understands he may have to pull a trigger sometimes."

"That won't be a problem," Noah said. He turned back to the phone and reactivated the microphone. "Aubrey? You want a job? Kinda like the job you had before you got jammed up—interested?"

There was quiet on the line for a moment, as "Aubrey" seemed to think it over. "I be working wit you?"

"Yep, you sure will. Good pay, and not much to worry about. I fell into something good, here, and I could use you. How soon can you get here?"

"You tell me where I come," Marco said, "I be dere tonight! We gon' be havin' fun, yes?"

Noah laughed. "You bet," he said. He told Marco to come to Berryville and call when he arrived, and had to hold the phone away from his ear when Marco let out a Cajun "*Oh, yez!*"

He ended the call and put the phone back into his pocket. "Aubrey's one of the few men in the world I think is tougher than I am," he said to Morgan, "but he seems to think the same about me. He'll always have my back, which means he's always got yours."

"Sounds good," Morgan said. "Now, let's get back on your trucker buddy."

Noah grinned. "Matt's out on a run for the next couple of days, but he called me back last night. I gave him kind of a vague notion of what I'm thinking, didn't want to say too much over the phone, but he's definitely interested. He'll be back at his place sometime in the next day or so, and then we can really talk about it."

"You're pretty sure he'll play ball? If we can get quality liquor by the truckload, it'll be worth spending the money to set up a warehouse."

"He will," Noah said. "After he got out, he and I kept in touch. I think I told you I almost went to work for him after I got out, right? I already knew his company was doing this kind of thing, but I was blown away when I saw just how big his operation really is. He's got a couple hundred trucks, and I bet twenty of them are always running hot trailers. I'd guess he could get us six or eight loads a week."

Morgan played with a calculator on his desk for a couple of minutes, then whistled. "If we could average thirty loads a month, that could be a clear profit of close to seventy million a year. Add that to what we make on the legitimate liquor sales, it'll probably get close to eighty or eighty-five million. That ain't nothing to sneeze at, Rex. You put this deal together, I'll cut you in for five percent."

Noah's eyebrows shot up, and he smiled. "Five percent? Geez, Jimmy, that's like four million dollars a year. For that kind of money, I may have to come up with a few more good ideas."

The two of them laughed together. "I'll be ready to hear them if you do," Morgan said. "Like I told you, I think you're exactly the kind of guy I've been looking for for a long time. You're smart, you're not afraid to do what has to be done, and you've already got some connections of your own. A guy like you can live real good, here, if you don't get too big for your britches."

Noah waved a hand in dismissal. "No chance of that," he said. "I'm not that great a businessman. The last thing in the world I'd ever want to do is try to run an operation even a tenth as big as this one. I know damn well I'd mess up and find myself right back in Bloody Beaumont, and that's the last thing I ever want. Me and Angie want to have kids of our own someday, and it just wouldn't work out for their daddy to be in the joint."

Morgan stared into his eyes for a moment, then smiled. "You stick with me, Rex," he said. "You'll go farther than you ever dreamed you could." He picked up his new phone and waved it at Noah. "Let's go get my phone turned on, okay?"

CHAPTER SIX

A s they left the Artel store an hour later, Morgan directed Noah to another building in town. "This is where Heather works," he said.

Noah parked the car in front of the little building that was marked only by a sign that read "Happy Maids." He looked at it for a moment, then turned to Morgan. "A cleaning service?"

Morgan laughed. "Not exactly," he said. "We do have plenty of girls that do cleaning, but a lot of these maids probably make more messes than they ever clean up. Most of their clientele are, let's just say, single men. They don't have a wife to clean house, but they also don't have one for other things, and that's where Heather and the girls come in. The men like it because all their neighbors see is a car with a Happy Maids sign pull up in front of the house and some pretty girl gets out and carries a bucket full of cleaning supplies to the front door. It's not really that big a secret, but everybody pretends it is. This is the main office."

He got out of the car, and Noah followed him into the building. He had seen Heather earlier in the morning, when she came to the house to pick up her new phone, and she gave both of them a big smile when she looked up from her desk to see them.

"Jimmy," she said. "And Rex, right? To what do I owe the pleasure this morning?"

"I'm just showing Rex around," Morgan said. "He's turned out to be a pretty bright guy, and I want him to get a good idea of everything I'm into. He's already come up with a couple of good ideas, like those phones we passed out this morning. The more he knows about what we do, the better the ideas he can come up with."

Heather turned her brightest smile on and aimed it at Noah. "Well, awesome," she said. "What would you like to know?"

Noah gave her a grin. "Well, I think I have a fair idea of what you do," he said. "On the other hand, it's not a business I've ever been involved with. Are there any particular problems that you run into?"

The pretty blonde made a nonchalant shrug. "Not a lot of them," she said. "Every once in a while one of the clients gets a little rough with one of the girls, or maybe forgets to mention that he doesn't have any money when she shows up. In either case we usually ask Jimmy to send someone out to visit the guy, and that seems to handle it. Of course, we never service them again."

"Okay," Noah said. "Have any of the girls been seriously injured?"

"Well, Jill got her jaw broken a couple months ago, and another girl got her arm broken once. Usually it's just a few bruises, though, nothing a little makeup can't cover."

Noah nodded. "How do you find out about these injuries? Is it after everything is already over, or do they have a way to let you know something is going wrong at the time?"

Heather looked at him blankly for a moment. "Well, it's after," she said. "I mean, we don't exactly have a way to watch what's going on inside the client's house, right?"

"Of course not," Noah said, "but each of the girls should have some way to call for help in a hurry if they need it." He turned to Morgan. "I'm thinking of something like a panic button, on a necklace, maybe. I'm sure I can find a way to get something like that, so all the girl would have to do is squeeze it hard, and it would show up on the computer here in the office that she was in trouble. If Heather had a man who could go to the rescue, it might keep things from getting out of hand."

Morgan grinned. "See what I mean? He's pretty bright."

Heather's eyes were wide, but she was smiling. "I actually like that idea," she said. "How about letting me keep Rex here, Jimmy?"

That got a laugh out of Morgan. "If I left him here," he said, "you wouldn't be paying much attention to the computer, or anything else. Don't let her fool you, Rex—Heather's just a bit of a nymphomaniac."

"Hey, there's nothing wrong with enjoying your work, now, is there?" The smile on her face told Noah that Morgan was probably correct.

"I think I need to keep Rex with me," Morgan went on, "but I'll have him look into these panic buttons. If we can find something and get it set up, I wouldn't have a problem with letting you have one of the boys for a watchdog. How's everything else going?"

"Pretty good," Heather said. "All of the offices are doing pretty well, right now, but I think Fayetteville is probably bringing in the most money. Of course, Fayetteville is a lot bigger than we are; they've got thirty girls over there. I've only got twelve out of this office, but they do stay pretty busy."

A door opened in the back of the building at that moment, and two women walked in together. They gave Morgan a wave, then turned into a room off the hallway that led to the back.

"That's Pam and Janine," Heather said. "They've already had a client each this morning, so they'll hit the showers and be ready for the next ones."

"Good," Morgan said. "It's all about keeping the inventory fresh." He laughed at his own little joke, and Noah offered a chuckle of his own.

They left a few minutes later, and Morgan told him to drive over into Eureka Springs. They'd gone more than halfway through the tourist town when he told Noah to take a right turn, and they went downhill into an area filled with very old storefront buildings. Morgan had him turn onto Springs Street and pointed to one, so Noah pulled into the parking lot beside it.

This particular building looked like it might have once been a furniture store, but the big glass windows had been painted over. It was a two-story building, but when they walked through the door it was instantly obvious that the second floor had long ago been removed. Noah was surprised to see dozens of slot machines and video gambling games. All of them seemed to be occupied, and there were scantily clad women walking around holding trays of drinks. A bar at the back of the large room seemed to be pretty busy.

"It isn't only the Indians around here who get to run casinos," Morgan said. "This little place makes me more than a million dollars every month, because there are several thousand people who convince themselves they can beat the games. They can't, of course, because they're all run by computers that are programmed to know when and how much to pay out. For every dollar somebody wins off one of these machines, it will take in almost five hundred dollars. That's what we call house odds, which means the house always wins."

A small man in an expensive suit came walking toward them. Noah recognized him as Leonard, another of the lieutenants he'd met that morning.

"Hey, Leonard," Morgan said. "Just showing Rex around. Everything going okay today?"

"It's going great, Mr. Morgan," Leonard said. "The hotels are pretty busy right now, and we're getting a lot of the guests coming over. Some of them even mentioned that they learned about us the last time they were here, and came back because they like our games."

Morgan turned to Noah. "An interesting little trivia fact about Eureka Springs," he said, "is that two of the most haunted hotels in the country are here, the Crescent and the Basin Park. People flock to them because they heard the ghost stories, but we make sure they find out about our little casino while they're here. Brings us in some new blood every day, right, Leonard?"

"Sure does," the little man said. "Right now, since it's fall, they're starting up the ghost tours again, and the guides are happy to pick up an extra hundred dollars a day for telling their groups about the casino. Keeps us pretty busy."

"That it does," Morgan said. "What do you think, Rex? Got any ideas how we can improve things here?"

Noah had realized as soon as they entered that, with the second floor gone, the room was more than just large; it was very tall. From the floor to the ceiling, he judged, was probably close to eighteen feet. That would have been reasonable if the store had once sold very large items of furniture, of course, but now it only meant there was a lot of empty space above all of the games and stools. "First thing I would do," he said, "is put in a surrounding mezzanine, like a second floor that's open in the middle so people can look down into all of this. Make it a VIP area and put in some soft, comfortable couches, someplace where your high rollers can get intimate with one of the girls. Put some special games up there, like real poker with dealers, real blackjack, a roulette wheel, maybe a craps table. If you tell your regular gamblers that they have to bank a few thousand dollars to get up there, it'll make everyone think they can win more if they get up the stairs." He looked at Morgan. "I haven't been around a lot of gambling, but I've read about how casinos use human nature to make people want to lose more money. If being a VIP means dropping more cash, those who can are going to do it."

Morgan looked around the high blank walls and nodded. "I can see it," he said. "Leonard, let's plan on closing down for a couple weeks next month for some renovations. Let all your regulars know that things are about to get a lot better here, all right?"

Leonard looked like he was about to hit a jackpot of his own, and Noah realized he must be working for a percentage of the house take. "I certainly will, Mr. Morgan. This is going to be exciting."

Morgan nodded and motioned for Noah to follow him, and they left the building. Instead of heading toward the car in the parking lot, however, Morgan turned and started walking down the street.

"There's a lot of history in this old town," he said. "A lot of famous people were connected to it back in the late 1800s, when it really got started. The story goes that one of the springs here, I don't know which one, had healing properties. Long time ago, they say an Indian princess who had gone blind was brought here by the tribe and got her sight back, and that story spread all over the place. I don't know who the first white man was to try it, but he claimed he got cured of some kind of ailment, and it seemed like lots of folks swore by it. There was a doctor who actually built a hospital where he claimed the spring would cure cancer, but I read where he got in trouble over that. The hospital is what we call the Crescent Hotel nowadays."

"It definitely looks old," Noah said. His eye was caught by a large neon sign that bore a surprising resemblance to male genitalia. "The Palace Hotel and Bath House," he read. "That sign..."

Morgan burst out laughing. "Every visitor to this town sees that sign, and they always have the same reaction. Yeah, it looks like a pecker and balls, but the interesting thing about that sign is that it was the very first neon sign ever installed west of the Mississippi River, and that it was made by the Frenchman who actually invented neon signs. It was sent on a ship from France to America, then on a train to Eureka Springs. Rumor has it that the reason it looks like that is because the place was actually a bordello at the time."

Noah looked from the sign to Morgan and back, then shook his head. "That is a bit of history I never would have imagined," he said. "I do like the architecture of these old buildings, though. Is that limestone?"

"Limestone blocks, yes. They were quarried just a few miles from here, in a place called Beaver. Some of the buildings also have dolomite blocks, but they've faded from the original red color, so it's hard to tell them apart from the limestone, anymore."

Morgan turned left and crossed the street, and Noah stayed right beside him. They entered a small building that looked like an antique store, and a gray-haired man looked up from behind the counter and smiled.

"Morning, Jimmy," he said. "Good to see you."

"Hey, Chuck," Morgan replied. "This is Rex—he's my new right hand. I'm showing him around so he knows everybody."

Chuck extended a hand, and Noah shook with him. "Good to meet you, Rex," he said, and then he looked back at Morgan. "What can I do for you fellers this morning?"

Morgan grinned. "Tell Rex what we do here, Chuck."

Chuck's eyebrows rose slightly, and his smile seemed to fade just a bit, but he looked at Noah without hesitation. "Why, we sell antiques," he said, but Morgan cleared his throat. Chuck relaxed a bit at that point, and his smile regained its brightness. "Of course, that isn't all we do," he said with a chuckle. "We make loans, Rex. Before I retired, I was a loan officer at one of the banks in town for almost thirty years, and people know me. I had been through a bad time not long before I retired—my wife had cancer, and passed away, but the medical bills just about wiped me out—so Jimmy offered to set me up in business and loaned me the money to open my little antiques store, here. I guess a lot of people thought I must've been rich, because they started coming and asking me if I could loan them some money, and we decided that it might be another good business for Jimmy to get into."

Noah nodded. "I can see where that would be profitable," he said. He reached up to adjust his glasses on his face again.

"It is," Morgan said. "People come from all over Northwest Arkansas to borrow money from Chuck, and most of the time they pay it back when they're supposed to. Every now and then, though, I have to send one of the boys to remind them to make a payment. It usually doesn't take long to collect."

Noah smiled. "I bet not."

That made Morgan chuckle. "Any ideas for this operation?"

Noah grimaced, then shrugged. "I'm afraid high finance isn't something I know much about," he said. "I'm guessing these are just signature loans? No collateral?"

"Yep. But don't get the wrong idea, this isn't the kind of thing you see in the big city with loan sharks. Chuck showed me that the way to make money by lending money is to let people make small payments they can afford, but keep the interest higher. Somebody borrows ten grand for his business, we charge him thirty-six percent interest, but he only has to pay it back at three or four hundred a month. With the interest, though, he's still paying me ten years later and I've made three and a half times what I loaned him."

With a grin, Noah said, "I think he probably knows a lot more about it than I do. I doubt I could really suggest anything he hasn't thought of."

Morgan chuckled. "That's okay, that's okay," he said. "I just want you to know all about the entire operation. You never know when I might need you to handle something, so you need to know exactly what I'm talking about if I tell you to come see Chuck."

From the corner of his eye, Noah saw Chuck's face pale just a bit. The man's smile never wavered, but Noah knew instantly that the old fellow was skimming some of the profits and was terrified Morgan might have found out. He turned and looked Chuck in the eye, then winked at him.

"I'll be happy to help anytime you need me, Chuck," he said. The old fellow nodded graciously, but his body language was screaming in terror.

Morgan didn't seem to notice, as he waved goodbye and led Noah back out of the building. They walked back toward the casino, where the car was waiting.

"The reason I'm giving you this little tour," Morgan said to him as they walked, "is because I want you to be able to think like I do. I've spent years knowing I was pretty much the smartest guy around here, and I've got high hopes for Ralphie because he ain't stupid, but I need somebody else I can trust who can pretty much figure out what I want without having to ask me. I think you might be that guy, Rex. What do you think?"

Noah thought about how to answer for only a couple of seconds, then looked directly into Morgan's eyes. "I've always known I was smart," he said. "I've always been able to look at things a little differently from everybody else, and that usually lets me see ways to improve something. Loans, that's not something I really know much about, but it did give me an idea for something else. Mind if I ask a blunt question?"

"Hell, no," Morgan said. "Spit it out. What do you want to know?"

Noah grinned. "Do you do anything in the insurance business?"

"Insurance? I'm not sure I follow."

"My sister, Katie, made a comment the other day that I thought was interesting," Noah said. "She said that she can go on vacation and leave her door standing wide open, because you don't put up with thieves and burglars in your domain. I'm thinking that some of the businesses around here are benefiting from that, and it seems to me they ought to be rewarding you for making them so much safer."

Morgan's eyes narrowed. "And how would you make that happen?"

Noah shrugged innocently. "I'd just have somebody pay them a visit and suggest they wanted to join the Morgan Mutual Benefits Association," he said. "Membership means nothing bad happens to their

business, and if somebody does break in or something, we do whatever it takes to find out who and shut them down. I think just about
any intelligent business owner would agree that protection like that
should be worth ten percent of their annual net, don't you?"

A light flared in Morgan's eyes as they suddenly got wider. "Holy
geez," he said. "Why the hell I ain't never thought of that?"

"Like I said," Noah replied, "I look at things a little differently.
You're already providing the protection, just because most other
criminal elements are scared to death of you. From what I gather,
there are probably thousands and thousands of businesses in Northwest Arkansas that should be members of the Association. I doubt if
many of them would be stupid enough to refuse to join, and you'd be
looking at getting ten percent of all the profits they make."

"We're talking billions," Morgan said, his voice hushed in awe.
"And if they don't join, of course, something really bad does happen.
Fire, something like that, maybe."

Noah just smiled at him as they walked into the parking lot and
got into the car. "That would probably work."

Morgan shook his head. "Man, I like the way you think," he said.
"I had never thought about something like that. I mean, I've heard
of the protection rackets that the mob used to use, and I guess this is
really the same thing, but I never considered just how much money
you can make with it." He looked over at Noah. "You ready for some
lunch?"

"Sure."

"Me, too. Cut out of here and take a left. I'll show you some of
the best food in all the Ozarks."

Noah drove back up the hill, where Morgan had him turn left
again. The winding road that went through town was busy with fall
tourist traffic, but it was only a few minutes before they came to the
hotel on the right and Morgan told him to turn in.

"The restaurant here serves the best fried chicken you'll ever eat anywhere," Morgan said. "You do like fried chicken, right?"

"One of my favorites," Noah said. He parked the car and locked it as he followed Morgan inside.

CHAPTER SEVEN

The woman in the lieutenant colonel's uniform was escorted into the office by one of the security guards, and Nick Weber looked her over carefully. She appeared to be in her early fifties, her hair a bit grayer than he would've expected a woman to allow, but she looked to be in good physical condition. He rose from his seat behind his desk and extended a hand, which she shook firmly.

"Colonel Hogan," he said. "We don't often see the Army here. What can I do for you?"

The woman who called herself Lieutenant Colonel Janice Hogan looked pointedly at the security guard, who glanced at Weber and waited for a nod before exiting the office. Once he was gone, she sat down in the chair just in front of Weber's desk and crossed her legs.

"Good to see you, Nick," she said, and Weber's eyebrows came down in the center. "I know, I know," she said, "the voice is familiar, right? Maybe this will help." She reached up with both hands and hooked her thumbs into what Weber had thought was a natural hairline. She lifted slightly and he suddenly saw the blonde hair that was tightly packed under the gray wig.

As she pulled the wig back down into place, Weber looked at her face again. "Allison? Allison Peterson, right?"

Allison smiled. "I didn't think I was that forgettable," she said. "You've come up in the world since I got transferred. Deputy Director of Analysis, and from everything I know, the job suits you well."

Weber grinned. "The pay isn't much better than it was when we worked in the Middle East room, but I don't spend as many late nights in the office as we did back then. What happened to you?"

"I got my own division," she replied. "I'm the director of E & E."

Weber's eyebrows suddenly shot upward. "Seriously?"

"Yep. You'll remember when I was called to the White House over my suggestion that a certain prime minister should be eliminated."

"Right, I remember."

"Well, the president and the joint chiefs decided to concentrate everything to do with assassination under a single agency and offered me the job of running it. Naturally, I took it. That's why, whenever your people want someone removed nowadays, you have to put in a request to my office. If I agree with that request, then I send one of my teams out to take care of it."

Weber leaned back in his chair and folded his hands across his belly. "I knew that somebody was making those decisions," he said, "but I didn't have any clue it was you. Congratulations. Now that I think about it, I think I'd have to agree that you're the right person for the job."

"Thanks, Nick," Allison said. "It's not always easy, but somebody's got to do it."

Weber nodded. "Somehow, though, I don't think you're here to reminisce about the good old days in the Middle East room. What can I do for you, Allison?"

Allison leaned slightly toward him. "Nick, there are very few people in this world I actually trust, and when it comes to the Company, I could count them on half of one hand. You're at the top of a very short list, and I need your help with something."

"Name it," Weber said. "Bear in mind that I'm only the deputy director, so I'm not certain how much good I can do you."

"I'm after intelligence. You've heard that the CIA has a mole, correct?"

Weber nodded again. "It's not exactly the best-kept secret around here."

"Well, that mole has been causing me a lot of headaches. A couple of months ago, my best team was almost compromised when one of its people was snatched and sold to the Chinese at the mole's direction. She underwent some pretty dramatic interrogation, but we managed to get her back before any real damage was done, and then we learned that the reason behind it all was that the Chinese were trying to identify that team's leader."

"Camelot," Weber said. "Right?"

"Well, I see you've done your homework. How much do you know about Camelot?"

"Not a lot, actually. We just see that code name come up from time to time. We've figured out that your organization uses mythical names for the teams, but Camelot seems to be one of your most active. There is enough chatter about Camelot in a lot of our information to tell me that the Chinese aren't the only ones trying to figure out who he is."

"True," Allison said. "He gave the Russians some fits a while back, and the Brits have tried to get information on who he really is, but it's the mole who almost accomplished it. Turns out there were several people in my organization who had been blackmailed into cooperation, but we've been able to identify them all, now, or at least we think so."

Weber scowled. "We've had a few of those in the Company, as well, which is one reason the very existence of the mole is not widely known. Our internal investigation wants to keep him from knowing exactly how much we've learned about him, so we never confirm or deny his existence. So far, most of our people think he's just a rumor."

Allison smiled. "Well, I can tell that you don't know much," she said. "I suspect we know considerably more than you do, in fact, because we set up a sting to try to catch him. Unfortunately, the only thing we've managed to learn so far is that he is a she."

Weber sat forward and put his hands on his desk. "A woman?"

"Yes. I'm here to see if giving you what I know will help us figure out together just who on earth she might be. Will you work with me on this?"

"Of course," Weber said.

"Good. The mole is a woman, approximately four feet and eleven inches tall, and appears to be in her late thirties or early forties. She would be considered trim and attractive, with the figure of a teenager. The one time she's been seen, her hair was blonde and her eyes were blue, and she went by the name of Monique. I've checked every roster of Company staff and employees I can get to, and nobody seems to fit that description. Any idea who she could be?"

Weber's eyes were narrowed as he seemed to be deep in thought. "Monique..." he whispered softly. "The name doesn't ring any bells, and I can't think of anybody who would fit that description. Hair and eye color can be changed, of course, but the size... Give me just a minute."

He got up from his chair and walked out of the office, leaving Allison where she sat. He was gone about five minutes, then came back in with a young woman following him.

"Colonel Hogan, this is Miranda Spillman. Miranda is one of my best analysts and the only one in my offices who knows that the mole exists for certain. That's because I assigned her to go through every bit of intelligence we've got on this person and report directly to me. I just told her what you shared with me, and I wanted you to hear her response for yourself."

Allison turned and looked at Miranda, who seemed nervous. "Mr. Weber says that you somehow determined that the mole is a woman who is slightly less than five feet tall, somewhere around forty years old, and who would be considered both fit and attractive, correct?"

"That's correct," Allison said.

"There's a woman who fits that description who has been seen several times in different situations that we know the mole was involved in. I do not have a name for her, but when I add her appearances to the information you've just shared with us, I suspect we may be talking about the same person. In each of the appearances I'm aware of, she has claimed only to be the representative of someone unknown, someone who seems to have sent her to influence a political action or decision. In some cases, she does so by seduction and blackmail. In others, she seems to appear shortly after a significant assassination, apparently to make sure the victim's successor is aware that no one is untouchable."

Allison rolled her eyes. "Well, at least she's been noticed. Do you have any other information about her at all? Anything I can add to the little bit we've got?"

Miranda pressed her lips together for a second, then nodded. "From what we can tell, she's an American. She is not, as far as we can ascertain, the employee of any government agency, but she seems to have some way to gain information from just about any of them. We know that she has used a threat of violence against loved ones to coerce others into doing her bidding, although none of the extortion victims we've identified has ever seen her face-to-face. All of the information we have on her comes from incidental eyewitness accounts, and until today, we would never have suspected that she was actually the mole, herself."

Allison looked at the girl for a moment, then smiled. "Okay, quid pro quo. I can see you're bursting at the seams to ask questions of your own, so go ahead."

The girl's eyes lit up. "How'd you gain your intelligence?"

"We knew that the mole was trying to get information about a particular operative, so we created a false dossier on that operative and allowed one of her victims to pass it off to her. She made contact with the operative using technology to conceal her identity and gen-

der, but agreed to a meeting because she wants this operative to perform certain work exclusively for her. This particular operative is the
most reliable eyewitness I have ever known, so we regard his description as completely accurate."

"Can another meeting be arranged?" Miranda asked.

"Not at this time, but we hope there will be one in the not too
distant future. Unfortunately, she arranges the meetings in such a way
that we don't have any advance warning. There's no way we can set
anything up ahead of time to try to capture her."

Miranda nodded. "Did your operative happen to notice anything
unusual about her hands?"

Allison's eyes narrowed suddenly. "No. What about them?"

"In one of the eyewitness descriptions, it was said that her hands
might be smaller than the rest of her body would suggest. They appeared to be about the size of a six-year-old child's hands. Being almost five feet tall, that means that her hands are slightly out of pro-
portion to her body. That would be a noticeable trait, so I was wondering if your operative saw it."

Allison frowned. "If he did, he didn't think it worth mentioning,"
she said, "and that would not be like him. He tends to report everything he sees. Is it possible that particular witness was simply incor-
rect?"

"Oh, certainly," Miranda said. "I've got three separate eyewitness
descriptions of this person, and only one of them mentioned the
small hands, so it could be nothing. That was why I asked you about
it."

"I'll make sure to tell him to look if he gets another opportunity.
If I find anything that corroborates it, I'll let Nick know, and he can
tell you."

"Thank you, Colonel," Miranda said. She glanced at Weber, who
nodded that she could go, and walked out the door.

"Well," Weber said, "at least that gives enough confirmation that we can now work on the assumption that the mole is a woman. My only real question is how she could be manipulating your people and mine if she isn't actually installed in one of our agencies."

"Yes," Allison said, "that is a pickle, isn't it."

THE REST OF NOAH'S day was similar, as Morgan directed him from one location to another, introducing him to even more of his top people. Noah managed to snap at least one photo of each, just by fiddling with his sunglasses from time to time. They made it all the way to a house in Fayetteville by midafternoon, where Noah was introduced to a man named David Walters.

When Noah adjusted his glasses again, Morgan looked at him and grinned. "Those things giving you a problem?" he asked. "I see you fiddle with them a lot."

Noah grinned. "They're new," he said. "I haven't got them broken in yet."

Morgan chuckled and turned back to Walters.

"Dave, here," Morgan said after the introduction, "handles special problems. He'll get all upset if I go into too much detail, but let's just say that if somebody comes to us and is having a serious problem with somebody, Dave is the guy I call to make sure that problem goes away. I think of it as a necessary service we offer, because most of the problems he handles involve removing somebody dangerous from a situation, if you get my meaning. Ex-husbands who tend to get violent, that sort of thing."

Noah had been briefed about Morgan's criminal activities and was aware that murder for hire was one of them, but no one had known who headed up that part of the operation. Noah smiled and shook Walters's hand while committing his name and face to memory.

"Good to meet you," he said. "Sounds like you're a good guy to know."

"For some people," Walters said. "Not for everybody."

Noah looked him in the eye as they shook, and he knew that the man was watching for him to flinch. After a couple of seconds, Walters actually smiled.

"I see a kindred spirit," he said. Noah gave a slight shrug, and they released each other's hands.

Walters looked at Morgan. "So, this is the new guy," he said, a statement rather than a question. "I've been hearing about him, and I was going to make a point of coming to meet him sooner or later. You might want to let me borrow him now and then. I think he might come in handy."

Morgan grinned but just looked at him. "You think so?"

Walters indicated Noah with a short nod of his head. "This guy's a killer, Jimmy," he said. "Make sure he's on our side, okay?"

"Hell, I know that," Morgan said with a chuckle. "First thing he ever did for me was kill the little sucker who tried to shoot Ralphie. Snapped his neck, what I heard."

"That's not that hard to do, if you can get the leverage. Not too many people really know how to do it, though." He turned to Noah. "How'd you learn it?"

"Beaumont federal prison," Noah said. "It was that or die."

Walters smiled. "My kind of guy," he said.

They gave Walters a phone and Noah explained it, then told him to go by the Artel store and have it activated on his number. "With these," Morgan said, "we can talk about anything right over the phone. No more having to speak in code, know what I mean?"

Walters nodded. "And you're sure it's secure?" He looked at Noah with this question.

"Absolutely secure," Noah replied. "These things were actually built for the government, but the guy I got them from had the encryption tweaked so that even the government can't break it. Nobody will be able to listen in on any call made between two of these phones, that's certain."

When they left Fayetteville, Morgan was ready to call it a day. Noah dropped him off at home an hour later and then headed for his place. He was almost back to the house when his phone rang, and he pulled it out to see that it was Marco calling.

"Hey," he said as he answered. "I'm all alone at the moment, and the line is secure."

"Cool," Marco said. "I'm about two hours out. Just wanted to check in and see how you want to handle this. Should I come see this fancy farmhouse of yours or just get a hotel room?"

"Come on to the house," Noah said. "I need to talk with you a bit before you meet anybody in the morning, anyway. I'll text you the address so you can come straight in."

"Okay, sounds good. Almost six thirty now, should I eat before I come?"

"I'll have Sarah save you some dinner. See you when you get here."

He ended the call, then used his thumb to punch in the address of the farmhouse and sent it off to Marco. When that was done, he tapped the speed dial icon for Sarah.

"Baby!" she said excitedly. "Are you headed home?"

"I am," Noah said. "I was calling to see if you want me to pick up something for dinner. We got company coming in a couple of hours, and we all know Marco's appetite."

"Nope, I'm making spaghetti. There'll be plenty, don't worry; we'll just keep it hot until he gets here. How was your day?"

"Pretty good. I've been meeting some of the top people, because Morgan has decided I'm his new right hand. I think things might just come together in the next few days."

"Cool. How long before you get here?"

"About five more minutes," Noah said. "See you then."

"Okay, baby, I love you."

"I love you, too," he said, and then he reminded himself that he needed to say that to her more often.

He dropped the phone back into his pocket and relaxed, watching the road ahead and occasionally glancing into the rearview mirrors. The sun was a little low in the sky, but it was still daylight, so Noah looked again when a car in the distance behind him suddenly flashed its headlights.

The car was gaining on him rapidly, and Noah kept flicking his glance to the rearview mirror to watch it, even as he was paying attention to the road. The car was black and wasn't one he had noticed before, so he eased his pistol from its holster and laid it in his lap.

It came up behind him and hung back a couple of car lengths, but he couldn't make out who was driving. The lights flashed again, and then he heard the horn honking. Somebody was definitely trying to get his attention.

His next turn was coming up, so he put on the signal and began to slow. The car behind him also put on a turn signal, so he made it around the corner and pulled over to the side of the road. His follower parked behind him, and then the driver's door opened.

The man who climbed out was Justin Haggard, allegedly the man who had hired Benny Smoot to try to kill Ralph Morgan a few days earlier. Noah gripped the pistol as the man walked toward his car, but he noticed that Haggard kept both of his hands out where they could be seen. He powered down the window and watched Haggard in the mirror on the door.

"Mr. Madison?" Haggard called while he was still approaching the car. "Mr. Madison, my name is Justin Haggard, and I need to talk to you. I'm unarmed, Mr. Madison. Can we just talk for a minute?"

Noah opened his door and stepped out, the gun visible in his hand as he did so. He didn't aim it at Haggard but made sure the man could see that it would take only a split second to do so. He quickly looked around to be sure that there were no other vehicles in the area and there was no place where any other people might be hiding nearby.

"What can I do for you?" Noah asked.

"You can just listen for a minute, please? Would you do that?"

"I'm listening. Go ahead."

"Okay, look," Haggard said. "I heard that the word is going around that I tried to pay somebody to kill that Morgan boy. Man, I swear to you that's not true. Everybody says Morgan has put out a contract on me, but I heard you were supposed to be the new second-in-command, so when I saw your car go by I thought—well, I thought maybe I could try to get you to listen."

Haggard was a big man, and Noah was struck again by his resemblance to Arnold Schwarzenegger. He had the same square face and iron jaw and was every bit as muscular as Schwarzenegger had been in his younger days. He had stopped about ten feet away and was still keeping his hands out in plain sight, but the sun was going down behind him and making it hard to see his face.

Noah used his left hand to reach into his pocket and pull out the sunglasses Wally had given him, then took them out of their case and put them on. They did help to cut the glare a bit, but it was the special features they had that he was most interested in at the moment.

"You didn't hire Benny Smoot to shoot him?" Noah asked.

"No, sir," Haggard said, "I sure didn't."

Still keeping part of his attention on Haggard, Noah watched the little orange dots. None of them changed color, and the text box did not appear.

"Why would somebody try to set you up for it?"

Haggard shook his head, his face reflecting bewilderment. "Mr. Madison, I'd say somebody wants me to get killed," he said. "All I know is that people have been telling me the last few days that Morgan wants me dead, and to be perfectly honest, I'm so scared I can't even think. I heard that you were working with him, and about your black Charger, and when I saw you go by a bit ago..."

Still no change in the dots, and Noah realized that the man was probably telling the truth. He slipped the pistol into its holster but kept his hand on the butt.

"Any idea who really did hire Benny?" Noah asked him.

Haggard suddenly looked nervous, and Noah watched the display in the sunglasses. "I—I might have an idea," he said. "I think it might've been some people I've been working with, but I swear I didn't know anything about it at the time. I'm not even sure, now, you understand, but I think I may have figured something out."

Still no sign of deception, so Noah relaxed a bit more. "Who is it you're working with?"

Haggard grimaced but said, "His name is James Cabot. He—he hired me a while back to try to set up a kind of competition for Morgan's drug operation, see if maybe I could move some stuff for him and make some fast money. It was just some pot and a few pills, nothing big, but I got told real quick that if I didn't stop, something bad was going to happen. I went back to Cabot and told him I was out, and that was the day that dumb-ass tried to kill the kid."

Noah looked at him for a moment, then reached a decision. "So, you're a drug dealer? Why didn't you just go work for Sneed, if you wanted money?"

There was another grimace. "I used to," he said, "but Ronnie got it in his head I was stealing money. I wasn't, but he wouldn't listen to anything I had to say about it, and he kicked me out." Noah noticed that the dots still did not change, indicating that Haggard was telling the truth. "I been trying to find work for the last couple months, but nobody would hire me for anything that could really make a buck, till Cabot offered to let me try to move some product for him."

"So, you think Cabot is the one who hired Benny?"

"Yeah, I do," Haggard said. "Benny, I've been knowing him for a few years, and he'd buy any dope off anybody. I know he bought some off Cabot, because Sneed cut him off a while back over not paying when he was supposed to. Hell, I sold him some myself a few days before all that."

Noah took out his phone and dialed Morgan's number, motioning for Haggard to stay where he was.

"Rex?" Morgan said as he answered the phone. "Everything okay?"

"Jimmy, Justin Haggard just flagged me down out here in the country," Noah said. "He claims he had nothing to do with hiring Benny, but that it was a man named James Cabot who was trying to muscle in on your drug territory. That name sound familiar?"

"I know who Cabot is," Morgan said. "You think Haggard could be telling the truth?"

"I've always been pretty good at telling when somebody is lying to me," Noah said, "and I get the feeling Haggard's telling me straight. How do you want me to handle this?"

Morgan was quiet for a moment, then spoke up again. "Haggard is worthless," he said. "Unless he's willing to give up Cabot, like in helping you kill the bastard, then just put a bullet in his head. If he'll help, then tell him I'll give him one more chance. He's not very bright, but he's strong as a damned ox. I can always use him out at the yard, if nothing else. Think you can handle it?"

"I'll take care of it," Noah said. He ended the call and dropped the phone back into his pocket. "Jimmy said to tell you that if you're willing to help me get Cabot, he'll give you one more chance with him. You might have to go work out at the junkyard, but at least you wouldn't be dead. What do you say?"

Haggard swallowed hard. "I know where he's staying," he said. "But, Mr. Madison, if he figures out I'm helping you, then he'll kill me faster than Mr. Morgan would."

Noah smiled. "He can't kill you if he's dead."

CHAPTER EIGHT

Cabot, according to Haggard, was living just a short distance across the state line in Shell Knob, Missouri. He was known to be a fairly large player in the drug business up around Springfield and Joplin, and had apparently decided to try to move farther south.

"He's got several people at his house," Haggard said. "I was up there once, and he had like five guys just hanging around, every one of them packing."

"Just tell me how to get there," Noah said. "I'll handle it."

Haggard gave him directions, and Noah made him repeat them twice so that he was certain he could remember them. When he was sure he knew the way, he asked, "Did you have a phone number for him?"

"Yeah," Haggard said. He pulled out his phone, moving very carefully as he did so, and found the number in his contacts. He read it off to Noah, who added it to his own.

"Here's my number," Noah said, scribbling it down on a scrap of paper and passing it to Haggard. "You call me tomorrow and I'll let you know if it's safe to go see Jimmy. Until then, just try your best not to run into anybody who might want to score on you. Just about any of Jimmy's people might figure killing you would get them some brownie points, right now."

Haggard took the number and got back into his car, and the man was gone only seconds later. Noah watched his taillights as they rolled north, then took out his phone once more.

"Babe?" Sarah asked as she answered the call. "Why aren't you home yet?"

"Something came up," he said. "I need to go and handle a situation for Mr. Morgan. May take me an hour or so, so keep some of that spaghetti hot for me, too."

Sarah sighed. "Okay," she said. "I'll see you when you get here."

"Okay, baby," Noah said. "I love you."

The smile was audible in her voice as she repeated those words back to him, and then the phone went dead.

Noah climbed back into the Charger and started it up, then spun it around and pointed it north on the two-lane blacktop. The house Cabot was staying in was only about thirty minutes away, but Noah decided to push the car and get there more quickly. It was only about twenty-two minutes later that he actually found the place, a big Victorian-looking house on one of the roads that worked its way around Table Rock Lake.

The sun was getting quite low, and there were lights on in the house and around it. Noah cruised past it sedately, trying not to draw attention from the two men he could see obviously standing guard near the base of the front steps. The house sat back about a hundred yards from the road, amidst a stand of trees. By the time he'd gone an eighth of a mile, it was invisible to him once again.

He traveled for another mile, then found a place to turn around and headed back. He stopped just short of where he would be visible to the guards and took out his phone. He scrolled through the contacts quickly until he found the one he had just added earlier for Cabot, then tapped it with his thumb.

"Yeah," a gruff voice answered.

"Mr. Cabot?" Noah asked.

"Who's asking?"

"Mr. Cabot, this is John Mackey. I was wondering if you might be at home this evening. I've got something I think you might want."

"John Mackey? I know you?"

"Not yet, sir," Noah said, "but I'm hoping you might have an opening for me. See, I've got a little piece of video that I think you might want to see. You know who Justin Haggard is?"

There was a moment of silence and then, "Yeah, I know him. What's this video about?"

"I sort of got some video of Justin Haggard telling Jimmy Morgan that you were the one who hired that junkie to try to kill Ralphie. I'm about fifteen minutes from your place on the lake, and I was wondering if I could bring it by and let you see it."

"That big son of a bitch," Cabot said. "You know where I live?"

"Yes, sir," Noah replied. "Like I said, I can be there in about fifteen minutes if you're there."

"I'm here. You get on up here and let me see that. We'll talk about a job while we're at it, okay?"

"Yes, sir, I'll be there shortly." Noah ended the call and dropped the phone back into his pocket, then put the car back in gear and let it idle slowly toward the house. He had turned off his lights and reached down alongside the seat to turn on the infrared display. The image of the road ahead was projected onto the inside of the windshield, which allowed him to see clearly even though the sun had finally dropped low enough that the trees made it dark.

Noah turned into the driveway of the house a few seconds later, and the two guards suddenly focused on him. He reached down alongside the seat and pressed the first button, and the cross hairs appeared on the video screen. Noah reached up and tapped on the image of the guard closest to him, then squeezed the trigger button on the steering wheel.

He held it for a full second, and a hail of 9 mm bullets shredded the guard. The second man was scrambling to aim a gun his way, so Noah tapped the screen again and squeezed the trigger once more. The man dropped like a stone, but suddenly two others came rushing out the front door of the house.

Noah reached down beside the seat again, pressing the second button that activated the high-explosive shotgun. The cross hairs changed color on the screen, and he tapped the image just beside where the two men were crouching down behind a pillar. When he squeezed the trigger, there was a loud *bang* and that section of the porch exploded.

Noah tapped again, centering the cross hairs on the front door of the house, then fired again. Another explosion blew out all of the windows on the front of the ground floor, and Noah took his foot off the brake and rushed the car up closer to the house.

Machine gun fire suddenly came from one of the blown-out windows, so Noah pointed the car toward it. Bullets were ricocheting off the car, flying in every direction as he tapped the screen again. This shot blew out a large section of the walls, and part of the second story began to sag. He tapped the screen again and aimed the shotgun toward the window on the opposite side, and when the explosive round went off, the second floor simply fell downward, sliding forward as the ground floor collapsed completely.

Noah waited for a moment, but there was no further gunfire and no other signs of life. The remains of the house were on fire, so he turned off the cross hairs, spun the car around, and headed back toward Arkansas.

As soon as he crossed the state line, Noah took his phone out of his pocket and dialed Morgan. "Problem is handled," he said. "Apparently, Mr. Cabot was messing around with something that was explosive, because I understand his house just blew up."

"Blew up?" Morgan asked, laughing uproariously. "Man, Rex, you have got to tell me how you managed that one. You carrying hand grenades or something?"

"Didn't need one," he said. "Just a few well-placed rounds was all it took. People really shouldn't mess with things that go boom, you know?"

Thirty minutes later, Noah parked the car beside Sarah's and climbed out. He could smell the spaghetti by the time he got to the front door, and his stomach was already rumbling for it.

"Hey, baby," Sarah said, throwing her arms around him and giving him a big kiss. "That didn't take long."

"Not very," he said. "Let's eat, and I'll tell you about it afterward."

Neil was sitting at the table with his computer and looked up at Noah. "Afterward? What's wrong with telling us while we eat?"

Noah shrugged. "I guess I can," he said. "I just had to go up into Missouri and blow up a guy's house."

Sarah froze in the act of putting spaghetti on a plate for him and turned to stare at him. As it turned out, he had to explain the whole thing before he got his dinner.

The spaghetti was delicious, and Noah made sure to say so more than once. Neil told him that he'd received a message from Molly, telling him that Allison had spoken with her contact at the CIA but that they had been unaware the mole was a woman. They had no idea who Monique might be, but it had been suggested that her hands might be unnaturally small. Noah stopped and thought about it for a moment, but shook his head. He hadn't paid enough attention to her hands to remember them.

Marco pulled in driving a pickup truck while they were still at the table, so Sarah opened the door for him and then handed him a plate. "Help yourself," she said. "There's plenty, and you really want to hear what Noah has been up to today."

Marco looked at Noah. "Oh-oh," he said. "Did I miss out on some fun?"

Noah told the story again, as Marco wolfed down two plates of the spaghetti. When he finished eating, Noah showed him the spare bedrooms and let him choose one, and then he brought in his bags.

"Man," Marco said as he sank onto the couch, "that is a long drive. I'm beat."

"Yeah, that's how I felt last night," Sarah said. "You made good time, though."

"Not bad. I had to talk my way out of a speeding ticket, but lucky for me the cop was a babe."

Sarah rolled her eyes. "Oh, come on, seriously?"

Marco laughed and took out his phone, poked at its screen for a moment, and then held it out so she could see. There was a selfie he had taken with a female Missouri state trooper, and it looked like the officer was having the time of her life.

"Geez, Marco," Sarah said, "what would Renée think right now?"

Marco looked at the picture on the phone, then looked back up at Sarah. "She'd think it was a good deal I talked my way out of a two-hundred-dollar speeding ticket." He suddenly started laughing. "I'm just playing with you," he said. "I've had that picture on my phone for months. I actually dated that girl for a while."

"You better get rid of it before Renée sees it," Neil said. "Women don't have a great sense of humor when it comes to pictures like that."

Marco looked at the picture sadly. "Yeah, I probably should." He turned his eyes back up to Sarah. "And thank you so much, by the way, because guess what she and I were doing last night. We were looking at engagement rings on the internet." He shook his head. "I guess I should've seen it coming, though. She's been awfully nice to me, lately."

Noah looked at Sarah, then turned to Marco. "Worse things could happen," he said.

MARCO RODE IN WITH Noah the next morning, letting out a low whistle when he saw Morgan's house.

"I do declare," he said, already in character, "dat be one big fancy house. You sure dey gon' let me in dere?"

Noah smiled at him. "Just be cool, Aubrey," he said. "Believe me, you're gonna fit right in."

They climbed out of the car and walked past the two men standing watch outside, who all but saluted Noah and watched Marco like a pair of hawks. Marco stopped just in front of them and looked from one man to the other.

"What you think," he said, "you don' never see a big Cajun before? Wait till I get settle in, I gon' make some gumbo what make your mout' think it die and go to heaven."

"Aubrey, come on," Noah said, standing at the door. "He's with me, guys, he's cool."

The two security men looked at each other, then shrugged as Marco walked past them and up the steps. Marlene was just opening the door when he got beside Noah, and Noah introduced him.

"Marlene, this is my friend Aubrey, from Louisiana. Aubrey, this is Marlene, and she's a better cook than you've ever seen."

Marlene grinned. "Rex, any friend of yours is welcome here," she said. "Breakfast is still on. You boys want some?"

Marco made a show of sniffing the air. "*Mon ami*," he said, "do dat be bacon I smell on de air?"

Marlene burst out laughing as she pushed the screen door open. "I guess that's my answer," she said. "Come on in, boys, there's plenty."

She let Noah lead Marco to the dining room, where Jimmy and Ralph Morgan were sitting with Scott Forney and another man Noah didn't know. Morgan looked up and smiled, a slice of bacon in one hand and a forkful of scrambled eggs in the other.

"Hey, Rex," he said. "This your buddy?"

"Yes, sir," Noah said. "Aubrey LeBlanc, I'd like you to meet Jimmy Morgan. Mr. Morgan is my boss, and he's the one who said I could hire you."

Marco stepped forward and bowed low. "Mr. Morgan," he said, his accent thick, "I do be one grateful son of a bitch. My frien' Rex, he tells me you a good man to work for, and I be yours to comman'."

Morgan laughed. "Hell, we need to get him to teach manners to the rest of the boys. Good to meet you, Aubrey. Now grab a squat on a chair and let Marlene bring you a big plate of eggs and bacon."

"Oh, Boss Man, you don' gon' have to tell me twice, no!" He pulled out a chair and sat down, then picked up the cloth napkin that was lying on top of the plate in front of him and tucked it into his shirt like a bib.

Morgan was still laughing, so Noah pulled out a chair and took a seat, himself. He laid the napkin to the side as Marlene carried a huge skillet full of eggs into the room and started scooping them on-to their plates. She was back a moment later with a plate of bacon and set it on the table between them. "Eat up, boys," she said. "There's plenty more if we need it."

Noah and Marco dug in, and Marco's face made it clear that he was enjoying one of the best breakfasts he had ever had. The conversa-tion around the table was mostly about Noah's encounter with Justin Haggard the night before.

"So, how sure are you that Haggard was telling you the truth?" Morgan asked.

"I'm certain, now," Noah said. "I had him give me Cabot's phone number and called the guy. I told him I had video of Haggard telling you that Cabot was the one who tried to have Ralphie killed, and he didn't deny that it was true. He just wanted to see it, and then he wanted to hire me to kill Haggard."

"Okay, so what happened?"

Noah had prepared for this question. "Cabot was living in this big fancy log cabin up on the lake, but he was stupid enough to have somebody making meth in the basement. I snuck up and snooped around, found that out and spotted the big propane tanks, so I just backed off a ways and started pumping bullets into them until they blew up. Took out the whole house and everybody in it. I stayed around long enough to be sure there were no survivors and then split."

Morgan had stopped chewing, and his mouth was hanging open. He stared at Noah for a moment, then burst out laughing. "Holy crap," he said. "Rex, you absolutely blow my mind. I don't know anybody else who would've thought of that."

Noah shrugged. "He had several people in the house, and I know at least some of them were armed. I didn't want to get into a shootout, so it seemed like the best move."

"Whatever, it worked. Now, as for Haggard, I said I'd give him another chance if he cooperated, and he did. I'll put the word out this morning that he's not to be touched, and we'll get a message to him to come see me at the yard this afternoon. Like I said, he strong as an ox. I can find somewhere to put him to work."

"I told him to call me today," Noah said. "I'll give him that message when he does."

The conversation turned to which aspects of the Morgan empire were most likely to need supervision that day, although Ralph did suggest to his father that it was time for Ronnie Sneed to be transferred to another division.

"I got something in mind for him," Morgan said. He turned to Noah. "Rex, did you get hold of your friend with the trucking company yet?"

"I'm afraid he hasn't called me back yet," Noah said. "I expect to hear from him anytime, probably today."

"Well, I hate to start the distributorship without confirming that he can bring us the kind of inventory you expect, but it might be smarter to go ahead and at least take the first steps toward it." He turned back to his son. "I'll come by and get Ronnie this morning. There's a building up in Blue Eye that's big enough, and it has a ten-bay loading dock. Belongs to that TV preacher, but he's not using it, and I've never met a preacher who didn't like money."

"Thanks, Pa," Ralph said. "He keeps trying to tell me how I should do things, but I've already got more product out the door than he ever did in a single week."

"And, speaking of product," Morgan said, looking back at Noah. "Shame about Cabot," he said, "and an even bigger shame about his wife—she was a looker, but that woman was colder than the bottom of a well." He winked. "You know, there's gonna be an awful lot of people in Missouri looking for a new supply of their drugs. Probably too much for Ralphie to handle, though, don't you—"

"Like hell," Ralph said. "Murkowski's probably going to take over Joplin, and I'd bet on Stinky Dupree doing the same in Springfield, but that leaves most of Southwest Missouri up for grabs. I'll have to send a couple people out there to hook up with the dealers, but most of the small-towners aren't going to want to deal with either of those pricks. I'll get them."

Morgan was chuckling. "That's how you handle a teenager, boys," he said. "You just tell 'em they can't do something, and they'll do it to spite you." He looked at his son one more time. "You're right about Murkowski; he was Cabot's lieutenant in Joplin, and he's got enough loyalty from the punks up there that he'll be able to hold on to it. Dupree, I don't think so. I know Cabot had him in charge up there, but from everything I hear, nobody liked him or trusted him. Duane Goodwin's the number two up there, and if he has a lick of sense, Dupree will be in the ground before the day is over."

Ralph was frowning. "Well, maybe," he said. "Dupree's gonna be expecting it, though. He might be hard to kill, and he'll probably send somebody after Goodwin just to try to show who's boss."

His father shrugged. "You just keep us out of it," he said. "My money is on Goodwin, just because the foot soldiers up there know what Dupree was like whenever Cabot wasn't keeping him under control. I don't care how much product you got, you can't scare your people into selling more of it if the customers just aren't there, but that's how Dupree likes to work. If his dealers don't sell as much as he expects them to, he picks one of them for an example and blows his head off." He shoved a forkful of eggs into his mouth and shook his head. "That's not how you motivate people."

There was a bit more discussion about the drug business, but then Ralph was ready to go. Forney got up to follow him, but the other man stayed seated as the two of them left. Once they were gone, Morgan pointed at the newcomer with his fork.

"Rex, this is Eric Carpenter," he said. "Eric is a lawyer, the good kind. He never tries to tell me what I can't do, and he doesn't try to tell me what I can do, either."

"No," Carpenter said with a grin. "What I do is ask him what he wants to do, and then I tell him how to get away with it."

Noah grinned but raised his eyebrows. "I wish I'd known you five years ago," he said. "You sound like the kind of lawyer I needed."

"Well, he's the kind I need, right now," Morgan said. "I'm thinking about making a couple changes, things that will make it a little easier to clean up the money that comes in. With all these rules the banks are putting on us nowadays, it can get pretty hard to get all this cash into the proper accounts. Eric's here to figure out a way to simplify that."

"I'm glad that's his job," Noah said. He shook his head. "I wouldn't have a clue where to start."

"Oh, it isn't really all that hard," Carpenter said. "The trick is to buy and sell. You buy up things that are easy to turn over, and you pay cash. When you sell, though, you insist on a check or a bank transfer. You'll end up losing a little bit or breaking even, at best, but it gets the money into the financial system so that you don't have all that Financial Crimes Enforcement BS hanging over your head."

"Which we don't need," Morgan finished for him. "I told Eric about your trucker buddy and what we're fixing to do on setting up a liquor distributorship, and he said this is ideal. We can send people out to buy booze in other parts of the state and then move it with our inventory. My bookkeepers can cook the numbers so it just looks like normal everyday business, but every load we drop at a bar or liquor store will mean some of that hot money gets washed and dried."

"Sounds like a plan," Noah said. "You want me and Aubrey with you today?"

"I'm not gonna be all that busy, today. Why don't you take your pal there and just show him around? And that reminds me, you said he just got out, too? What kind of paper problems you got, Aubrey? Probation with the feds?"

"Oh, no, sir," Marco said. "I been de bad boy in de feds, dey keep me almos' all de whole time in de hole. When you like me, you don' get no good time. I done did every damn day o' my time, all nine years. I got no paper, no probation, no parole, no nothing."

Morgan nodded. "That's good. You need a gun?"

Margo grinned, and his eyes seemed to hold an evil glint. "I got me a gun de same day I got out," he said. "Me, I keep two guns. One for shoot anybody I don' like, and one for shoot his friend if he got any."

Morgan laughed. "You know, Rex," he said, "it just about sounds like you've got your hands full with this one."

Noah chuckled and shrugged. "Aubrey's cool," he said. "Like I said, he's always got my back."

Morgan started to speak, but Noah's phone suddenly rang. He pulled it out and glanced at the display, then got to his feet. "Gentlemen, please excuse me," he said. "I need to take this call."

He moved to the far end of the dining room and put the phone to his ear. "Hello?"

As Noah had expected, the next voice he heard was Monique's. "I have a job for you," she said without preamble. "You'll need one or two days away from your mission, and I need you to be available to me within the next two to three hours. You may be gone overnight, so prepare for it."

"Hey, Matt," Noah said. "I'll have to ask if I can get away, but we definitely want to get this show on the road. Hang on just a minute, let me check with my boss."

He turned and looked at Morgan, who was watching him curiously. "Jimmy, this is Matt, the trucker. He wants to know if I can go and meet with him to discuss the whole thing in person." Noah grinned sheepishly. "Matt just doesn't like to talk about things over the phone—that's how they busted him last time."

"Yeah, that's no problem," Morgan said. "How long you gonna be gone?"

"Probably just a couple of days," Noah replied. "Thing is, we might be able to get this happening pretty quick, and that would help with what Mr. Carpenter is doing, too, right?"

Morgan nodded. "Yeah. Okay, do what you gotta do, but try not to be gone any longer than necessary. I need people to get used to seeing you around here, and they can't do that if you're gone all the time."

"Trust me," Noah said, "I'm ready to stop doing all this traveling." He put the phone back up to his ear. "Okay, it's all set. Where you want to meet up?"

"Go to Memphis and straight to the airport. Call me when you get there, and I'll give you further instructions then. Make sure that nobody knows where you're going." The line went dead.

"Okay, that sounds good," Noah said, pretending the conversation was still going on. "I'll be in touch this afternoon." He put the phone back into his pocket and walked back over to the table. "He's gonna meet me about halfway, in Indiana. Do you have anything you want Aubrey doing while I'm gone?"

"Not that I know of," Morgan said. "Just let him take it easy till you get back, I guess. You can start showing him around then."

"Yes, sir. Aubrey, you done eating yet?"

Marco said he was finished, said goodbye to Morgan, and then went into the kitchen to give Marlene a hug. When she finished laughing and blushing, he let her go and followed Noah out the front door. As he passed the two security men, he suddenly spun around and pointed his fingers at them, his thumbs up in the air in the classic hand symbol for guns, and yelled *bang*! Both of the men stared at him like he was some kind of an idiot, and Marco launched into a long belly laugh as he got into the car.

"Oh, but did you see de faces on dem boys? Dey almos' piss deyselves..."

CHAPTER NINE

"That was Monique on the phone," Noah said as soon as they were out on the road. "She wants me in Memphis, at the airport, as soon as possible. I'm going to leave this morning."

"Want me to go with you?" Marco asked.

Noah shook his head. "No. Whatever it is she wants me to do, I have to go alone."

The Charger rolled rapidly through the countryside, and Noah saw Sarah step out onto the porch as he pulled up to the house. He and Marco got out of the car and walked up the front steps, where she was holding the screen door open for them.

"Monique called," he said. "I'm supposed to go to Memphis right now."

Sarah stared at him for a moment, then nodded solemnly. "Do you think she knows..."

"We can only hope not," Noah said. "If she does, I'll deal with it however I have to." He walked into the bedroom and grabbed his overnight bag from the closet, tossed it onto the bed, and started packing. Sarah went into the bathroom to get his shaving kit and brought it out to him.

"I hate this," she said. "This woman is pulling your strings like a puppet, even though she really has no power over you at all. I wish you could just kill her and get it over with."

"If I get the chance, I will," Noah replied. "I think Allison would rather have her in custody, but being dead would put an end to her influence just as thoroughly."

Neil stepped into the room and handed Noah something wrapped in paper towels. He glanced at the bundle and pulled one of the towels away to see a stack of four black, eight-inch-long knives, each of which bore a single bright red number.

"I made those for you the other day," Neil said, "but I forgot all about them until I heard you say you were going to Memphis. A metal detector won't pick them up, so you should be able to carry them right onto an airplane. And yes, before you ask, each one has a detonator chip embedded in it. Give me your phone and I'll program the codes into it. Just be sure you know which one you want to set off before you tell it to go, and be careful because they're sharp as hell."

Noah handed him the phone and went back to what he was doing. Packing took him only a few minutes, and then he took a few more minutes to hold his wife. When he let her go, Neil handed him his phone.

"I marked them 'knife 1, knife 2,' etc. They're at the top of your list."

"Thanks," Noah said. "This was a very good idea." He turned and looked at Sarah again. "I'll be back," he said. "You can be sure of that. Keep Marco here until I get home, just in case any problems arise. And keep your guns handy, you and Neil. If she does know I've gotten rid of her little bomb, this could be a ruse to make you vulnerable. Anybody tries to come in this house, you shoot first and ask all the questions later."

"No one will get in," Sarah said. "Neil's been working on security, you might say. He's got some little toys from the printer scattered around the yard, and he's memorized which ones are where so that he can set them off if he needs to."

"Good thinking. Tell him not to hesitate if the time comes." He tilted her chin up and kissed her, then picked up his bag and headed for the door. Sarah followed him out onto the porch, with Neil and Marco right behind her.

"Come back, boss," Neil said. "And if you can bring that bitch's head with you, so much the better."

"I'll definitely try," Noah replied. "You guys take care of Sarah for me." He kissed her one more time and walked down the steps and got into the car. The big engine fired up, and the car backed into the yard, turned around, and was gone.

"He'll be back," Sarah said. "He will."

Noah waited until he was through Berryville and on a stretch of open road, then took out his phone and called Allison. She answered on the second ring.

"Camelot," Noah said. "Monique called almost an hour ago. I'm en route to the Memphis airport. No idea where I'm going yet; she'll let me know when I get there."

"Damn," Allison said. "Any idea whether she's planning to meet you?"

"I don't know anything yet. Just that I'm supposed to call her when I get to the airport. I'm assuming she's planning to send me somewhere, and I'll let you know where if I get the chance."

"No, don't. She'll undoubtedly have someone watching you at the airport, so don't risk making a call from there." She sighed. "I'm tempted to have someone of our own there, but I'd have to use someone from the FBI, and I can't be certain she wouldn't know about it. That would blow your cover with her, and we just can't risk that right now. Do whatever you have to do, Noah. If she does meet you, try to get any additional information you can that will help us identify her. In this day and age, it seems like it would be impossible for anyone to stay hidden, but she's managing it. That has to come to an end, somehow."

"I agree. If I get the chance, I plan to terminate her."

"I prefer to take her alive, if possible, but you make the call. Dead or alive, we need to figure out who the hell she is so that we can try to determine just how much damage she's done to national security."

"Yes, ma'am," Noah said. "So far, though, she seems to be more interested in wealth and power than actually engaging in serious espionage. If she's using us to make herself rich, it might not be that hard to clean up the mess once she's been put down."

"You could be right, but I have to assume the worst. She's obviously got some kind of connections to the intelligence community, or she couldn't possibly know some of the things she knows. Just the fact that she's been able to identify operatives of various agencies, including our own, and subvert them means that she has access to some of the most secret information in the world. I don't know about you, but that makes me pretty nervous."

"I can't disagree. I'll let you know more as soon as I have anything to report and feel it's safe to do so."

"Very good." As always, the line went dead as soon as Allison was finished speaking.

Noah set the phone on the console and concentrated on the road ahead. Memphis was about a five-hour drive, according to his GPS. He tapped the display on the dashboard to turn on the stereo, and the strains of an old Beatles tune filled the car.

"WHEN DO YOU EXPECT to be back?" The man who asked the question was sitting in the back seat of a limousine, looking at the tiny woman who was about to get out of the car. "I'll manage, but I don't like it when you're far away. Sometimes I think you're the glue that keeps me together."

Monique smiled at him, her hand on the door handle. "Relax, sweetheart," she said. "I'll be back later tonight, or by sometime tomorrow night at the latest. Surely you can survive without me that long, can't you?"

He smiled back. "Survive? Yes. Actually feel alive? Well, that may be a little more difficult, but I'll be waiting with open arms when you get here."

He leaned toward her, and she gave him a passionate kiss. "I love you, Charles," she said. "Don't worry, I'll be back before you know it." She turned and stepped out of the car, then waited while the chauffeur got her bags from the trunk and handed them to the redcap. The car pulled away, and the redcap followed her into the airport.

Monique didn't bother with commercial flights, which is why she'd had the chauffeur drop her at the charter terminal. The woman behind the counter glanced at her ID and smiled.

"Ms. Lancaster," she said, "welcome. Your plane is ready to go. If you'll just follow the yellow line to the exits, you'll find it waiting for you on the tarmac."

"Thank you, Kelsey," Monique said. The girl had been at the counter almost every time she had flown for the past few months, and they had become familiar with each other.

She turned away from the counter, and the redcap followed, carrying her two bags as if they weighed nothing. As soon as she stepped out the door, a man in a charter company uniform was waiting to take them onto the plane, while the pilot escorted her into the cabin. She was the only passenger, even though the plane was designed for a group of ten or more, and she sat down in the first pair of seats. There was a small table in front of her, and she laid her phone on it as she buckled her seat belt.

"Good to see you again, Ms. Lancaster," the pilot said. "We'll be leaving in about ten minutes. Flight time should be just about two hours, and I understand the weather in Memphis is warm and clear."

"Thank you, Lester," she said. "I'm glad you were available today. You are absolutely my favorite pilot."

Lester broke out into a big grin. "Well, you're undoubtedly one of my favorite passengers. All comfortable?"

She said she was, and Lester went into the cockpit. The flight attendant—the man who had taken her bags—pulled the door, shut and she heard the engines start to whine as they were started.

Ten minutes later, exactly on schedule, the plane leapt into the air.

IT WAS ALMOST TWO O'CLOCK when Noah got to the airport. He put the car into long-term parking, locked it and set its alarm, then carried his bag into the terminal. He had left his gun locked in the trunk, inside the safe with his money, although he had a couple of thousand dollars in his pockets. He glanced up at the sun and then pulled the sunglasses out of his pocket and slipped them onto his face. They cut some of the glare but weren't so dark that he would have to remove them inside.

Once inside, he found a chair off by itself, took out his phone, and called the number Monique had used. It rang twice, and then her voice came on the line.

"Good timing," she said. "Do you know where the charter desk is?"

Noah looked around. "I see a sign," he said.

"Good. I'm waiting for you there. I prefer to fill you in on the details of this trip in person."

The call ended, and Noah got up and followed the signs toward the charter counter. It was about a ten-minute walk, hampered at times by crowds of people, but he saw her as soon as he entered the area. She was sitting all alone, in a chair near the windows that looked out over the airport. He sat down in the chair beside her and let his peripheral vision focus on her hands. They were indeed quite small, and noticeably smaller than he would've expected.

"We're going to Nassau," she said without looking at him. "This job will be very simple. I have to take care of some business there, and I need someone I trust to make sure I am not interfered with."

"I'm a bodyguard?"

She looked up at him then and smiled. "Yes. Is that a problem?"

Noah shrugged. "I work for you," he said. "I do what you tell me."

Monique nodded. "Very good," she said, still smiling. "Relax, Noah. If you'd chill out a bit, we might even get to be friends."

"Friends aren't a luxury a guy like me can afford. I'll settle for just being an employee, okay?"

She made what could be considered a facial shrug. "Suit yourself," she said. "Come on, I've got the plane waiting. I think the flight is only about two, two and a half hours." She got up from her chair and started walking, and Noah picked up his bag to follow.

They stepped outside and she pointed at the plane, a small Learjet that was sitting only a couple of hundred yards from the building. A flight attendant was standing beside it. He smiled as they climbed inside, then followed them in and closed the hatch behind him.

"Jordan," Monique said to the flight attendant, "this is Mr. Fox. He's an associate who travels with me from time to time."

Jordan smiled at Noah. "Mr. Fox," he said. "It's a pleasure to meet you. Just let me know if you need anything during the flight."

Jordan turned away, and Noah looked at Monique. "You have your private jet?"

"Oh, no," she said with a smile. "I use JetBlue. They can get a plane to me within four hours, just about anywhere in the world I might want one. Costs a whole lot less than buying my own, and I don't have to worry about having my own flight or maintenance crews. Besides, you have to jump through so many hoops when you own an airplane that can travel internationally. Being a client of JetBlue allows me to remain more anonymous, but I can still go anywhere in the world on very short notice."

Monique took a seat, and Noah took the one facing her. He buckled his seat belt and waited, and then the engines came to life. The flight attendant took a seat and buckled his own belt, and then the plane began to taxi toward the runway. Noah took the opportunity to reach up and adjust his sunglasses, snapping a photo of Monique by doing so.

Once they were in the air and had accepted soft drinks from the flight attendant, Monique looked at Noah. "So, here's what's going on," she said. "I've got some accounts in Nassau that I manage, and I need to transfer money to a few other locations. There really isn't a lot of risk involved, but the particular bank I use is one that gets a lot of, shall we say, international business."

"Espionage or criminal?" Noah asked.

Monique laughed. "Both, I'm sure," she said. "Anyway, I don't think it's necessarily prudent for me to go into such areas without backup. Did you bring weapons with you?"

Noah frowned. "I didn't know if I was going to be flying commercial," he said, "so all I have at the moment are some knives that can get through metal detectors."

"That's no problem. I have an extra Glock in my bag." She took a sip from her glass and then looked him in the eye. "I was expecting a bit more animosity from you."

"What good would that do me? It's not going to change anything, is it?"

The look she gave him reminded Noah of the look a mother might give a mischievous child, part annoyance and part amusement. "Well, no," she said, "but it might make me feel better if I knew you were at least irritated with me. After all, it's not often somebody just takes over your life, is it?"

Suddenly, the dots that had appeared over her face blinked red, and the text box appeared. "Deception detected," it read.

Noah cocked his head to one side and looked at her. "That's interesting," he said as the display cleared itself. "You have no problem manipulating people's lives, ordering deaths and orchestrating God only knows what kind of political disasters, but you need my anger to justify to yourself the things you've done to me on a personal level."

"You're surprised? I'm human, aren't I?" She looked at him for a moment, then shrugged. "I learned something a long time ago, Noah. People are crazy, pretty much all of them. That also includes me, but I have the advantage of being aware of my craziness. That allowed me to put it to work, to use it, and it didn't take me long to realize that the biggest difference between me and everybody else is that I didn't bother trying to hide my craziness. Most people, they don't want anyone else to know just how crazy they can be, so they put on an act for the whole world to see. They act the way they think other people expect them to act, because that's how they expect to be judged. I could frankly give a flying fig what anyone else thinks I should do, because I'm only going to do what I believe is of benefit to me."

The dots had remained orange and steady until the final sentence. They blinked red, and the text box said, "Deception probable."

Noah was quiet for a moment, then went on. "And you think that makes you crazy?" he asked. "Take a look at the animal world. You'd be hard-pressed to find any other creature on the earth, other than humans, who worry about what other creatures think. The only exception is when it comes to mating; there are many animals that participate in some sort of courtship ritual that is designed to attract a mate, but other than that the only thing they want other animals to think is that getting into a fight with them might not be a good idea. Genuine self-interest is not a sign of insanity; it's simply a natural instinct we all possess."

"So that's why you're not angry?" Monique asked.

Noah gave her his most vicious grin. "I never said I wasn't angry. I simply asked you what good it would do me to express any anger, and we both agree that it wouldn't do me any good at all."

She looked at him for a long moment, then shook her head and chuckled. "Then I guess everything is okay with the world," she said. "I'd feel like I was doing something wrong if you didn't want to kill me. You do, don't you?"

"Yes. I most definitely do want to kill you, but you're not the only one who can govern your own actions according to self-interest. You offered me a way out of a life I don't want to be in; you offered me the chance to have a family and perhaps even find some kind of happiness. For now, your survival enhances my chances of achieving the goals of my personal self-interest, so my own desires get put on the back burner."

There was something in her eyes that Noah couldn't quite interpret. It almost looked like she was in awe of him. "What an amazing man you are, Camelot. No wonder your superiors consider you their best asset. You seem to have the ability to analyze a situation almost instantly. How did that happen?"

Noah laughed. "Everybody asks me that," he said, "but nobody ever wanted to believe my answer. Did you ever watch *Star Trek*? Well, I was always fascinated by Mr. Spock. He could, as you say, instantly analyze any situation he went into. I spent most of my childhood and teenage years learning to act like him, and that led to a study of logic and psychology. Between the two, I can usually get a fair idea of what makes people tick and what's likely to happen from a given scenario when it's applied to particular personality types." He leaned forward with a conspiratorial smile. "In high school, I even used to put on this mentalist routine, where I could make people think I was reading their minds. It was a lot of fun, because all I was really doing was watching how they reacted to the things I said."

Once again, she simply stared into his eyes for a time. "You, Noah, are probably one of the most dangerous men I have ever known. I'm quite glad that I have you under my control."

ALLISON LOOKED UP FROM her desk when Donald Jefferson walked into her office. "Anything new?"

Jefferson plopped into the chair in front of her, shaking his head. "Everyone at R&D has been vetted with the deception-tracking glasses," he said, "and absolutely no flags went up. I took Elaine with me and we each wore a pair while we interviewed everyone, and the only indicators of deception we found led us to determine that a couple of the men are hiding the fact that they're gay, and there are at least six couples who are dating in violation of the stated policies of the department."

Allison threw the pen she was holding down on the desk. "Then how the hell has this bitch been getting materials out of our research facility? That little bomb they took out of Noah's arm had our freaking detonator microchip in it. Wally said there's absolutely no doubt that it came from the ones his people made right here."

"I know, I know," Jefferson said. "Allison, I don't know what to say about this. There has to be some other way that it got into her hands, because there's nobody working out there who's been compromised. I'd bet my life on it."

"That's wonderful, Donald, but it isn't your life we're betting. It's Noah's. If she's got someone inside R&D that we haven't found, then she undoubtedly knows we got that bomb out of him." She glanced at the clock on the wall. "He would have gotten to Memphis more than an hour ago, so he's probably in the air right now, headed into some kind of a situation that she's in control of. If we're wrong, he may not come back alive."

Jefferson pinched the bridge of his nose between his fingers. "Then we need to figure out how that chip could possibly have gotten away from us. If we can find any other reasonably feasible answer, then there's still a good chance she doesn't know." He closed his eyes and sat quietly for several seconds.

"Okay," Allison said. "Assuming for the moment that everyone in R&D is clean, what other possible way could she have gotten hold of that chip?" She leaned back in her chair and looked at the ceiling for a few seconds, then suddenly blinked. "Wait a minute," she said. "Donald, have you asked Wally that question?"

Jefferson's eyes popped open, and he stared at her. "I was under the impression you were going to be the one speaking with Wally," he said.

"I did," Allison said, "but all I was thinking about was finding out who might have stolen a chip and given it to her. It never occurred to me to ask if there was any other way one might have left his facility." She picked up the phone on her desk and dialed the number from memory. "Wally," she said when he answered, "it's about those detonator chips. Besides you guys at R&D, who else has access to them?"

Allison's eyes seemed to glaze over for a moment, and then she leaned back in her chair with a sigh of relief. "Thank you, Wally," she said. "No, no, it's okay. You couldn't have known that I would forget to ask the right questions. Just relax, everything's okay. I'll talk to you soon." She dropped the handset back into its cradle and looked at Jefferson with a weak smile.

"I'll bet you couldn't guess in a million years," she said.

Jefferson stared at her, his mouth partly open as he tried to think of something to say. "Um... I give up."

"Senator Charles Wiggins heads up a senate committee on counterterrorism. Six weeks ago, the president authorized him to visit Neverland, and Wally in particular, to discuss the adaptation of some of Wally's inventions for use by Delta Force and the Navy SEALs. Among the things Wally showed him was the bomb printers and the detonator chips. The son of a bitch put in a requisition for two of the printers and a thousand chips while he was here, and I guess I authorized it without even really paying any attention. Wally got the order to ship them the next day, and he had enough made up in stock so they went out by UPS that afternoon."

Jefferson narrowed his eyes for a moment. "Delta Force and the SEALs only do CT work when they're under the direction of CIA.

That's how she would have learned about the chips." A look of relief began to spread on his face, but then it stopped. "Wait a minute," he said. "She would've also learned about the explosive 3-D print material, but the microbomb we pulled out of Noah was made of low-grade explosive in a soft plastic shell, with a separate pressure sensor and a common miniature battery. Why wouldn't she have simply had the whole thing made in the bomb printer? Those chips are powered by an ultra-miniature diamond betavoltaic battery that can last for thousands of years, and the pressure sensor could have been tied right into it. Why wouldn't she have used all of the new technology?"

Allison's eyes were wide and bright. "That, Donald, is an excellent question. Obviously, she didn't get access to everything, or didn't understand exactly what it was. This could be important, Donald."

"Yes, but I'm also thinking that we now know she has some connection to the CT operation of the CIA. That's the only way I can think of that she might have gotten hold of one of these chips."

"And yet, nobody at CIA has any idea who she could be. That's what blows my mind. How could she be so close to the counterterrorism groups and still have nobody know who she is?"

Jefferson leaned his head back, puffed up his cheeks, and blew air. "Could we be looking in the wrong direction? What if it isn't the CIA she's connected to?"

He could see Allison's mind racing, and he imagined it scurrying along many different tracks, like a dog sniffing for a scent it knew was there, somewhere. Her eyes were scanning the room, but he was certain that what she was seeing was something far away.

"Who else would have access to the counterterrorism committee's intelligence? I suppose the joint chiefs, possibly even the various branches of military intelligence. Who else?"

She sat there for another moment, then reached over and picked up the phone again. Her fingers flew over the dial pad, and she smiled a moment later. "Molly? It's Allison. I need your brains."

CHAPTER TEN

Noah stood quietly behind Monique as she sat in front of the desk of the director of the Caribbean Royal Bank of Nassau. His presence seemed to unnerve the man, but he was making every effort not to let it show.

"I believe that's everything," Monique said. "How long will it take, do you think, to get all of these transfers completed?"

Mr. Dunlevy, the director, glanced at Noah for a split second before he replied. "The Australian banks will take the longest," he said. "I would expect both of those to be completed in about three days, but everything else—the ones in Berlin, Abu Dhabi, and Johannesburg—will almost certainly be finished within twenty-four hours."

Noah had been watching his face and wasn't surprised when the sunglasses indicated he was being deceptive.

Monique frowned. "Well, I suppose there's no help for it. I'll try to plan further ahead for any future transfers to Melbourne." She shook off the frown and replaced it with a smile. "Now, I had also requested a substantial withdrawal in US dollars."

Dunlevy matched her smile with his own. "Yes, and I have it ready." He pressed a button on his desk and a voice came from a speaker in the ceiling.

"Yes, Mr. Dunlevy?"

"Have Mr. Washington bring in the parcel for Ms. Lancaster, please," Dunlevy said. A moment later, a large man entered the office with a briefcase, which he set on the desk. He opened it and then turned it so that Monique could see its contents.

"And it's all there?"

"Yes, Ms. Lancaster," Dunlevy replied. "Two million, four hundred thousand US dollars in one-hundred-dollar bills."

Monique nodded, and Mr. Washington closed the briefcase, then set it on the floor beside her chair before turning and walking out of the room.

"I suppose that's all I need for today, then," Monique said. "I thank you for your time, and for taking care of everything so promptly."

Dunlevy stood and bowed stiffly. "As always, Ms. Lancaster, it has been my pleasure."

This time, the "Deception detected" was in glowing red.

Monique got to her feet and picked up the briefcase, which she then handed to Noah. "Goodbye, then," she said. She turned and walked out of the office with Noah on her heels, which clicked across the marble floor. A doorman opened the front door for her, and they stepped out onto the street.

A limousine was parked at the curb, and Noah opened the rear door for her, then climbed in beside her after she entered. The driver put the car into gear and pulled away, sliding smoothly into the traffic.

Monique turned and looked at Noah. "See? This was an easy job."

"Too easy," Noah said. "I was watching closely, and absolutely no one paid any attention to you whatsoever. I'm not sure what this was really all about, but you didn't need a bodyguard."

Her smile spread across her face. "You might be surprised," she said. "Did you consider the possibility that your presence is the reason no one paid attention? Even for those who don't know who you truly are, you cut quite an imposing figure. I recognized three faces inside the bank, and I can assure you that any one of them would be pleased if something bad would happen to me."

"Why? What have you done to them?"

Monique laughed. "It isn't so much what I've done to them," she said, "as what they revealed to me about themselves. I seduced them, Mr. Wolf, and in so doing I learned that they are men of socially unacceptable tastes. Since they would greatly prefer not to have anyone learn of their proclivities, they grudgingly grant me whatever I require of them."

"Blackmail?" Noah asked. "Oh, wait, that's your stock in trade, isn't it?"

"If it works, it works. I used to think that being so small made me weak and vulnerable, but the truth is actually quite the opposite. Men like those, they see my diminutive stature as a way to exercise their most secret fantasies. I play along, and then I simply send them an email. One look at the video that I attach to it is usually enough to ensure their cooperation, because I've learned to use camera angles and software that make me look much younger than I truly am."

Noah nodded. "They're pedophiles, then," he said. "They pretend that you are a child?"

"Which is something they don't want anyone else, particularly their wives and business associates, to ever find out. It's absolutely amazing to me how many men fall for that trap." She let her eyes roam over Noah. "But you wouldn't."

"No. But if you ever decide you want them eliminated, please feel free to hand me that assignment."

She lowered her eyebrows. "Why? Despite their fantasies, we were all consenting adults."

"Because the day might come when pretending with a small woman won't be enough to satisfy those fantasies. Eliminating them might very well prevent a child from ever suffering at their hands."

"Well, well," Monique said. "Perhaps I'll let you do just that, one of these days."

"So, what's next?" Noah asked. "Where do we go from here?"

"Back to Memphis. I'll drop you there, and then I have to go home."

They arrived at the airport a few minutes later, and the chauffeur took them directly to the area where the Learjet was waiting. Noah followed Monique through the gate and onto the plane, stowed the briefcase under her seat, and reclaimed the seat that would be facing her. The flight crew took care of their last-minute details, and the plane was in the air only a few minutes later.

Monique was leaning back in her seat with her eyes closed, and Noah took the opportunity to look more closely at her hands. They were perfectly proportioned in themselves, yet they seemed smaller than the rest of her body would indicate. Monique was about the size of an average twelve-year-old girl, but her hands looked like they would fit better on a six-year-old.

He looked up at her face and let the dots find the various points on her features. "Where are you from, originally?"

Monique's eyes opened and she looked at him. "Why do you ask?"

Noah shrugged. "You said something earlier about how we could be friends," he said. "I've been thinking about it, and I guess if I had to be honest, today you don't seem so frightening or evil. Makes me curious about you."

She let a slow smile spread across her features. "I'm an American," she said, "just like you. Small-town girl who ended up in the big city and found out how the world really works."

"Everyone thinks you're part of the CIA," Noah went on, "but I don't think so. I'm not sure exactly who or what you are, but I know you can pull a lot of strings. Seems to me that if I'm going to be working for you, now, it couldn't hurt to let go of my anger and see if we can't develop some mutual loyalty."

"You mean, I could let my guard down around you? Not have to worry that you might shove a knife in my throat?" There was a small increase in the upward curvature of her smile.

"Can you really arrange for me to vanish from E & E?" He focused on the orange dots and watched them carefully.

"That's surprisingly easy to do," she said, and the dots indicated she was telling the truth. "Some of the people I control are quite capable of producing bodies that would convince anyone you were dead. I also have people who can alter the DNA records that I know are on file for you, so even DNA identification would pass. As far as Neverland would know, you would be dead and buried."

There was still no change in the display.

"And I'm right, aren't I? You're not part of the CIA. Whatever you do, you have a much greater reach than that."

Monique only looked at him but said nothing.

Noah grinned at her. "I figured it couldn't hurt to ask."

"It never hurts to ask a question," she replied, "but sometimes it can hurt to answer one. You surely don't want me to start wondering why you want these answers, do you?"

"It's just simple curiosity," Noah said. "I don't expect you to tell me anything that could actually identify you, and I wouldn't ask questions like that. To be honest, though, I'm wondering how someone who obviously has no actual connection to the government could be as powerful as you seem to have become. The guy you had me kill back at Neverland? Randy Mitchell? I knew him. If there was ever a man I would've trusted, it would've been him. Somehow, though, you managed to subvert him and, I'm guessing now, get him to get you all the information you needed on me. Right?"

She winked at him. "Touché," she said. "Obviously, he knew too much. If he decided to work against me, he could have blown things for both of us. His death was a good thing, beneficial to our mutual interests."

"I'm not going to completely disagree," Noah said, "but I'm a little concerned that you were done with him so easily. What happens if you decide you don't need me any longer? Am I going to get a visit in the night, the way he did?"

Monique simply looked at him for several seconds, then cocked her head slightly to the right. "If I reach the point of being unable to trust you," she said slowly, "then that is obviously a possibility. However, that little gift I gave you, the one under your arm, pretty well ensures that won't happen, don't you think?"

The glasses indicated no deception, and Noah shrugged. "I'll admit to a certain determination not to get on your bad side, and some definite interest in your personal well-being."

"Then you have nothing to worry about. Camelot, I'm going to answer a couple of your questions. This is one of those quid pro quo things, where I give you something because I want something in return. Ready?"

Noah gave a quick nod. "Sure."

Monique smiled. "Okay, then," she said, "here's the answer to your last question. No, I'm not directly connected to the CIA. My connections are actually much higher than that. I can honestly state that I have access to and control over personnel in every major intelligence agency in the United States, as well as having a few people scattered around other agencies throughout the world."

Noah let this run through his mind for a moment. "Okay, I can see that," he said. "Quid pro quo. You answered my question, now I'll answer one for you."

"Good, because I've got one," she said. "A couple of days ago, you went to Neverland. You spent several hours at R&D the afternoon you arrived, but you didn't pick up the phones until the following morning. What was going on out there for those hours?"

Noah thought quickly and then smiled. "Don't you already know?"

"Yes," she said calmly, "but I want to see if you'll be honest about it."

The dots on the inside of the lenses turned red, and the display lit up with "Deception detected." In less than a second, Noah thought through the implications, but he could not be certain whether the detected deception indicated that she actually did not know or if she truly did not care about his honesty.

"Wally has come up with some interesting new toys," he said. "A few of them appealed to me, and I wanted to take the time to check them out. I ended up bringing some back with me to Arkansas, something he calls a 'smart gun' that can be hidden just about anywhere and will watch for a particular target. When someone comes into view, it uses facial-recognition technology to decide whether that person is the target or not. If it is, the gun aims and fires instantly."

Monique's eyebrows rose slightly. "Interesting," she said. "The report that I got indicated that you spent some time alone in a highly secure area of the facility. Why was that?"

The glasses indicated that she was telling the truth. "That was because certain items I was shown are so new and highly classified that only a team leader is allowed to see them. The rest of my team had to go put up with Wally trying to entertain them for an hour or so."

Monique watched him for a moment, then inclined her head toward him in acceptance. "Okay," she said. "I got two in a row, so I'll give you one more."

Noah looked directly into her eyes for five seconds, then smiled. "What's your ultimate goal?" he asked. "You've got an incredible amount of power, but something tells me you're not out to rule the world. What is it you're really after?"

"Wow," she said with a chuckle. "Straight to the finish line, right? I'll tell you what, I'll give you the short version for now. If things progress smoothly, then eventually I'll fill in the details. Acceptable?"

Noah nodded once. "Acceptable."

She leaned her head back against the seat for a moment, then sighed. "Noah—you don't mind if I use your first name, right?"

"Why not?"

"Good. You see, Noah, our world is managed by groups of people who, to me, personify evil. Innocent people are sacrificed every day so that these groups can build and maintain their power, and I find that unacceptable. Unfortunately, many of them are so well insulated that there's no way to strip them of that power, short of killing them." She raised her head again and looked him in the eye. "Some years ago, I came to realize that power is like a chess game. If you can maneuver your pawns into positions of strength, but without letting your opponent realize what it is that you're trying to do, you can eventually surprise them with a checkmate. Once I understood that, and managed to make certain connections that would allow me to see what my opponents' future moves were likely to be, I decided to try to play against them. Unfortunately, it soon became obvious that I would have to be every bit as ruthless and cunning as they were, which is why you and I are having this conversation today."

She chewed on her bottom lip for a couple of seconds, then smiled at him. "You want to know what my goal is? It's to completely undermine the power of the oligarchs, the groups that run the world from the shadows. I don't give a damn about ruling the world; I think that should be a matter of the will of the people. The problem is that there are so many of these groups that the will of the people is never truly known. I'm preparing an endgame that I hope will topple at least some of those groups, and expose others." She shrugged. "Maybe then the people will have a chance to run their own world."

The dots stayed orange. Monique was telling the truth.

"You are an altruist, then?" Noah asked. "You'll forgive me, I hope, if I find that just a bit hard to believe."

"An altruist? Probably not. I definitely have some selfish motives in mind. I want to be protected and safe when all this goes down, and

I don't want to have to worry about my own personal future. There might even be a few people that I genuinely care about, so some of this is for them rather than for just everybody. No, I don't think I'm being altruistic; I think I'm just being coldly and ruthlessly practical. The only thing these groups can understand is the same kind of power and force that they use, so I have had to learn to express myself in their language."

Noah chuckled. "You seem to have achieved a significant level of fluency."

"Well, it came at a high price. Would you believe, I used to be the kind of girl who cried over homeless kittens? I had an almost perfect attendance record at Sunday school until I was nineteen, and I had a very hard time accepting my role in all of this. It took the better part of ten years for me to get up the nerve to do some of the things I have to do. The first time I used sex to get information, I spent hours crying and begging God to forgive me, but I learned what a powerful tool it really is. Now, it's just another weapon in my arsenal. When you sacrifice innocence in the pursuit of power, it's hard to decide whether you've won or lost, you know?"

"I'm sure you sacrificed more than that," Noah said. "Family, children—if you've honestly committed yourself to the path you're describing, then your life is undoubtedly far from what you expected it to be."

Monique giggled suddenly, and Noah had a brief mental impression of what she must've been like as a child. "The key to success in any endeavor," she said, "is knowing how to insulate one part of your life from another. Would it surprise you to learn that I'm a happily married woman?"

"A bit, yes. I suspect your husband might be surprised if he knew who his wife really is."

"That's why he doesn't know. He can never know. That's one of many reasons I'm so careful about who knows who I really am, and why I make sure that I have their absolute loyalty, no matter how I have to get it."

"Which explains this little gadget in my arm, right?" Noah asked.

Monique nodded. "An unfortunate but necessary measure. I actually have hopes that you'll become a genuine and trusted ally, but until that time..."

"I suppose anything is possible," Noah said. "At the moment, you still present enough of a threat to me and my family that I'm not sure we'll ever reach that point. Once we're out of E & E, that might change."

She shrugged and smiled. "One can only hope."

"You got two questions in a row, so I get one more. How does selling American secrets to our potential enemies benefit your plan to eliminate oligarchy? When you had Sarah captured and sent to the Chinese, they were trying to identify me and prove the existence of E & E. Had they been successful, it could have done significant damage to American national security."

Monique laughed. "But they weren't," she said. "I'm sorry that your Sarah had to be used in the way she was, but it wasn't about helping the Chinese identify you. It was about getting all the intel on you that I possibly could for myself. I first learned about you almost a year ago, but you were wrapped in such a shroud of secrecy that I couldn't even get your real name. All I knew was Camelot, and that you were considered America's number one assassin. You'll find that I always employ the best, because only the best are going to help me achieve my goals." She leaned back in her seat and sighed. "I stumbled across Mitchell about a year ago and was able to learn enough to identify his family. I got him to cooperate by proving to him that I could reach them at any time, and for the most part all I needed him to do was keep me apprised of the missions his team was involved in. Knowing who was going to be taken out allowed me to adapt and modify any existing plans I might have, you see. Then, when he let me know that he was working with the famous Team Camelot, I required him to give me particular details of the mission. All he knew at that point was that a female operative who was part of your team had been abducted from an undercover operation in the Bangkok Hilton, but it wasn't hard for me to find out who had snatched her. I got a message to them explaining just how valuable the blonde girl was and arranged for them to profit substantially by turning her over to those who would transport her to China. Once the Chinese had her, I simply waited for you to make your move."

"You expected me to go after her," Noah said, a statement rather than a question. "But what was the point?"

Monique leaned her head forward, and her eyebrows rose. "Well, the point was to make sure you were really as good as your PR. I knew just enough about you to know that you'd go to any lengths to get her back. I had my people watching when you took down the safe house on Hong Kong Island, and I have to tell you that they were impressed." She settled back again. "After that, I just pressured Mitchell to get me any information he could find on you. Anyone who could not only get past all of the Chinese intelligence community to find her, but then manage to get out of the country without being caught? I knew right then that I definitely needed you working with me. How did you get out of China, by the way?"

"I stole an antique airplane and flew it into Vietnam. It was a little tricky, especially when we had to shoot down a fighter jet along the way."

The eyebrows went up another notch. "Impressive," she said. "That wasn't in your file."

"I think the Dragon Lady decided to keep that out of the after-action report. It had the potential to cause several different kinds of international incident."

"The Dragon Lady? That's what you call Allison Peterson?"

Noah grinned. "Kind of our internal nickname for her. If you knew her, you'd understand."

"I'm just surprised I hadn't heard it before," Monique said. "I've had someone almost on top of her for the last eight months, but they never mentioned that nickname."

The orange dots didn't flicker.

"That's interesting," Noah said. "I would never guess you could've gotten that close to her. I know you had Randy Mitchell, and there was that girl in Korea, but I guess it just never occurred to me that you might go for the average office worker. It's her secretary, right?"

Monique only smiled.

After a moment, Noah chuckled. "Of course," he said, "you're not going to tell me anything yet. First you have to be sure you can trust me, right?"

"There are a few people I trust completely, Camelot," Monique said. "None of them, however, have any idea who I can get to. I'd prefer you not speculate about it, just in case you were to accidentally let something slip that would complicate things for me."

The display lit up. "Deception probable."

She's trying to make me think I hit it on the head, he thought, *but I haven't. It's not the secretary, so it has to be one of the top staff. Of course, most of them would have been able to tell her that the bomb was removed, but she doesn't seem to know that.*

"Okay, I'll let it go. Any idea when I'll hear from you again?"

"Oh, it probably won't be long. I've already got things started on your extraction, but that will take some time. I'm guessing a couple of weeks, at least, but probably more like a couple of months. How's your mission going?"

Noah shrugged. "I'm just about ready to execute it," he said. "Unless there's a reason you'd like me to delay?"

Monique laughed again. "No, no need for that," she said. "I've actually been quietly doing you favors behind the scenes, hoping you could get this one wrapped up quickly. How do you think you happened to be at just the right place at just the right time to save Morgan's kid?"

The dots indicated no deception, but Noah looked at her as if he was confused. "Are you trying to tell me you had something to do with that?"

"James Cabot has been useful to me in the past," she said, "but he had outlived that usefulness. I told him to arrange for something to happen to the Morgan kid, but not to allow it until I gave him the word. Once I knew you had arrived on the scene, I had him keep tabs on you. As soon as his people saw you enter the bar where he knew both the Morgans were waiting, he called that boy and gave him his orders."

"Wait a minute," Noah said. "Are you saying that you knew I would stop Benny from killing Ralph Morgan?"

"Well, I didn't know if you'd manage to save him or not," Monique replied, "but I knew you'd be looking for an opening. Considering everything I know about you, I was quite certain you wouldn't just sit by and let it happen without taking some kind of action. I actually just expected you to take the shooter down after the fact, but you made it work out even better than that."

"Why? What got you so interested in this particular mission?"

Her eyebrows rose once more. "Didn't you understand what I was telling you earlier? Morgan and his cronies are completely undermining what our society is supposed to be. He rules that whole region like some little tin god, like some sort of self-proclaimed king. Granted, it may be on a much smaller scale than the people I normally deal with, but his activities were brought to my attention several months ago. The reason E & E got this mission is because I pressed my contacts at DOJ to request it."

Noah shrugged. "Killing Morgan and his top people might eliminate his criminal organization, but it won't stop crime in the area."

"Noah, Noah," Monique said. "Crime is nothing. Crime is something that will always be a part of society. Letting Morgan continue to act like he owns that entire region, however, would be far worse than any crimes he might commit. The people in that whole area are scared, and they have every reason to be. The government, whether you're referring to the federal, the state, or the local, has no power against a man like Morgan. Once you've done what you were sent to do, then the parasites that were feeding off him can be rounded up. There won't be anyone to kill off witnesses or intimidate them into not speaking. The people can start to breathe again, and that's what counts."

"But why do you care? There has to be something in it for you."

"Oh, there is," she said. "Eliminating a hydra like Morgan is the first step toward restoring the values of our society in that area. Granted, it's not a huge step, but it's a necessary one. Once he's gone, the local authorities can sort out the rest of the situation. Corrupt officials can be prosecuted, the people can start to feel like they are more than just subjects, always at the whim of some false king. That's what I want to see—I want to see people breathing free once more." She took a deep breath. "Morgan isn't the only little tin king in America, and I've got operations working to shut down several others even now. As soon as I learn about them, I take action. Morgan was just the first one I couldn't eliminate through normal channels, so your people had to be involved."

Noah shook his head. "You are really a strange woman," he said. "Do you know that?"

"I'm not that strange," she said, "I'm just somebody who is willing to act on what I believe. Isn't that what we should do?"

"I killed James Cabot," he said. "When I found out he was the one behind the attempt, Morgan asked me to take him out."

"Yes, I read the police report last night, a couple of hours after it happened. Pretty impressive, actually. Don't worry, Noah—remember Mr. Haggard? I arranged for someone to suggest to him that going to you was his best chance at survival. There was no doubt in my mind Morgan would order the hit, and as I said earlier, James Cabot had outlived his usefulness. Having Haggard come to you so that you could tell Morgan what Cabot had done was a no-brainer. Morgan would want him dead, and would send you to take care of it—that was logical. I knew you'd handle it quickly and efficiently, which only puts you in tighter with Morgan."

Noah simply stared at her for a moment. "As I said, you're a very strange woman." He grinned suddenly. "On the other hand, you're not always cautious. Has it occurred to you that, if I were not already under your control, I'd be able to track you down through this airplane? If it belongs to JetBlue, it wouldn't be a bit difficult to find out where the flight originated and who the customer was."

She actually stuck out her tongue at him. "And you think that would do some good? I have a number of identities, Noah, and only one of them deals with this company. If you were to track it down, you would find that it leads to a perfectly complete dead end. On top of that, I employ some of the best computer hackers in the world. Even if you got into the company's records on this flight, you would be surprised. This airplane was nowhere near Memphis and never went to the Bahamas today. The client who hired it has a special arrangement with the company that requires the flight crew to deny any knowledge of the flight or its passenger. Tracking the flight wouldn't get you any closer to knowing who I am."

Monique leaned her head back and closed her eyes, and Noah sat quietly until they arrived in Memphis. He adjusted his glasses twice more, snapping a couple of extra pictures as he did so.

CHAPTER ELEVEN

"I think I may have something," Molly said as she walked into Allison's office. She was carrying a tablet with her and turned it around to show Allison the screen. "This might be our mole. I set up a program to scan for the general description we had heard, including the small-hands issue. The program found a few references that seemed to fit, all of them on Facebook. When I got to looking at them, I tracked them back to this profile."

Allison reached out and took the tablet, staring at the small blonde woman in the photo. Her hands were remarkably tiny compared to the rest of her body, but it wasn't the hands Allison was looking at. It was the three children in the photo with her. The two girls looked to be in their very early teens, but the boy was probably only nine or ten.

She looked up at Molly. "Who the hell is this?"

"Her name is Monica Lord," Molly said, "and at first glance she appears to be nothing more than your average housewife and mother. It wasn't until I really got to digging into her background that I found enough evidence to suspect her. Publicly, she seems to be a typical entrepreneur; she owns a company that sells health and beauty products under her own label that are carried in stores all over the world. I think, however, that she only uses that to cover her occasional need to travel. See, most of the time, she's just your average mom, taking the kids to soccer practice and things like that, but she takes short jet trips around the country about twice a week and an occasional one to other parts of the world. Go back twenty years, though, and you'll discover that she used to be an executive assistant to a freshman senator named Charles Wiggins. Some of Wiggins's people apparently objected to the way she ran his offices, claiming that she was literally forcing them into actions they didn't want to take, and there were rumors that they were having an affair. As a result, she voluntarily resigned after three years with him, and she was married to Jonathan Lord, a local businessman, a little more than a year after that."

Allison's eyebrows were trying to crawl over the top of her forehead. "As soon as you mentioned Wiggins," she said, "I was sold. This has to be Monique. I mean, even the name is similar. Add in the description and the fact that she's connected to Wiggins and I'm convinced. Is she still connected in any way to him now?"

"Not that I can prove," Molly said with a grin, "but I can tell you that the two of them have a tendency to turn up in the same city from time to time. That could be coincidental, until you notice that they always stay at the same hotel. I'm pretty sure Mrs. Lord is having an ongoing affair with Senator Wiggins."

"Which would give her plenty of access to a lot of things he knows. She could be blackmailing him, or it's possible he's just one of those men who talks in bed."

"It might also have given her a start in knowing just who to blackmail," Molly said. "If this is the mole, we know that she's got tentacles reaching into at least our organization and the CIA, but there's probably a lot more."

Allison's phone rang, and she held up a hand to tell Molly to wait. "This is Allison," she said as she answered.

"Camelot," Noah said on the other end of the line.

Allison hurriedly hit the speaker button on the phone and set the receiver back in his cradle. "Camelot, report," she said. "Molly is here with me, and we may have an identity on Monique."

"I just left her," Noah said. "All she wanted me for was a bodyguard on a trip to Nassau, to a bank. We just flew back in, and I'm driving out of the airport now."

"Very good," Allison said. "Here's what we've got. Monique appears to be Monica Lord, wife of Jonathan Lord, who is a DC-area businessman. She runs a business of her own, selling some kind of beauty products that she came up with, but we think that's just a front to allow her to travel a lot."

"She just told me a while ago that she is a happily married woman," Noah said, "even though she uses seduction and blackmail regularly to manipulate men. From what she said, she's very good at pretending to be a young girl and can often get some pretty damning video of her liaisons."

"Well, we know she won't stop at anything to get what she wants," Allison replied. "I gather you did not feel it was the right time to eliminate her?"

"To be honest, I don't think there's going to be a right time. There's a lot more to Monique, or Monica, than meets the eye. Yes, she can be ruthless, but I got her to talk to me about her motivation, and I was able to determine that she was telling me the truth. Her purpose in life seems to be to expose the men behind the curtains, the shadow governments that run things while people think their elected officials are actually in charge."

Allison and Molly looked at each other, both of them with wide eyes. "And you're saying she's telling the truth about that?"

"Yes," Noah said. "Considering what she knows and the influence she's got, I'm beginning to think she could be an asset to national security."

"But, Noah," Molly blurted out, "this is the bitch who sold Sarah to the Chinese. You can't seriously be saying you'd be willing to work with her?"

"I'm saying that she could be valuable," Noah said. "I'll confess that a part of me wants to put a bullet through her brain, but if that brain can be used to help secure America's position in the global political quagmire, I have to think that she's more valuable to us alive than dead."

"Well, well," Allison said. "This is quite a conundrum. How would you propose to bring her in from the cold?"

"I think the best idea," Noah said, "would be to start with a supervisory group made up of representatives from all of the relevant agencies. Let her share with them what she knows, and then perhaps we might establish an entirely new agency, one designed to do exactly what she's been trying to do."

"I can't say I think that's a bad idea," Allison said. "The only problem is getting it set up without those very 'men behind the curtains' finding out about it. Whoever they are, I'm certain they enjoy the power and anonymity they have, and they're not going to give it up willingly."

"I agree, and that's why I think it's important. Hold on a moment. I took a couple of pictures of her, and I'm sending them to Molly right now. Take a look and tell me if it's the same woman you found."

Molly's phone chimed and she snatched it out of her pocket. She brought up the images Noah had sent, and a smile appeared on her face. She turned it around to show it to Allison, saying, "It's her."

"Definitely the same woman," Allison said. "Now, what have you got in mind?"

"Turning the tables on her a bit. She'd have no idea that we have figured out who she is, so she won't expect me to show up on her doorstep. I think the shock of seeing me appear in her daily life, combined with a logical argument that she would better serve the country and her purposes by coming in with us and serving as an advisor might be enough to do the job."

Allison looked up at Molly. "Any sign of serious security around her in her personal life?"

"She lives in a gated community on the edge of Reston, Virginia, and it's patrolled by private security guards. There is a standard electronic security system in her home, but she and her husband don't employ bodyguards, nothing like that."

"Noah, how soon could you get to Reston?"

"If I fly, I could be there in a couple of hours, probably. If I drive, we're probably looking at twelve hours, maybe a little more."

"She might know if you got onto a plane," Allison said. "I think you should drive, but I don't know if you should try to get there in one stretch. You can stop and get a room somewhere, get some sleep, and then surprise her tomorrow."

"It's only little after seven, right now," Noah said, "so that would make it a little after eight in DC. I'm not that tired, and I'm sure I can drive straight through. That would put me close to her by eight, nine in the morning."

"It's your call, of course," Allison replied. "We'll send you her address, and I'll put some very clandestine observers on her place right now, since she's probably still on the plane, anyway. Incidentally, she apparently has children, two teenage girls and a younger boy. You check with me in the morning before you make contact, and I'll know who's in the house with her. That's an order, by the way."

"Yes, ma'am," Noah said. "By the way, is there anyone else in the room with you right now?"

"No, just me and Molly. Why?"

"Because Monique says she's got someone watching you very closely, and she tried to imply that it's your secretary, but I don't believe her. I'm pretty sure it's someone in your inner circle, someone who was subverted by her about eight months ago. Molly's been with us almost a year, and while I'm personally certain it isn't her, you can't afford to take any risks. I would suggest sequestering Molly from this moment until at least after I make contact with Monique tomorrow. I would further suggest that you not reveal any of this conversation to anyone else at this time. Whoever she's got, she certainly knows a lot about how our organization is run."

Allison looked at Molly, who shrugged. "Looks like you got a roommate for the night," the younger woman said. She handed Allison her cell phone and tablet, then turned out all of her pockets.

"I don't believe it's Molly, either," Allison said, "but you're right about not being able to take the risk. She's going home with me for the night. All anyone else needs to know is that we decided to hang out and watch chick flicks together. No one else will be aware of your current mission, so get to it."

"I'm on the way to DC," Noah said. This time he ended the call before Allison could.

"I like chick flicks," Molly said hesitantly.

"I hate them," Allison replied. "How would you feel about watching some old *Three Stooges*? I've got some that haven't been seen in more than sixty years."

NOAH STOPPED FOR GAS and then turned the car east on I-40. He set his cruise control at eighty-five and maneuvered through the traffic carefully, only rarely having to tap the brake pedal. Once he got out of Memphis, he raised the speed up to ninety and let the miles fall away underneath him.

He took out his phone and called Sarah, and she answered on the first ring.

"Baby?" Sarah asked, and Noah could hear the tension in her voice.

"I'm fine," he said. "Allison and Molly have identified Monique, and I'm headed for DC to have a talk with her in the morning. I don't know how long I'm going to be, but there are some strange things going on."

"Strange things? Like what?"

"I just told Allison that I think Monique could be an asset," Noah replied. "She isn't in this just for money; she actually sees herself as fighting for the people. Her goal is to expose the people and organizations who actually run the governments, and she's apparently amassed a lot of knowledge and information that could be of great benefit to national security. All I have to do is convince her to come in from the cold."

"Oh, God, Noah," Sarah gasped. "Don't you think this could be a trap?"

"Actually, I don't. At the moment, I'm quite certain she has no idea that we've identified her, or that we've removed her little bomb, so I'm hoping that taking her by surprise will disarm a potentially volatile situation. She flew me down to the Bahamas today to act as her bodyguard, but I think the real reason was just so that she and I could talk. I think she actually wants to get me on her side, but I'm counting on being able to turn it the other way."

They talked for a few more minutes, and then Noah told her that he loved her and ended the call. The phone went back into his pocket, and he continued on his journey.

THE PLANE LANDED AT Dulles Airport, and Monica Lord walked off with her simple carry-on bag. It had been an interesting day, and she was congratulating herself on making inroads with Camelot. She was convinced that he was, underneath everything else, the kind of man who would support her actions. If she could get him to be voluntarily on her team, there was honestly a chance she might be able to make a difference in the world.

Of course, the biggest problems were right here in her backyard. Washington was a snake pit, and no matter who sat in the Oval Office, it only got worse every year. It wouldn't be long, she knew, before she would have to start cleaning up at home, the way she'd already been doing in other capitals.

She checked her personal phone for messages. Jonathan knew that she kept it turned off whenever she was traveling, and he accepted her explanation that business required all her attention. A phone was nothing but a distraction, but she always checked it periodically to see if he or any of the kids had left a message.

There was a new one. "Hey, sweetheart," Jonathan's voice said. "I was just informed that I've got to go to Los Angeles right away. I'll probably be a couple of days, but we can switch our date night to Friday, if that's okay. I love you, and I'll see you as soon as I can get home. Hope everything went well today. Bye."

She couldn't help smiling. Jonathan was one of the sweetest men she had ever known, and she admitted to herself that she had been looking forward to having the house all to themselves that night. Britney and Alisha were going to spend the night with one of their friends, and Junior was on a school band trip to Philadelphia and wouldn't be back for a couple of days.

Of course, having the evening free wasn't necessarily a bad thing. She took out her other phone and scrolled through the contacts, then hit the Dial button on one of them.

"Charlie," she said in a singsong tone. "Guess who's back in town a little early?"

"Already?" There was a huge smile in his voice. "Are you busy tonight?"

"Oh, I've got a few hours. The usual place?"

"I'll be there in an hour," Charles said. "Can't wait to see you."

"Ditto, sweetheart. See you soon."

She put that phone away as well and then made her way to the taxi stands. She walked past the first two cabs and started to get into the third, then turned around and walked back to the first one. She opened the back door and slid inside, and the driver turned his head to look back at her.

"The Saint Anthony Hotel," she said. The driver nodded and started the meter, then put the car in gear and they were off. The ride took almost twenty minutes, and she was happy to tip the driver an extra twenty dollars for getting her there so quickly.

She walked inside and went to the front desk, and the clerk smiled at her. "Ms. Lancaster," he said. "I don't think we were expecting you tonight."

"No, but I've had a problem that requires me to stay overnight, and you know I couldn't stand the thought of staying in any other hotel. Have you got a room for me?"

"Of course," the clerk said. "The Overlook Suite is available. Would you like it?"

She smiled. "That would be perfect," she said. She handed over a credit card and received her key cards only a moment later. She had been a guest at the hotel often enough that the computer could complete the registration from her credit card alone.

She turned and carried her bag into the elevator, then used the key card to tell it to go all the way to the roof. The Overlook Suite was a penthouse on the southwest corner of the building and commanded a fantastic view of the White House and the National Mall. She took out her second phone and sent a text message to Charles. "Overlook Suite. Call me when you get into the elevator and I'll bring you up."

She got into the suite and dropped her bag on a chair, then kicked off her shoes. The deep pile carpet felt good on her stockinged feet, but her phone rang before she had a chance to truly enjoy it.

"Hello?"

"I'm here," Charles said. "I'm getting into the elevator now."

"Fantastic," she said seductively. "Just ride it up. I'm calling it now."

She hurried out the door and to the elevator, then inserted the key card into the slot that would call the elevator all the way up to her. She heard it ascending, and then the doors opened. Charles stepped out and she jumped up to throw her arms around his neck and her legs around his waist.

"Oh, Daddy," she said. "I thought you'd never get here."

Senator Charles Wiggins kissed her passionately and carried her through the open door into the suite.

Their affair had begun twenty years earlier, when Monica Simmons had come to work in his offices. She started out as a receptionist, then quickly moved up to secretary. That was when Charles actually began to pay attention to her, fascinated by her diminutive size. At first he was only mildly flirtatious, but it hadn't taken long for Monica to realize that he was one of those men who harbored fantasies about young girls. Being as small as she was, she had known many of them and had learned not to let her disgust show on her face.

Charles seemed different, however. While he was definitely flirting, he didn't make any of the usual comments she'd grown accustomed to. He had never offered her candy, for instance, nor asked if he could buy her some new toys. Those seemed to be common opening gambits for most such men, but Charles only hinted that he would like to take her to dinner.

It was her curiosity about him that finally got her. When he invited her to dinner with him after a late night at the office, she accepted, and her only precaution was to make sure she had a stun gun in her purse. If things got out of hand, she wasn't a bit bashful about shocking her boss into sleepy time. If nothing else, she figured, it would definitely result in some serious job security. He'd be terrified of what she might say if he ever let her go.

He was a perfect gentleman throughout dinner, though, and she finally figured he wasn't going to put "the move" on her until it was time to take her home. When dinner ended and he had his chauffeur stop at her apartment building, she actually had her hand in her purse and holding the stun gun, but all he did was thank her for a lovely evening and say he would see her the following morning at the office.

She had gotten out of the car and walked halfway to the front door of her apartment building before that same curiosity overcame her completely. She stopped, turned around, and walked back to the car, and he powered down the window with a smile on his face.

"Would you like to come in for a drink?" Monica asked him, and she put all the sultriness into it that she could manage.

CHAPTER TWELVE

"O h, er," he stammered. "Monica, I—I'd honestly love to, but it might seem a bit inappropriate."

He was just too freaking good to be true. The curiosity mixed with frustration, and she reached down and opened the door. "Why? You're not married, are you?"

"Well, no, but..."

"Senator—Charles, you've been flirting with me for weeks. You've offered to take me out for dinner a dozen times, and this is the first time I ever accepted. Are you honestly going to sit there and turn down the chance to come into my apartment alone with me?"

"Monica," he said readily, "I honestly don't know what to do. Do I want to come in there with you? Absolutely. But you hear things nowadays is about sexual harassment and how powerful men are forcing themselves onto the women who work for them. I don't want anyone to get that kind of idea about me, and I certainly don't want them talking about you."

And that was when she burst out laughing. "Charles," she said, "you can either get out of that car and come in with me, or I can guarantee you that I will do everything in my power to drive you completely out of your mind at work. I will dress so sexy that no one will even notice you at all, because they'll be too busy staring at me. I will tease you every possible chance I get, I will sneak up behind you and run my fingernails across your neck, I will do everything possible to make you want me so badly that you will be unable to even think about what you're supposed to be doing. Now, which one will it be?"

The man actually managed to sit there for another thirty seconds before letting out a sigh and climbing out of the car. He wasn't that much older than her, and he was certainly an attractive man. Monica was willing to accept that she might have been wrong about him, that maybe it wasn't about her size at all. He had followed her in, and they sat on the couch and enjoyed a cocktail together before she finally wrapped her arms around his neck and pulled him down for a kiss.

That had been the beginning, and it had gone on ever since. There was something about Charles that she simply couldn't walk away from, and it wasn't long before he was telling her that he loved her. She would always shush him at that point, because she actually detested politics and couldn't imagine herself as a senator's wife. She told him that she loved him, as well, but that it would never work out if they were to be married, and he finally accepted.

A few months later, he promoted her to office manager, and that's when the trouble began. Other staff, aware of their relationship but unable to prove it, were undoubtedly jealous. Complaints were filed against her, and after a couple of years of putting up with snide comments and pure rudeness, she finally told Charles that she was going to quit.

"I'm only quitting the job, though, sweetheart," she said. "I'm still your girl, and that won't change."

Change always comes, though, and it was about a year later that she met Jonathan Lord. He was running a business incubator at the time, and she was just preparing to launch her beauty products business, something that Charles had invested in. Jonathan helped her get it started and created the marketing program that had been so successful. They began dating, and she finally had to tell Charles that she was going to be married.

They had actually been in this very suite at the time, and Charles had almost fallen to tears. He told her that he would always love her but would always want the best for her, and so he would let go and vanish into the woodwork.

"The hell you will," she said. "I mean, I really don't want to give you up, not completely. Sure, getting married might mean I'm not always available, but I promise I will make time for you."

"I can't ask that of you," Charles said, but she had shut him up with a kiss. He couldn't resist her, and she knew it, and he had given in to her rather quickly.

It was after that time that she noticed how he was caressing her, and it suddenly dawned on her that he had always done it just that way. He was gently rubbing her shoulders and upper arms, not allowing his hands to roam anywhere else. He always kissed her on the forehead, as well, but it had always seemed so perfectly natural with him. It had never bothered her, the way it had with other men she had been with.

She admitted to herself that she had always subconsciously known that he wanted that particular fantasy, and that she had forced herself to ignore it because she was afraid it would sully their relationship. Suddenly, however, it actually seemed like something she would enjoy. She turned on her side and cuddled up to him, playing with the hairs on his chest, then raised her eyes to look into his.

"If I ask you to do something," she said softly, "will you promise not to get upset with me?"

"I could never get upset with you," he said.

She licked her lips, suddenly finding it difficult to say what she wanted to say. "When we—when we're together, in bed, I mean, would you mind if I—if I call you daddy?"

His sharp intake of breath had told her that she had scored, and he assured her that he would never be upset if she did so. They had made love again, and it was the first time she ever pretended to be a little girl with him, and she was absolutely shocked at how much she enjoyed it.

Charles, on the other hand, had been so enthralled that she almost worried he was going to have a heart attack. Their affair became one of fantasy, and Monica looked forward to the times when she would be with him.

And then he had started confiding in her, telling her things that would normally require a serious security clearance. Monica filed it all away in her memory, at first only thinking of someday writing a book about Washington, but then some of the things she was learning started her thinking about other possibilities. Armed with the information he shared in their beds, she began slowly creating her plans, and it wasn't long before she no longer had any compunctions about using seduction to get what she wanted.

Some of the people Charles worked with were into far greater perversions than his, and she learned quickly to play along with them. She always made sure she arranged the room and got there before the men and women she targeted. That allowed her to plant small cameras she acquired, some of them disguised as clocks and other common, everyday items that would go unnoticed.

She collected photographs and videos until she was finally ready to make a move, and then they were carefully sent to her victims. They always seemed to come from some foreign intelligence agent, and by using a voice-changing device and a fake accent, she could soon give orders to some of the more powerful people in DC. Through them, she made contact with other agencies, eventually even gaining control over powerful people and operatives from other countries.

Surprisingly, a few of them seemed to actually enjoy her domination and became loyal helpers. It was one of those, a man named Eric, who devised the little explosive that could be implanted into a human body, and he even taught her how to do it herself. The very first one she implanted was into him, and he seemed proud to be so permanently marked as her own.

Since then, she had implanted only a few more, and had convinced him to create the device that monitored her heart rate. He'd been very proud of that one, since it had to be powerful enough to send a signal through a cellular tower, and had to be rechargeable. She had a small, soft device that she could plug into a wall socket and wrap around her neck, a cordless charger that would keep the little battery going for many, many years. The battery in the device could last up to two weeks, but it needed to be charged for at least six hours every now and then.

Jonathan thought it was some kind of New Age healing device that she used because of the constant sore throats she claimed to get every week or so. He was always kind and gentle when she had to use it, and she loved him for it.

But Jonathan wasn't here, and Charles was. Not only was she about to have a great time, but there was no telling what he would talk about after.

As always, it paid off. When the loving was finished, Charles lay there with her and told her about all of his concerns, about the sudden increase in terrorist activity around the world, about the various agencies his committee had to oversee. This was how she had first learned of E & E and a few other agencies that were kept hidden from the public eye, and she had learned to listen closely in these moments.

It was also how she learned about some of the special devices that were used in counterterrorism. Charles had told her about the little microchip detonators he had acquired from one of the agencies, and how it could be controlled by something as simple as a cell signal. She had told Eric about them, and his position with the CIA allowed him to get his hands on a number of them. He had immediately started using them in the little implantable bombs, and Noah had actually gotten the first of those.

And then her reveries came to an end, as Charles said something that put a chill through her. The director of the CIA had come to see him that very day, and the committee had finally been made aware of the existence of a mole within the US intelligence community. Jointly, the CIA and FBI had created an operation to try to uncover this person's identity, code-named Witchfinder, but so far all they had learned was that the mole was most likely a woman.

"They say she's apparently got her claws into just about every agency," Charles said. "They already linked her to a number of assassinations, and she's been instrumental in revealing some unimaginable state secrets to some of our potential enemies. According to the director, she's known to have been colluding with North Korea and China, possibly even Russia." He shook his head as he cuddled her. "When they find her, there won't even be a trial. She'll simply be terminated, and the whole thing will stay buried forever."

Monica fought the urge to ask questions, because even Charles was not immune to suspicion. No matter how much he loved her, there was no doubt in her mind that he would hand her over if he learned about her clandestine activities. Instead, she simply lay there awake as he drifted off to sleep, and when he woke in the morning she was gone. She left him a note, telling him that she loved him and would see him again soon, but that she needed to get home.

It was time for damage control, and she knew that she had to move fast if she was going to survive. Somewhere in the halls of Langley, there was a young woman who was in charge of Operation Witchfinder, and Monica needed to know who she was immediately. This woman had to either come under her control, or she had to die.

It was just before six when she got to her house, already exhausted from not being able to sleep all night. She walked inside and locked up, setting the alarms automatically, and then decided that a couple of hours' sleep would do her more good than making a pot of coffee. She climbed the stairs and entered her bedroom, dropped her clothes into the hamper, and went into the bathroom for a quick, hot shower.

Fifteen minutes later, her hair still wrapped in a towel, she slid into her bed and forced herself to think about her children for a few minutes. That always helped when she needed to relax, and soon she was breathing deeply as she slept.

If she hadn't been tired and worried about what this unnamed young woman in the CIA might actually know, she would have noticed the utility van that was parked two doors down.

CHAPTER THIRTEEN

The Charger rolled into Washington, DC, at just before eight in the morning, and his GPS directed him to the gated, secure community where Monica made her home. There was a security fence that went around the entire subdivision, and Noah cruised along its perimeter as he took out his phone to call Allison.

"Camelot," he said when she answered.

"Where are you?" Allison shot back.

"I'm just outside her subdivision. There are two entrances, both of them with gates that only open with a code, and I can see a security car roaming through the streets. A lot of video cameras are scattered around, but I think I can avoid them."

"I can fix that for you," Allison said. "Molly was able to get Jonathan Lord's gate code. It's five-one-seven-nine-eight and then the pound sign. He's out of town on a trip to Los Angeles, and apparently her children are gone. My people say she's alone in the house, but she didn't get in until five forty-nine this morning."

"I'd been under the impression she was coming straight home after she dropped me at Memphis," Noah said, "but apparently she had other things on her agenda. That's fine—if she's a little tired, then she'll be less likely to try to put up a fight before she hears what I've got to say."

"All right. You are authorized to proceed." The line went dead, as always, and Noah dropped the phone into his pocket as he circled around to the main entrance of the community. He pulled up to the gate and powered down his window, then reached out and entered the code. Three seconds later, the gate began to swing open, and Noah drove through it.

The GPS directed his turns, and he parked the car on the street in front of the house across from Monica's. He got out of the car and walked directly to her front door, then rang the doorbell.

A couple of minutes later, he rang again. He considered the possibility that she might have seen him and run out the back, but he was counting on her natural intelligence to realize that he wouldn't have rung the doorbell if he was coming to do her harm.

From inside the house, he heard faint sounds of motion. It sounded like bare feet on the hardwood floor, and then the small curtain on the window in the door moved aside and Monica's face peered out at him. There was no look of shock or surprise, just a wariness that kept her eyes locked on his for about five seconds, and then he heard the dead bolt click as she unlocked the door. She swung it open and stood there in a bathrobe, just looking into his face.

"I'm here to talk," Noah said.

Monica nodded slowly. "I thought as much," she said. "I suppose you might as well come in. I've got coffee on. Would you like a cup?"

"That sounds good," Noah replied, "but I'll pour it myself if you don't mind."

She actually managed half a grin as she reached out and unlocked the storm door. Noah pulled it open and stepped inside, and she turned her back to him as she led him toward the kitchen. When they got there, she pointed at a cabinet over her coffee maker. "Cups are up there," she said.

She sat down at the table and picked up her own cup as he chose one and filled it. A moment later, he sat down across from her and sipped at the hot liquid.

"Do your bosses know what happens to you if you kill me?" Monica asked.

"I had your device removed two days ago," Noah replied. "It wasn't that hard to do, actually."

She narrowed her eyes and looked at him. "I've got a little detector that says you're lying," she said.

Noah shook his head. "We caught the little transmitter, and I've got one implanted in the same spot that puts out the same coded signal. Your detector only checks to see if it's receiving the signal, and it is. Unfortunately, it can't tell whether it's coming from the original device or a simple mockup, like mine."

Monica's face was pale, but she wasn't letting the fear into her expressions. "So," she said, "you said you wanted to talk. What about?"

"About bringing you into our organization as an advisor," he replied. "Monique—sorry, Monica—you've been working alone and trying to accomplish so many things for a long time, but you had to have known that you'd almost certainly be discovered sooner or later. If it was anybody but us, you'd already be in a top secret holding cell, and someone would be doing everything possible to make you tell everything you know. When that was over, you'd simply disappear, but I think you're much more valuable than that. Allison authorized me to try to convince you to work with us."

"And if I refuse," she said, "then I'm sure your orders are a bit more final, am I right?"

"Yes. If you refuse, I am under orders to terminate you."

She looked directly into his eyes for several seconds, then cocked her head slightly to the right. "So, if I accept, how would this work?"

"You would remain free, using your contacts and knowledge to provide information to a very small group of representatives from several agencies. CIA, E & E, DHS, NSA, maybe FBI and a couple others. They'd be like a committee, and you would answer to them. Your true identity would be kept secret, and your operatives would never know that you are working with the US government."

"I'd have to have the freedom to continue doing the things I do," she said. "It's how I maintain control over these people."

"I expected as much, and I can guarantee that you can do so."

She leaned back in her chair, looking a great deal like a nervous child. "My husband never knows? My kids?"

"Not unless you end up telling them," Noah said. "That would only hamper your benefit to the government. Of course, when you retire, there will probably be a medal in it for you, so they might find out then that you were working for the government."

She sniffled. "Sorry, I seem to be getting a cold. Who all would be on this committee?"

"I don't have names, but they would probably be intelligence analysts. They would ask you questions, and you provide the answers. What they do with the information after that is up to them."

"And who above them would know about me?"

"Their top supervisors, of course, and there may be a few others, but your actual identity would be classified Top Secret with special restrictions. Even the president would not know who you are, only that someone in your position exists."

"What happens when they're done with me? Is that when you pay me another visit?"

"I sincerely doubt it. Monica, if you had found your way into the CIA and shown your capabilities there, you would be considered a national hero. Even now, by coming in with us, you can count on absolute amnesty for everything you've done in the past. Your value to our national security is that great."

"And what if I don't want to?" she said suddenly. "Don't you understand that our own government is little more than a puppet to the people I've been working against?"

"I do," Noah said. "That's precisely why I'm here. Allison agrees with me that we need an organization that can do exactly what you have been trying to do, and setting you up with this committee is the first step in that direction. All of your activities will remain top secret, restricted, so that you can continue your work to expose and eliminate those puppet masters."

Her eyes opened slightly wider, and Noah suddenly saw a twinkle in them. "Are you saying I could possibly run such an organization?"

"I know of no one else better qualified. Monica, this is your chance to achieve your goals, while putting an end to all the efforts currently going on to figure out who you are. If you agree to this, you will be in a position to make a serious difference. If you don't, all you're going to do is leave your children motherless."

A flash of anger flew across her features and vanished as quickly as it came. "You don't pull any punches, do you?"

"That's not my job," Noah said. "My job, right now, is to convince you to take this offer while you still can."

"Of course I'm going to take it," she said. "It's not like you're leaving me any choice, now, is it?"

"Not really. And before you try to get all sneaky, don't even think about agreeing to take it unless you're willing to actually commit. If you try to disappear or turn this against us, it won't be me they send. It'll be someone you'll never expect, and it will happen so fast that you won't have any chance to see it coming."

"My children are young enough that they need their mother," Monica snapped. "I don't plan on disappearing, and I'm certainly not going to risk getting one of your kind set on me. Noah, I'm not going to lie and say I'm thrilled that you found me out, but I'm also not going to be stupid enough to get myself eliminated now that you know." Her expression softened over a half-dozen seconds, and finally she gave him a slight grin. "I guess, in a way, I appreciate this. You giving me a chance, I mean, when it would be so easy to just kill me and get it over with. Of course, a part of me wonders why you're doing it."

Noah looked at her for a couple of seconds, then came to a decision. "The file you were given on me was completely fake. It was designed primarily to try to set you up to be caught, but you are actually smarter than we thought you were. Every trap we set for you failed to track you down, and it wasn't until I actually saw you face-to-face yesterday that we managed to get the one detail that would confirm who you were."

"And what was that?"

"Your hands," Noah said, pointing at them as they were wrapped around her coffee cup. "When our intelligence department found out about how small your hands are compared to the rest of you, they actually found a reference to them on Facebook that led them back to you. Once we compared the photo on your profile to one that I had taken of you, we knew we had the right person."

Monica stared at him for a moment, then chuckled. "The sunglasses, right? Camera built into them?"

Noah nodded. "Yes. I snapped a couple pictures of you yesterday with them and sent them back to my HQ. That's how we confirmed your identity, and what led to me making you this offer."

"Okay. Then who are you, really?"

"I'm a man who suffers from something called histrionic affect disorder. What that means is that I have no normal emotions, and nothing that would normally be considered to be a conscience. You made the comment that I seem to be able to analyze the situation instantly, and that's because I really do operate on logic, but I also have learned to mimic normal human behavior in order to fit in. That's given me an insight into human nature that allows me to predict what people will do fairly accurately."

"I should've known it was stupid of me to want to recruit you," she said. "But that's me, I have to have the best. So, what happens now?"

"When are your children due home?"

"The girls will be home later today, but Jon Junior won't be back until tomorrow. Why?"

"Because I need you to meet the Dragon Lady. She's the one who will actually put this group together, and she needs to know that you're ready to come on board."

"Okay," she said with a sigh. "Jonathan won't be home for a couple of days, probably, and I can arrange for the girls to stay where they are another night. They'll be thrilled. Can I be back home by tomorrow?"

Noah took out his phone and dialed Allison, then put it on speaker and laid it on the table. She answered in the middle of the first ring.

"Camelot, report," she said.

"I'm sitting at the kitchen table with Monica Lord," Noah said, "and you are on speaker. I've made my presentation, and she has agreed. I think the next step is to put the two of you together so you can begin assembling the supervisory group."

"I agree," Allison said. "Monica, hello."

"Hello, Allison," Monica replied. "I've heard a lot about you."

"I could say the same," Allison said with a chuckle, "and probably neither of us has heard a lot of good about the other. Noah says you accept his proposition?"

"Well, I'll be honest enough to tell you that it beats the alternative."

"I'm sure it does," Allison said, "but I have to say that I'm looking forward to the chance to work with you. How soon can we get together?"

"Noah just explained that we need to do it as soon as possible, so I'm going to make a couple of calls in just a moment. I've got to arrange for my daughters to stay with their friend another night, and then I can arrange a flight and be out there probably by lunchtime."

"Excellent. Have Noah give you my number, and you can let me know when your flight will be in. I'll make a point of meeting you myself at the airport. We'll talk then, and I'll buy lunch."

The phone went dead, and Noah picked it up and put it back into his pocket.

"She doesn't waste any time, does she?" Monica said, grinning. "My kind of person."

"She definitely knows what she's doing," Noah said. "Make your calls, and I'll take you to the airport."

Forty-five minutes later, Noah dropped Monica off near the charter entrance of Dulles Airport, then drove directly to a nearby hotel and got a room. As soon as he was checked in and inside the room, he called Sarah to let her know that he was going to get some sleep before heading back.

"How did it go?" Sarah asked.

"The only way it could. She accepted my proposition, and she's on a plane to Kirtland right now. Allison is going to meet her at the airport, and my curious side wishes I could watch."

"I just hope she doesn't try to pull anything," Sarah said. "Allison wouldn't hesitate to have her killed if she thought it was necessary."

"I'm pretty sure Monica knows that. Baby, I'm going to get some sleep and get back on the road this afternoon. I'll be back there by tomorrow evening. Everything going okay there?"

"It's fine," she said. "Neil and Marco have been playing a lot of video games, and Kate and I are going shopping this afternoon. With those two around, the groceries are getting low already."

"All right," Noah said. "Just be careful."

They each pledged their love and then ended the call. Noah took a quick shower and got into bed, and was asleep within two minutes.

CHAPTER FOURTEEN

Allison watched the Learjet touch down, sitting on a bench just outside the entrance to the terminal. Kirkland's airport wasn't huge, but it boasted a couple of the longest runways in the state outside of Denver. Officially, that was because of the secret military base nearby, the one that wasn't really all that big a secret to the locals, but the reality was that it allowed any size jet aircraft to land at or take off from the facility. Air Force One had made an occasional appearance there, and hadn't that been a nightmare, trying to manage the security necessary for the president of the United States to visit his most clandestine operation?

The Learjet taxied up to the terminal, and the side door opened. The steps were folded down, and a moment later Allison got her first look at Monica Lord.

The woman was genuinely very small, and Allison could understand why she might be mistaken for a child at times. She walked across the tarmac with her eyes focused on Allison, who got to her feet as she approached.

"Well, well," Monica said, "the famous Dragon lady." She held out her hand, and Allison shook it.

"That's what they call me," she said. "I hope it has more to do with my tendency to breathe fire than any reference to my scaly skin."

"You don't look all that scaly. So, you said something about buying lunch?"

Allison laughed. "My car's out front," she said. "Is that all you brought with you?" She pointed at the small overnight bag hanging from Monica's shoulder.

"That's it. As I said on the phone, I'm hoping to be home by morning."

"Then let's go eat." She led the way through the airport terminal and out the front door, where she had exercised the privilege of her rank to leave her car parked at the curb. It was a year-old Cadillac, and she used her remote to unlock it.

"I arranged us a table at a local place that understands the need for privacy, sometimes. They have some small private dining rooms, and I felt it would be better for us to talk alone."

"That's fine by me," Monica said. "Do they serve drinks at this place?"

"There's a bar," Allison replied with a grin. "If there weren't, I'd probably pick somewhere else."

She started the car and put it in gear. The drive to the restaurant took about fifteen minutes, and the two women continued to chat along the way.

"So you've got kids?" Allison asked.

"Yes. Twin girls who are fourteen and a son who is ten. They keep me busy."

Allison barked a laugh. "Obviously not busy enough," he said. "You've managed to have something I never dared. I would've given anything to be a mother, but my career simply wouldn't allow it."

"Then you just told your first lie. If you honestly would've given anything, the career would've had to take second place to the family."

"Oh, goodness, don't get logical on me. I have to put up with enough of that from Noah."

"Yes, I can imagine. He explained to me this morning about his condition, and it amazes me that I didn't spot it."

Allison chuckled. "He's very good at hiding it, when he wants to. Of course, it's the same thing that makes him the best at what he does. He doesn't stop to think about things emotionally; he simply does what he believes is right, and that generally turns out to be exactly what needs to be done."

"Which is probably why I'm still alive," Monica said. "Am I right?"

"There might be some truth to that. I had wanted to take you into custody originally, but you were reaching into areas that were potentially devastating, whether to us or to national security. I told Noah to arrest you if possible, and terminate you if not. He was the one who decided you'd be more valuable as an asset than either imprisoned or dead, and he sold me on the idea." She glanced over at the smaller woman. "I'm glad he was able to sell you on it."

"I'd be lying if I told you I wasn't nervous about coming here," Monica replied. "For all I know, I could disappear into one of your dungeons and never be seen again. The problem is that Noah didn't give me any choice. It was either sign on or die, and I'm just not ready to give up living yet."

"That's what he was counting on. That, plus the fact that you have kids; he didn't think you'd want them to feel your loss. Noah himself is an orphan, so despite having no emotions, he does tend to think about such things."

They pulled into the restaurant a few minutes later and went inside. Once they were escorted to the private dining room and had given their drink orders, Allison took a pair of glasses out of her purse and put them on, then turned to her guest. "The first thing I want to know from you," she said, "is the names of every person inside my organization that you have subverted."

Monica looked at her for a long second. "Okay," she said. "And when I do, what happens to them?"

"That depends on how you got to them. If it was through blackmail, then we'll consider letting them live. If not, they'll be terminated."

"Ouch. Well, there are only two. Jack Miller works in your equipment supply department, and he managed to get me a few items that your R&D came up with. I got him to cooperate by threatening his mother. The other one is Carol Porter. She's in your..."

"She's our NSA liaison," Allison said, and Monica nodded. "Now, who else is there?"

Monica's eyebrows rose. "That's it, just those two," she said. "Why would I lie to you?"

"Because there's someone you're trying to either protect or keep for yourself. Now, Noah told me that you have someone watching me. I'm assuming this is the person you're trying to keep from revealing, but you might as well understand now that the cost of your survival is going to be absolute honesty. If you lie to me again, your children will be orphaned before this day is over."

Allison reached up and took off the glasses she was wearing, then passed them over to Monica. "Put them on," she said.

Monica looked at the glasses for a moment, then slid them onto her face and looked at Allison. Instantly, the little orange dots settled onto the prominent points of Allison's face, and Monica's eyes grew wide.

"I'm going to give you a pink elephant for your birthday," Allison said, and the text box lit up.

Monica snatched off the glasses and stared at Allison. "These glasses just told me that you were lying," she said with awe. "How in the world is that possible?"

"You'd have to talk to our Research and Development people," Allison said with a grin as she reached out and took the glasses, then put them back on. "They came up with the technology, but I understand it's based on something that was already available. The point I wanted you to see is that I know when you lie to me. Now, who else do you have in my organization?"

Monica shot her a sour look but then lowered her eyes to the table in front of her. "Is it absolutely necessary for me to tell you? I can assure you that he's going to know I'm no longer a threat to him, and..."

"What part of don't lie to me did you not understand?" Allison asked. "I cannot trust anyone in my upper circle that has already been subverted once. Tell me who it is, now."

Monica sighed but then looked up into Allison's eyes. "His name is Donald Jefferson."

DONALD JEFFERSON STEPPED into Allison's office and immediately noticed the small blonde woman sitting across from her desk. "You wanted to see me?"

"Yes, Donald," Allison said. "I wanted you to meet someone. This is Monica Lord. Monica, Donald Jefferson."

Jefferson smiled and stepped into the room, extending a hand toward Monica. "Pleased to meet you," he said.

"I sincerely doubt that," Monica replied.

Jefferson looked at her quizzically, then turned back to Allison. "Am I missing something?"

"Donald, Mrs. Lord is the mole we've been looking for."

Jefferson looked at her for a moment, then turned back to look at Monica. "You?" The incredulous sound in his voice made her look up at him. "Seriously?"

Monica stared at him for a moment, then turned to look at Allison, who—against all logical reason—had a smile on her face.

"I suspect it's me that's missing something here," she said. "I'm going to guess that you knew?"

"Of course," Allison said. "Donald came to me immediately after you contacted him and threatened his wife and daughter. Unlike some of the others in my organization, he knew that cooperating with you without my knowledge would be the biggest mistake he could ever make. Instead, he chose to let me in on it so that I could help him decide what information to share with you. It was necessary, of course, to keep you believing that he was firmly under your control, but the fact of the matter is that he was working against you the entire time."

"And you couldn't have told me this over lunch? Do you have any idea how miserable I felt after I gave him up to you?"

"A little misery is good for everybody, once in a while," Allison said. "The reason I didn't tell you is because I wanted to see your reaction when you met him. After all, there was always the possibility that he was playing us both, but there's no doubt in my mind now that his loyalty is to me and this organization."

"If there was one thing I knew for certain," Donald said, "it was that Allison would do everything in her power to protect my family. If you ever found out that I was playing double agent, you would have found it almost impossible to get any of your people near them. Meanwhile, I was another ace in the hole in our efforts to identify you. I'm sure you understand."

"Understand? You can't imagine how relieved I am. There's nothing worse than having to let someone know that their most trusted friends and associates have betrayed them."

"She must've liked you, Donald," Allison said. "She tried every possible way to avoid giving up your name, but I wasn't having it." She turned and smiled at Monica. "On the other hand, she now knows the futility of trying to deceive me, and I felt it was important that she learn that lesson the hard way."

Monica shook her head. "You people are disgusting, you know that?"

Donald and Allison both laughed. "Join the club, sweetheart," Jefferson said. "You've been at the top of every dirty list in the country for months now."

She managed a grin. "Yeah, yeah, tell me about it. No, on second thought, don't tell me about it. Just tell me where we go from here?"

Allison leaned forward and clasped her hands on her desk. "First, there are a couple of things I need to make clear. Under no circumstances am I going to trust you anytime soon. For that reason, you are going to be under twenty-four-hour surveillance. Any problem with that?"

Monica shrugged. "It's exactly what I would do with someone in my position," she said. "Am I going to get a new assistant or something? Somebody who has to go everywhere with me?"

"No need for that," Allison said. "As I'm sure you're aware, our R&D is one of the most advanced in the world. You'll be paying them a visit this afternoon, where you'll be getting another implant. This one will record every sound around you, even down to picking up the other end of a phone call. Periodically, it will upload the recordings into a highly secured server that will then provide copies to my analysis department. We'll know everything you do, everywhere you go, and everything you say."

"I think I like the assistant idea better."

"Yes, I imagine you would," Allison said, "but that is not an option. It's too easy to slip away from someone assigned to watch you, but you can't get away from yourself. This is part of the price of your survival. Take it or leave it."

"I'll take it, I'll take it. Geez, you people drive a hard bargain."

Allison smiled at her. "Just remember," she said, "we're doing things the easy way. You don't want to know what the hard way would have been."

"Hey, I'm in," Monica said. "You don't have to beat me up over it."

"Sorry, but I'm enjoying myself a bit. You almost cost me some of my best people, remember? I might be willing to extend amnesty, but not without putting a few marks on you of my own."

"Almost?"

"Can I tell her?" Jefferson asked, his voice filled with childish excitement. Allison nodded, and he turned toward Monica. "Remember Randy Mitchell? You had him under your thumb for quite a while, as I recall, and then you ordered Noah to kill him."

Monica's eyes narrowed again. "Yeah," she said cautiously.

"Well, Noah is pretty devious. He decided that he would prefer not to kill Randy, if there was any way to convince you he was dead, so he and his team came up with a way. Poor Randy was given an injection that made him appear to be completely deceased, to the point that the medical examiner was willing to certify it. In reality, though, he was just in the state of suspended animation, so we sent him out to R&D to get a new face and created a whole new identity for him. He'll be back to work within a week."

"And of course," Allison added, "if anything were to happen to his sisters, our entire deal with you is off. You understand that, right?"

"Understood," Monica said. "They are in no danger from me."

"Well, okay, then," Allison said. "Donald will take you out to R&D for your little procedure, while I get started on putting together your supervisory committee. They'll be based in DC, so you might plan to spend the next month or so bringing them up to date on your activities. I've got it set up so that you will speak to them only on a conference call, so that they will not know who you are. Once you get finished here, you can go on home. I'll give you a call sometime in the next few days to let you know when the committee will be ready for you."

Monica just looked at her for a long moment, but then Donald chivalrously offered her his arm. "Shall we go?"

Allison managed to hold on until they had gotten into the elevator before she cracked up laughing.

CHAPTER FIFTEEN

"So," Monica said as they rode down the elevator, "you were playing me the whole time?"

Jefferson smiled at her. "Just doing my job," he said. "Allison and I decided together what items of information I should pass along, and a lot of it was very real. I'm sure that you gained some genuine benefit from the things I gave you, but only so far as we were willing to allow."

"She was right, you know. I did kind of like you. That's why I tried hard not to give you up, even though I knew you'd find out I had accepted this deal and would know you are free of me."

"Yes, and there's a part of me that appreciates that," Jefferson said. "On the other hand, you should know that Allison is probably one of the most shrewd and cunning people I have ever known. Even attempting to refuse her what she wants could be suicidal. That applies to everyone who works for her, as much as it does to you. If she ever thinks for a minute that I'm genuinely disloyal, she would not hesitate to send Noah or one of the others to pay me a visit."

The elevator door opened in the parking garage, and Jefferson led Monica to his car, which turned out to be a new Tesla. He opened the passenger door for her like a gentleman, and she slid in. She had her seat belt buckled by the time he got behind the wheel, and then they were pulling out of the garage.

"I'll confess I'm a little excited," Monica said. "I never thought I'd actually get to see the inside of your R&D, or meet Wally. Does he know that he's quite a legend in the entire intelligence community?"

"I think he knows," Jefferson said with a chuckle, "but Wally is the kind of guy it wouldn't matter to. He's not so much interested in being famous or legendary as he is in coming up with his newest creation. He's shown me things they're working on that literally blow my mind. Maybe I'll ask him to let you see a few of them while we're there."

"Are you getting me that good a clearance? I know that most of Wally's work is TS/R."

"Allison says there's no point in trying to keep any secrets from you. You probably already know a lot of this stuff, but there's also the fact that you may sometimes need us to provide you information or equipment in order to do what we are asking you to do. If we went through normal channels, you'd probably never get a true top secret clearance, but these are not normal circumstances. Allison has the authority, granted by the president, to activate anyone she chooses in any capacity. She's chosen to activate you."

"Thank God for small favors. And yes, I'd love to see anything Wally has come up with. Like I said, he's a legend."

They arrived at R&D a short time later, allowed through by the security guards on Jefferson's authority. As second-in-command of E & E, he was allowed to override normal security protocols. His own ID was carefully examined and scanned, but none of the guards questioned Monica's presence.

When the security officer at R&D had finished scanning his ID, he handed it back and then notified Wally that Jefferson was there with a guest. Monica's eyes went wide when they heard running footsteps, and then Wally came skidding around the corner into the foyer. He stared at Monica for a moment, then motioned silently for the two of them to follow him back to his office.

As soon as they were inside and the door was secured, Wally turned to Monica with a huge smile and held out both hands. She reached up to shake with him, but he wrapped her right hand in both of his and brought it to his lips, then kissed it gently before releasing it.

"Allison briefed me this morning," he said. "I cannot tell you what an honor it is to finally meet you face-to-face. Mrs. Lord, you have done some incredible things, and the fact that you did most of them alone simply speaks to what a genius you must be. I am humbled to be in your presence."

Monica stared at him for several seconds, then turned to Jefferson. "Has he flipped?"

Jefferson laughed. "Monica, you need to understand something. Even the most seasoned espionage agents have never given our intelligence agencies half the headaches that you did. To Wally, you are the one who is a legend."

She rolled her eyes and turned back to Wally. "The honor is mine," she said. "Every intelligence agency in the world wishes they had you designing their equipment. I understand I'm here for what might be an unpleasant procedure, but there's a little bit of pride I'm feeling in the fact that it will be a Wally Lawson device that's being implanted in me. I understand it'll be something that can actually keep track of every sound around me, is that right?"

Wally started laughing, and his laughter was so high-pitched that it sounded like a slightly insane giggle. "Oh, I've come up with something better than that," he said. "When Allison told me you were coming in and that she wanted me to fit you with a monitoring device, I called a couple of our bright kids and asked them for something special. It took them almost three hours to put it together, but it's awesome." He turned to one of the tables and picked up something that looked like a thin blank quarter. "We're going to put this just under the muscle above your left breast. It's got a miniature diamond betavoltaic battery that will last for—well, pretty much forever, and it will deftly record every sound around you, but it does even more than that. Every couple of seconds, it will send out a burst of UHF sound waves that act like super-sophisticated radar. Those waves won't even be slowed down by the tissues of your body, but they'll echo back a clear image of everything around you. It'll be in black and white, of course, but we'll actually be able to see who you're talking to, where you are, everything. Isn't that great?"

Monica's smile turned into something of a grimace. "Absolutely fantastic," she said sarcastically. "Are those sound waves going to cause me any harm? What about cancer risk, things like that?"

"Oh, the risk is very low," Wally said. "We calculate that there's less than a ten-percent chance it'll ever cause cancer, but you might experience a little loss of bone density. You probably want to start taking calcium supplements now, instead of waiting for menopause."

Monica made a face. "Only ten percent, huh? Oh well, I guess I'll take whatever good news I can get. Is this gonna hurt?"

"Oh, you'll be sore for a few days. The doctor will actually make the incision up under your armpit and insert the disk from there. That way, you won't have a visible scar. Are you ready?"

Monica swallowed and looked at Jefferson. "Um, Mr. Jefferson suggested that you might show me around a little bit before we get started. He said you've got some really great new things that you like to show off."

Wally spun and looked at Jefferson, his smile getting even bigger. "Can I?"

Jefferson, doing his best not to burst out into belly-busting laughter, nodded his head. "Sure, Wally," he said. "She's one of ours, now. Allison says we can show her anything."

Wally spun back around and grabbed Monica by her left hand, then yanked the door open and took her out into the hallway. He was moving quickly, and it was a little hard for her to keep up, but she managed.

"First thing I want to show you," he said, "is something that no-body else has seen yet—well, except for Allison and Donnie and a couple of people who work here. You're going to get the biggest kick out of this, I swear you will. Come on, it's right down the hall."

Jefferson followed along, and they turned and entered a workshop on the left of the hall. Wally closed the door behind them and then pointed at a young woman who was sitting behind a desk.

"This is Esmeralda," he said.

Esmeralda looked up at Wally, then turned her face toward Monica. "Well, hello," she said. "What can I do for you today?"

Monica put on a smile. "Hello, Esmeralda," she said. "I'm Monica. Wally says you've got something interesting to show me?"

Esmeralda looked at Wally, and her eyebrows went up. "I do?"

Wally nodded. "Yes. Show her sequence twenty-seven."

Esmeralda smiled at him, then pushed her chair back away from the desk and got to her feet. She came around the desk until she was standing just in front of Monica and held out her hand. Monica took it and shook with her; then her eyes dropped to the hand she was holding.

She was literally holding it. Esmeralda had pulled her arm back, leaving the hand gripped in Monica's own. Monica stared at it for a couple of seconds and then squealed when the hand squeezed. She tried to let go and drop it, but it held on, and she raised her eyes to look at the end of the girl's arm.

Esmeralda raised the stump so she could look closely at it, and Monica saw that it was some sort of mechanical device. There were wires and connectors inside, and she looked up in shock at Esmeralda's face.

"Is this some kind of bionic arm?"

Esmeralda smiled. "Oh, no, it's mine," she said. "I'm a robot, you see. I'm not a true automaton, however. Everything I do is the result of programming designed to respond to particular words, situations, or stimuli. May I have my hand back?"

Her eyes wide, Monica nodded and held the hand out toward her. Esmeralda took it in her left hand and snapped it back onto her wrist. The artificial skin around it seemed to vibrate for a second, and then the seam was almost completely invisible. Monica looked at her other left wrist and saw that it also had a nearly invisible seam.

"But—but you seem so alive," she said.

Esmeralda smiled, and Monica noticed the first thing that looked artificial. There appeared to be no moisture inside her mouth at all, and the teeth that showed in the smile were unnaturally dry and white.

"Oh, thank you," Esmeralda said. "I was designed to pass as human under simple visual inspection. Of course, if someone got very close to me, they might notice a few things that didn't quite look right."

Monica nodded, still somewhat in shock. "Yes, your smile looks a little fake," she said. "Your eyes seem awfully dry, too."

"Yes, but I understand my designers are working on correcting those issues. Before long, it will be possible to tell me from human except with technological equipment."

Monica turned to Wally. "You've built a robot?"

"No. Well, yes, she's a robot, but not the way you would normally think of a robot. Esmeralda is not intelligent; there's no AI involvement. She can't think for herself; she can only respond in ways she'd been programmed to respond. She's actually been designed as a weapon-delivery device." He beamed, proud of his accomplishment.

"Weapon-delivery device?" Monica asked, her eyes wider than ever. "What kind of weapon?"

"Oh, chemical, explosive, maybe a biological weapon. Theoretically, we could even build a small nuclear device that would fit inside her. She would go to whatever destination she was told to go to and then release a chemical or germ agent, or detonate an explosive or nuke."

Monica's eyes were bouncing back and forth between Wally and Esmeralda. "And have you never heard what Stephen Hawking and

Elon Musk say about robots? What would you do that she decided she didn't want to cooperate?"

"Oh, she can't. She can't decide anything. All she can do is follow her programming, which requires her to accept spoken instructions and adapt them into that program. If I told her to go to, for instance, the Grand Canyon and jump in, she'd start walking. She'd keep going until her batteries ran down, which they never will, or she receives different instructions from someone who's authorized to give them to her. The only other way to stop her would be to break her to the point that she could not proceed. I mean, if you ran over her with a car, that would probably do it."

Monica looked Esmeralda up and down, then shook her head. "Esmeralda, what would happen if I told you to do something?"

Esmeralda smiled again. "If it was something simple, such as to get something for you, I would probably obey. If you told me to do something that falls under my higher-functions programming, I would simply apologize and tell you that I could not comply with your request."

Monica turned to Wally. "Her speech and mannerisms seem almost completely human. How did you manage that without artificial intelligence?"

"We assigned over a hundred different programmers to work on code modules. One programmer would write the code that enables her to smile and tells her what situations call for it, while another handled the parts that allow her to frown. Every human mannerism and function has been programmed into her, even those that are considered rude or socially unacceptable. She has over three thousand separate programs for facial expressions alone, almost seven thousand that control body movements and body language. We actually took her to Denver and put her on a commercial flight to Los Angeles and back a couple of weeks ago, and nobody paid enough attention to realize she wasn't human. She even had a couple of guys flirting with her, and engaged in several small-talk conversations with other passengers. From what we could tell, nobody even suspected she wasn't exactly what she appears to be, just a pretty young woman."

"You mean she didn't leave anybody holding her hand?"

"Nope. She kept everything attached, just the way it's supposed to be. Of course, we sent a couple of our people on the same flights to keep an eye on her, but it was actually unnecessary. She checked herself in, boarded the plane, chitchatted with the passenger beside her on the way to LA, took a taxi to an address we told her to visit, took another taxi back to the airport, and got on her return flight without a hitch. Once we iron out a couple of tiny little wrinkles like the dry-eyes thing, we could send her to just about anywhere in the world. The only problem we might run into is if she had to go through one of the X-ray scanners."

"Wait a minute," Monica said. "How does she get past the metal detectors?"

"Her skin," Wally said. "It blocks the metal detectors from sensing any of the metals inside her. That's something else we came up with here. Pretty cool, right?"

"Does anybody else know about this? Outside of here, I mean?"

"Nope. Esmeralda is all ours. She'll only be deployed as a last resort, if there's no other way to handle a mission."

Monica shook her head again. "Wally, this is incredible. I mean, I am literally blown away. I've seen all the robots on YouTube, and none of them actually look as real as Esmeralda does."

"Yes, I know," Wally said. "I'm pretty sure she's the best there is, although I know the Chinese and the Russians are both working on robots that can pass. I'd love to see the results of their work, if you ever run across any information on that."

"I'll be sure to let it be known I'm looking," Monica said. "Frankly, this scares me to death. What possible use could there be for a robot like her?"

"Oh, the possibilities are endless. I mean, what if you had a hostage situation and there was no way to take out the bad guys? We dress Esmeralda up as a nurse, maybe, and send her in to help somebody who's injured or sick, and then she just lets out a gas that puts everybody to sleep. Or maybe there's a madman in control of a country, and nobody can get close to him except a pretty girl he thinks he can, you know, put the moves on. Esmeralda can smile and flirt her way right up close, then detonate the bomb inside and he's gone, just like that. Or maybe she just gives him an extreme sepsis infection. He thinks he's fine, but half an hour later he falls ill and is dead within ten minutes. Pretty wild, huh?"

Monica swallowed hard. "Pretty wild, yeah. What else you got to show me?"

Wally snapped his fingers and motioned for her to follow him, leaving Esmeralda standing where she was. Monica looked at the robot for another second, and then she and Jefferson followed Wally out the door.

They went down the hall to another room and stepped inside. A couple of technicians were working on something on a table at the back of the room, but all Monica saw was the row of what looked like large model cars and airplanes on a table just inside the door.

"These are also robots," Wally said with pride. "Just like Esmeralda, they can be packed with explosives, chemicals, or bioweapons and sent just about anywhere. The cars can drive, the airplanes can fly, and we've got some that are built like boats, too. All we have to do is input a GPS location and turn them loose, and they go where they're supposed to go. Once they get there, they either do whatever job they were sent for, or they notify an operator that they are in place. Then the operator can decide when to set them off."

Monica grinned. "Well, I've got to say these are a little easier to handle than Esmeralda," she said. "Although, it might seem a little odd to see a toy car driving itself around, or a toy plane flying."

"No, we've done some testing. Most people simply think it's some kind of remote-controlled toy, and that some kid somewhere is behind. Nobody really pays them any attention, although we did have a couple of cases where somebody tried to grab one and run off with it. After that, we designed them to give a shock to anybody who even tries to pick them up."

"Have you used any of these in an actual mission"? Monica asked.

"No, not yet. Only in testing. Allison wants to be absolutely certain that they'll only go where they're supposed to go before we turn them loose in the field." He leaned toward her conspiratorially. "The planes can actually fly straight into a target, like a miniature guided missile. We make them out of a proprietary explosive that has almost thirty times the explosive power of an equivalent weight of TNT."

Monica looked at him. "I've heard of that explosive," she said. "That's the stuff you can use in a 3-D printer?"

Wally nodded, his smile close to splitting his face. "Yes, yes," he said. "That's how we make these. The frames and bodies and everything are made right in one of our printers, and all we have to do is add our detonator chip if we wanted to be able to explode. If not, that stuff is so stable that you can toss it in a fire and it won't explode. You can run over it, shoot it with the gun, whatever, and it still won't explode without that detonator."

"How do you manage that? I didn't know you can make an explosive that was that stable."

"It's our proprietary compound. It has lots of power when it goes off, but it takes extreme heat to make it explode. All we've got to do is put that extreme heat to one tiny part of a piece made with our material, and the whole thing will go boom all at once."

"And when you say extreme heat..."

"Well, if you were to hit one of these with an acetylene torch, that would get it hot enough to go off. The average fire can't get that hot, though, so it's highly unlikely anybody would ever manage to blow one up by accident."

Monica stared at him for several seconds, then shook her head again. "Wally," she said, "you are every bit the evil genius I've heard you called." She turned to Jefferson. "Can we just get this implant done so I can leave? This place is starting to scare me just a little bit."

Wally burst out laughing and led them to another part of the building, where the medical team was waiting. Dr. Reed, the surgeon who had removed the bomb from Noah, was waiting to implant the disk, and Slocum was there to handle anesthesia. They wasted no time in getting Monica ready and performing the procedure, though she noticed that neither of them seemed inclined to chat.

Two hours later, with her armpit still numb, Monica got to watch on a computer monitor as they activated the disk. She was absolutely amazed at how clear the images were, as echoes from the ultrasound pulses generated by the disk were recorded and interpreted. The pulses went out in every direction, allowing the computer to build a three-hundred-and-sixty-degree image of what was happening around her.

"That is absolutely incredible," she said after a few minutes. "Donald, I can actually recognize your face. Yours, too, Wally."

"Which means we'll be able to identify anyone you come into contact with," Jefferson said. "Is there anybody you want to tell us about now?"

Monica looked at him for a few long seconds, then nodded. "I think maybe we should go back and see the Dragon Lady again."

When they arrived back at Allison's office, Jefferson told her quickly that the operation had been a success and the disk was doing exactly what it was supposed to do. "I made a point of letting Monica observe just how well the computer can interpret the echoes, so she thinks it might be a good idea to share a few names with you."

Allison turned to Monica, smiling. "Good girl," she said. "Who are we talking about?"

"Well, there are a few names I need to give you," Monica said. "However, the main one—I want to ask you not to let anything bad happen to him. Is that possible?"

"It might be. I'd say it depends on who we're talking about and the circumstances."

Monica bit her bottom lip for a second, then frowned. "I've been having an affair," she said. "It's gone on for many, many years, and unfortunately, it's been the source of some of my information."

"You're referring to Senator Wiggins?" Allison asked.

Monica's eyebrows rose. "You already knew?"

"One of our analysts discovered that you and the senator tend to visit the same places and stay in the same hotels, so it wasn't that big a stretch. Is he aware of what you do?"

"No! No, I swear, he knows nothing. He's just accidentally let a few things slip, and it was enough to get me started. Kind of told me who to focus on when I started trying to gain power over people, you know?"

Allison nodded. "Does your husband know about your clandestine activities? Any of them?"

"Oh, goodness, no," Monica said. "Jonathan is a businessman and nothing else. I'm not going to say he doesn't love me or the kids, but his first love is business. He helps other companies get started, and that's his passion. And before you ask, he doesn't know about Charles, either."

"And you don't want to give up your affair?"

Monica looked at Allison for several seconds, then lowered her eyes to the floor. "I love my husband, Allison," she said, "but in the way that you love a familiar friend. I was never 'in love' with him, but being his wife offered me some camouflage I felt I would need. First, it was just about keeping my affair with Charles a secret, but later I realized that being Mrs. Lord afforded me a certain amount of anonymity. Sure, I own Monica's Beauty Secrets, but that's run by a board of directors in California, not by me. Being Jonathan's wife keeps me out of the spotlight, and that gives me the freedom to do everything else I feel I need to do." She sighed. "As for Charles? If I have to admit it, Charles is the one that I truly love. If he weren't in politics, I would've married him a long time ago, and I might have even left Jonathan for him. Hell, I'm pretty sure the twins are his, anyway, so no, I don't want to give him up."

"I'll keep your secret about Senator Wiggins," Allison said. "Just remember that we'll know everything the two of you talk about from now on."

Monica raised her eyes to meet Allison's. "Believe me," she said. "That's something I'll never be able to forget."

CHAPTER SIXTEEN

Noah awoke at two in the afternoon, checked out of the hotel, and picked up his lunch at a drive-through. By two thirty, he was on the interstate and headed back to Sarah. Once he finished eating his sandwich, he took out his phone and called her to let her know he was on the way, then set the cruise control at eighty and watched the road ahead.

After two stops for gas and another run through a fast-food place for dinner, he finally decided to stop again at midnight. He had made it to Louisville, Kentucky, which put him about eight hours out from Berryville, so he pulled into a motel and got a room, took another quick shower, and was asleep within minutes.

He rose the next morning at seven and took off again, a couple of egg-and-sausage biscuits and a large, incredibly hot coffee for breakfast. The big engine in the Charger sang to him as he rolled along, the cruise back on eighty and the stereo cranking out his favorite country music.

I-64 took him all the way to St. Louis, where he picked up I-44, then followed it to Springfield. From there he went south on Highway 65 until he got to Highway 86, then followed the now-familiar back roads into the state of Arkansas and on to Berryville.

It was just after three when he pulled up to his house, and Sarah came running out the door to greet him. She threw her arms around him and kissed him passionately, until he finally just picked her up and carried her into the house.

Neil and Marco were on the couch, playing a video game on the big TV. When he entered, they put down the controllers and followed as he carried Sarah into the kitchen and set her in a chair. He took another one for himself and stretched out his long legs as the other men sat down.

"Okay, so give," Neil said. "What's the deal with Monique?"

"I talked to Allison just a little while ago, and Monique—her real name is Monica, by the way—is now firmly under E & E control. She'll be reporting to a supervisory committee next week in DC, where she will begin her work as a clandestine agent of the government."

"You mean she gets away with it?" Neil asked, seemingly in shock. "All the stuff she did, they're just going to sweep it all under the table?"

"Believe it or not," Noah said, "pretty much everything she was doing was because she loves this country. Once we identified her, I suggested that it might be better to put her to work rather than kill her or lock her up, and Allison agreed. She's now sporting one of the embedded monitors like the one we used on Randy Mitchell, and Molly is in charge of the team that is keeping tabs on her. She slips up even once, Molly will catch it."

"And what about what she did to Sarah?" Marco asked. "We just gonna let that slide?"

"Hey," Sarah interrupted. "I trust Noah's judgment. If he thinks she can be an asset, then I'm behind him on it." She looked at Noah. "Just don't ever expect me to have to deal with her personally. I'm afraid my inner Noah might come out and decide to rip her head off."

"I doubt either of us will ever have to deal with her at all," Noah said, "unless she makes a big mistake."

The two men grumbled for a moment, but Sarah shushed them. "Now," she said, "what about this mission? Where do we stand on it?"

"I'm ready to execute," Noah said. "I thought about it on the way back, and there's no reason to put it off. I'll go see Morgan in the morning and try to get him to call a meeting of everyone we identified as a target. As soon as we can be certain they're all together, I'll detonate."

"Damn," Neil said. "This will be the biggest one yet."

"Yes, but it's necessary. Strangely enough, it was Monica who actually made me understand just how necessary it is. My only concern is to try to minimize any collateral damage. Some of these people have children, and I'd hate for them to be caught in the blast."

Sarah reached across the table and laid her hand on his. "I almost wish there was another way to shut him down," she said. "Some of these were probably good people, once, but I can tell you from past experience that money can corrupt anybody. I saw what it did to my dad, and it was even getting to me by the time I got busted. I loved having the money to do anything I wanted to do, and I didn't care what I had to do to get it, so I can sort of sympathize with some of these people."

Noah looked at her for a moment, then squeezed her hand. "I don't know how to sympathize," he said, "but I understand what you're saying. The problem is that these people, if I let them live, might have the wherewithal to resurrect the Morgan Mafia. This organization needs to be shut down, and it needs to be shut down now."

"Then we do it," Marco said. "Simple as that. What do you want me to do, boss? Hell, I didn't even get to play my Cajun part properly, not yet."

"You and I will go to Morgan's in the morning," Noah said, "just as if nothing was going on. I'll give him some BS about the liquor operation I was supposedly working on and then suggest that we need to get everyone together for a meeting. As soon as we know when and where, I'll start planning for the execution."

"Okay. What about after?"

"After a blast like this, it'll be pretty obvious that something went down. Feds will be coming in to round up the dirty cops and prosecutors, and I'm sure the state investigators will get involved, as well. It probably wouldn't be wise for me to show my face around here after it all goes off, because there will be plenty of people who were dependent on Morgan who are going to be extremely pissed that the gravy train has come to an end. Last thing I need is one of them trying to put a bullet in me out of revenge, so I think Neil and Sarah should pack up and head out before it happens." He turned to Sarah. "How much stuff will you need to pack?"

"Not really that much," she said. "Most of the stuff we brought with us was actually from Supply. My own real personal stuff will fit into one big suitcase."

"I can't leave the printer behind," Neil said, "or my computer, of course. I only brought one bag of clothes, but the printer is a big item."

"That's not a problem," Sarah said. "Everything will fit in the back of the Explorer. Should we go ahead and start packing now?"

"Not just yet," Noah replied. "We don't want to take the risk of tipping anyone off about what's going on. If they see us preparing to leave town, it could blow the whole operation."

The four of them sat at the table and looked at one another for a moment, and then Sarah took a deep breath. "Well," she said, looking around the kitchen. "This was kind of nice while it lasted."

"It's a nice little house," Noah said. "Once Morgan is gone, this will probably be a pretty decent little town again. Somebody will want this place."

"I wish we could keep it," she said softly. "It would be a great place to retire to, someday."

Noah checked himself just before commenting that they would probably never live long enough to retire. To him, it was simple logic; to Sarah, the thought would be devastating.

"It's a nice thought, anyway." He took out his phone and dialed Morgan's number. The man answered after only a couple of rings.

"Rex? That you?"

"It's me, Jimmy," Noah said. "I just got back in, and I'm pretty beat. Mind if I just get with you in the morning?"

"Normally, I'd say that's fine," Morgan said, "but something's come up. Can you get on out here now? I won't keep you very long, but we need to talk."

"Yes, sir," Noah said. "I'll be there in just a few minutes." He disconnected and looked at Sarah and the guys. "Morgan says there's something happening and that we need to talk."

"Oh, God," Sarah said. "What if he's found out you're not who you're supposed to be?"

Noah thought about it for a couple of seconds, then shook his head. "I think he wouldn't have waited till I got back," he said. "The way he operates, he probably would have sent someone out here to try to grab you, put me at a disadvantage. I'll go see what he wants, but I don't think it's anything that's going to blow up in my face at the moment."

He got up and walked out the door, then opened the driver's door on the Charger and got in. He fired up the engine and backed around into the driveway, then headed out to the road.

When he pulled up at Morgan's house, he was surprised at the number of cars parked close to it. There were six men standing outside in the front, and he could see a few more on the south side. He got out of the car and walked toward the house, paying careful attention to the men who were obviously on guard duty.

One of them was Shawn, and he gave Noah a mock salute. "Sure glad you're here," he said softly. "I don't know if you're going to be able to fix what's going on, but the boss is having fits in there. Scott says he needs you to come straighten it all out."

Noah gave him a nod and walked up the steps. When he knocked on the door, it was Scott Forney who opened it, rather than Marlene.

"Thank goodness you're here," Forney said. "We got a big problem, and Jimmy says he needs you to figure a way to sort it out."

"What's the problem?" Noah asked.

Forney looked nervous. "It's Ralphie," he said. "You know, there's some things you just don't do, even when your daddy is the most powerful man in the whole state, you know?"

Noah let out an exasperated sigh. "What now?" he asked.

Forney shook his head, a scowl on his face. "You know he was dating the mayor's daughter, right? Well, I guess some high school jock decided he wanted to get into her pants, and Ralphie found out about it. He gave us the slip this afternoon and went after him, and now I guess the kid's turned up dead. He was the star of the football team, and the whole damn town is in an uproar. Sheriff called Jimmy a couple hours ago and said he's got no choice but to arrest the kid."

Noah stared at him for a couple of seconds, then turned and headed toward the dining room, where he could hear a number of voices speaking loudly. Ralph was sitting at the table, his head down and his hands clenched between his knees, while Jimmy was standing over him.

"Everything I built, everything I've done to try to make life better for you than it was for me, you may have done thrown it all away," he shouted. "And for what? Some little tramp who let you get her pants down? How many times have I told you, boy, women ain't nothing but trouble. You find one, you keep her till she's used up, and then you kick her ass to the curb and get another one. If she goes out and plays around on you, just count yourself lucky that you found out and move on to the next one."

"But, Pa," Ralph said, but he didn't get a chance to say any more. Jimmy backhanded him across his left cheek.

"Don't you ever say 'but' to me, you little son of a bitch! I am the one who tells you how it's going to be—you don't get a say in anything until I tell you so. You got that?" Jimmy looked up and saw Noah, and the rage in his eyes toned down slightly. "Thank God you're here," he said. "Rex, I screwed up when I took you off Ralphie. This stupid little bastard has done gone and messed up everything."

"I heard a little bit," Noah said. "Somebody's dead, I heard. Who is it?"

"Dave Pritchett," Morgan said. "Just the freaking star quarterback of the football team, that's all."

Noah glanced down at Ralph, but the boy was keeping his eyes on the tabletop. He looked back up at Morgan. "Jimmy, did Ralph kill the boy?"

Instead of answering, Jimmy turned and backhanded Ralph again. "Open your mouth and speak, boy," he yelled. "Answer the man."

Ralph raised his face, and Noah saw the tears streaming down his cheeks. "I—I—I didn't mean to," he said. "I just told him to stay away from Darlene, and he started yelling about who did I think I was, and then he threw a punch at me, and then I went to hit him back—and the next thing I knew he was down and there was blood, like, everywhere. I tried to make sure he was okay, but he didn't answer, he didn't even look like he was breathing, so I just got out of there and ran. I got to a gas station, and then I called Scott and he came and got me..."

"Do we know for sure that the boy is dead?" Noah asked.

"Oh, he's dead all right," Morgan said. "Sheriff called a couple hours ago. This all happened out behind the high school, and a half-dozen kids found him as they were trying to cut class. Cops went to check it out, and it seems like half the school claims they saw Ralph and this kid go out behind the football stadium." He shook his head. "And if that wasn't enough, the kid apparently tore the pocket on Ralph's jacket, where he kept his wallet. They found it right beside the body."

"Okay," Noah said, "then we've got to figure out how to handle the situation. What did the sheriff say?"

"He says the whole town is screaming for blood, and it's Ralph's blood they want. He said he's got to come and arrest my boy, but there's no way in hell I'm gonna let that happen."

Noah looked at the man for a moment, then turned back to Ralph. "Was anyone else with you when this happened?"

Ralph shook his head. "Was just me and him," he said. "All I wanted to do was tell him to back off. I didn't mean none of this to happen."

Noah stared at the boy for a couple of minutes and was surprised that no one else bothered to speak the entire time. When he felt he had pushed the limits of Morgan's patience, he looked the man in the eye. "The way I see it," he began slowly, "we've only got two options. One—and hear me out, you're not going to like this—we let the sheriff take him in and put him in a cell for tonight, then we find someone else to pin the killing on. Number two..."

"Hell, no," Morgan yelled. "They get my boy in the jail, with the whole town out to hang him, we'll be finished around here. I've had the sheriff in my pocket for years, but if enough of these people want me shut down so Ralph can go up for murder, he's gonna be looking out for himself. Next thing we know, feds will be all over this place and we'll all go down."

"Not if we can convince everyone that someone else did it," Noah said. "Maybe even make it look like a deliberate frame-up. If you can give me a name of someone that's expendable, I guarantee I can make it look like that's what happened."

Morgan stared at him, his face still red with anger. "What's the other option?"

"Your only other option is to stand your ground," Noah said. "Call in everybody you've got and get ready for war. It won't save Ralph, though, and it'll probably bring down the very feds you're worried about now. I know this isn't what you want to hear, but you pay me to be blunt with you, right?"

Morgan stood there, one hand on the back of Ralph's chair and the other clenched into a fist. He kept silent for several seconds, then suddenly slapped Ralph up the back side of his head. "Damn you, boy," he said. He looked up at Noah again. "You absolutely sure you can find somebody else to pin this on?"

"Just tell me who," Noah said. "I'll go get him and make sure there's evidence pointing his direction."

"And how you gonna do that? Cops are all over the place where it happened."

Noah gave him an evil grin. "Just trust me," he said. "I can handle this."

Morgan watched him for a couple more seconds, then narrowed his eyes. "You done something like this before?"

Noah shrugged. "Remember I told you they never could figure out who killed that DEA agent?"

Morgan sat down at the table and put his elbows on it, resting his face in his hands. "Rex, this boy is all I got. If you can't pull this off, he'll go down for murder and we're probably all headed for prison, somewhere. If the sheriff turns against me, every other cop in the region is gonna follow him."

"Which is exactly why we've got to help the sheriff save face. If we don't, it's all going to fall apart. If we do, then he's going to be so deep into you that he can't possibly let anything go wrong."

Morgan leaned back in his chair and dropped his hands to his lap, then looked at his son. "You understand what's going on here, boy?"

Ralph nodded his head but said nothing.

"Ralph," Noah said, taking a seat beside the boy, "here's the way it would go down. Your dad calls the sheriff and tells him it's okay to come pick you up, because we're certain that we can prove your innocence. When they get here, you go with them peacefully and you keep your mouth shut. No matter what they say, no matter what they do, you don't say a single word. Understand me?"

Once again, Ralph nodded.

"What about a lawyer?" Morgan asked. "Should I get one now for him?"

"No, not yet. If you do, that makes everyone around here think Ralph must be guilty, so we want everyone to see that you're not the least bit worried about that. Once the sheriff picks him up, you should go out to dinner, go have a few drinks. Let people see you laughing about this and talking about how stupid the sheriff is going to feel when the truth comes out tomorrow. A lot of this is about perception, and the story going around right now is that Ralph is a monster of some sort. You need to get out there and start changing the story. If people see you acting unconcerned, most of them are going to think you know something they don't. That's exactly what we want them to think, because that will cause rumors to spread, rumors that maybe Ralph didn't do it, after all."

Morgan clenched his jaw a couple of times but then finally nodded his head. "Okay, we'll play it your way. But, Rex, if this goes sour..."

"It won't. Trust me, Jimmy, I know what I'm doing here. Now, you got a name for me?"

Morgan looked around the room, as if searching for an answer. "I don't know," he said. "Scott? Any ideas?"

Forney was leaning against the wall, but now he stood up straight. "What about Pete Wesley? He's a punk and a drunk, and he's always getting into some kind of trouble."

"Yeah, but what would he be doing behind the high school?" Morgan asked. "We need somebody who wouldn't be considered out of place, there."

"He hangs out there, sometimes," Forney said. "He's been known to supply booze and pot in exchange for a little bit of sweet young thing."

"That's perfect," Noah said. "This guy ever been known to be violent? Especially with his hands?"

"He's beat up a few people," Morgan said. "But don't you think somebody would have noticed if he was hanging around the high school, today? He's about thirty years old, and he's been around here his whole life."

"That's not a problem," Noah said. "Where does he work? What kind of stuff is he into?"

Forney looked at Morgan, then turned to Noah. "He doesn't have a regular job," he said. "Just mows lawns and does odd jobs. He's on disability or something and gets food stamps. Drinks, and I mean a lot. Now and then he decides to get stoned, especially if there's any girls around, and he's been known to use meth."

"He'll do," Noah said. "Scott, take a couple of your boys and go find him. Load him up and head for my place, and then give me a call. I need to have a chat with him as soon as possible." He turned to Morgan as Forney turned and walked out the door. "You need to make that call to the sheriff, Jimmy. Tell him that you found out what's really going on, and you'll make arrangements for him to know tomorrow. Tell him it's okay to come and get Ralph, because you'll be able to prove he didn't do it."

"And you want me to act like I'm cheerful about this, right?"

"No, you can be as mad as you want," Noah answered. "Your position is that you are putting up with this only because you want to see the truth come out and justice done. It doesn't matter how many people around here know the truth about you, everybody wants to believe that the people with the power have their best interests at heart. If you are cooperating, that makes it look like you are out to protect everybody else, not just your son."

Morgan shook his head again, but then he nodded. "Okay," he said. "I'm trusting you on this, Rex." He took his phone out of his pocket and called the sheriff, and Noah was amazed at how skillfully he pulled off his act.

Noah turned to Ralph. "Tomorrow, as early as I can arrange it, the sheriff is going to be handed a new suspect. He's probably going to ask you a few questions, like how this guy got hold of your wallet. The only thing you say when he asks that question is that you ran into him yesterday, but that's all you know. You didn't know your wallet was missing until you heard they found it near the body. You got that?"

Ralph nodded but didn't say anything. Noah patted him on the shoulder and then turned to listen to Morgan as he spoke with the sheriff.

CHAPTER SEVENTEEN

Noah stayed until the sheriff came and arrested Ralph, then headed back out to the farmhouse. He didn't know how long it would take Forney to find this Wesley character, and he was definitely tired. Even an hour's nap would help.

Unfortunately, he didn't get it. Forney called just before he got to his driveway, and Noah told him to bring the man out as soon as he could. He drove past the house and up to one of the outbuildings, then walked inside the house to explain what was going on.

"Apparently," he said, "Ralph Morgan beat another boy to death today. I understand there's been rumors in the past that he might've done something like this, but this is the first time anyone has been sure. Marco, I need Aubrey to help me out tonight. We are about to convince somebody that he wants to confess to the killing."

Sarah looked at him, confused. "But, why? If you're going to complete the mission in the next day or so, anyway, why would you go along with this?"

"That's precisely why," Noah said. "In order to get Morgan to call everyone together, I have to keep his confidence. This will be the second time I've saved Ralph's ass, so when I suggest it in the next day or two, Morgan is almost certain to agree."

"And what about this guy?" Neil asked. "Is he going to go down for a murder he didn't commit?"

"No. Once the mission is complete, I can arrange for Allison to send a message clearing him. The FBI will be in charge here, by then, anyway."

"Okay," Sarah said reluctantly. "I guess it all makes sense."

"If it don' make sense," Marco said, his Cajun accent flaring, "den dis man, Rex, he don' be doin' it. He do everyt'ing what make sense, 'cause dat how he tinks!"

"Oh, geez, Marco," Sarah said, chuckling. "I will never get used to you talking that way."

"Good thing you didn't know me when I was young, then," Marco said, grinning. "That's the accent and patois I grew up with. If anything, I speak it a little more clearly now than I did then."

Headlights flashed across the front window as Forney's car turned in to the driveway. Noah kissed Sarah, and he and Marco headed out to the shed he'd chosen. He stood in the driveway so that Forney could see him, and waited until he pulled the car up close.

Forney and another man got out, and then Forney opened the back door of the car. He reached inside and took the arm of Peter Wesley, who looked a lot like a frightened Southern hillbilly. The man wore bib overalls with a T-shirt and had a John Deere hat on his head. It had obviously been some time since he had either showered or shaved, and Noah simply pointed toward the door of the shed that Marco was holding open.

Forney and his helper, a man named Lindell, dragged Wesley inside, and Noah and Marco followed. Noah found a small barrel and set it in the middle of the floor, then ordered Wesley to sit on top of it. Noah stepped in front of him while the other three took up positions around him.

"Found him at that little trailer he lives in," Forney said, "down by the chicken plant. Took us half an hour just to get him awake enough to come with us."

Noah looked at the man on the barrel. "You're Peter Wesley?" Noah asked, and the frightened man nodded vigorously.

"Yes, sir, yes," Wesley said. "Can I ask what this is all about?"

"Where were you at one o'clock this afternoon, Mr. Wesley?" Noah asked.

"One o'clock? Me? I—I was at home. Why?" He looked around at each of the faces, obviously trying to figure out where this was going.

"Was anyone with you? Did you talk to anyone this afternoon?"

Wesley looked Noah up and down. "Are you the police?" he asked. "I ain't done nothin', I really ain't."

"Just answer my question," Noah said. "Was anyone with you at home this afternoon, or did you talk to anyone?"

Wesley swallowed hard. "No, sir," he said. "It was just me. But I ain't done nothin', I promise I ain't."

Noah glanced up at Marco, who shrugged. He looked back at Wesley. "You don't remember, do you?"

Wesley looked around at all of them once again, his eyes showing panic. "Remember what? What is it I don't remember?"

"You don't remember killing David Pritchett this afternoon, behind the high school?"

The little man's eyes were as wide as they could be, as he frantically looked around at all of their faces again. Each of the men nodded at him, and he finally turned back to Noah. "I didn't kill nobody," he said, whining. "I didn't kill nobody, I know I didn't."

"Several people saw you," Noah said. "They all said you got into an argument with him and started beating on him. When they saw you leave, they went to look and found him dead."

Wesley stared into his face, and a moment later tears began to pour down his cheeks. "But I wouldn't do that," he cried. "I wouldn't, I never hurt nobody. I got my check yesterday, and I just went and got me a couple bottles, and all I been doing is sitting home and drinking. I ain't gone nowhere where I could hurt nobody."

"But you did," Noah said. "You left your place this afternoon, and you went down by the high school. You were talking to some girls there, they said you wanted them to come over and party at your place, because you said you stole Ralphie Morgan's wallet and had a lot of money. Dave Pritchett, he tried to tell the girls not to listen to you, and that's when you got mad. Everybody saw you and Dave get into an argument, and then a bunch of them saw you beat him to death."

Wesley was shaking his head, still crying. "No, no, no," he said over and over.

"Mr. Wesley, I'm trying to help you out," Noah said. "Right now, the sheriff has an innocent boy in his jail, and they think he did it. When they find out the truth, they're going to come after you. You don't want them to come hunting you down, do you? You know how the sheriff is—he'll shoot first and ask questions later."

Wesley just sat there and cried, and Noah motioned for Lindell to step outside with him. He handed the man a hundred-dollar bill and told him to run down to the liquor store and get a couple of bottles of whiskey. When Lindell left, Noah stepped back inside.

"Mr. Wesley, it's going to be okay. We're going to help you. Would you like a drink?"

Wesley had been blubbering, but at the mention of a drink, he looked up at Noah with his eyes wide again. "A drink?"

"I sent my friend to get you a bottle of whiskey," Noah said. "As soon as he gets back, you can have it. My friends are going to stay here with you tonight, and then tomorrow we'll help you explain it all to the sheriff. Okay?"

The blubbering began again, but Wesley nodded his head. The three men stayed with him, and Noah kept telling him how he had stolen Ralph's wallet, then went down to the high school looking for girls and killed young David Pritchett, until Lindell returned with the whiskey. Noah handed him a bottle, and Marco found some old blankets and made him a pallet on the floor.

"I want you two guys to stay here with him tonight," he said to Forney and Lindell. "Keep him drinking, and keep telling him how sorry you are that this happened to him. Tell him over and over again that you know he didn't mean to kill the boy, and that we are all going to help him explain this to the sheriff."

Forney looked over at Wesley, then looked back at Noah. "You've got him believing he did it," he said quietly. "How in the world did you manage that?"

Noah shrugged. "When you told me he drank a lot, I figured there was a good chance you might find him drunk. If he was, well, a lot of people don't realize that alcohol induces a state of suggestibility. You can take someone who's truly drunk and tell them something over and over, and they'll believe it. It'll probably wear off when they sober up, but by then it'll be too late."

"And the cops will believe he's confessing because he was too drunk to lie his way out of it, right?"

"That's how a policeman's mind works, yeah," Noah said. "There's an old saying, *'in vino, veritas.'* It's Latin, and it means 'in the wine is the truth.' Comes from the old Romans, who firmly believed that somebody who drank enough wine was incapable of telling a lie. I think a lot of cops nowadays would have fit in real well, back then."

Forney laughed. "Ain't that the truth? Okay, we got this. Why don't you go on and get you some sleep?"

"That's exactly what I'm going to do," Noah said. "And if he starts yelling, just try not to let him get too loud, okay? I've had a couple of rough days, and I need some shut-eye."

Noah turned and headed toward the house, and Marco followed him. When they were out of earshot, Marco said softly, "Man, that was pretty slick. You really got that fellow thinking he did it."

"Yeah, it's not hard when somebody's that deep in a bottle. Do me a favor tonight and just kinda keep an eye on them. I doubt they'll come near the house, but you might peek out the window now and then, anyway."

They got inside the house, and Noah passed on dinner. Sarah followed him back to the bedroom and lay down beside him as he quickly drifted off to sleep.

When morning came, Noah got quietly out of bed and showered quickly, then dressed and walked out to the kitchen in search of coffee. Marco was sitting at the table drinking a cup. "I just made that half an hour ago," he said. Noah picked up a cup and poured some for himself, then joined Marco at the table.

"You been up all night?"

"Well, you told me to keep an eye on them, so I did. Forney and the other guy took turns napping, just sitting up against the wall, but Wesley is sleeping the sleep of the thoroughly wasted."

"You know that kind of sleep when you see it, do you?"

"I should," Marco said with a chuckle, "I slept that way many times."

Noah raised an eyebrow and looked at him. "I wouldn't have taken you for much of a drinker," he said. "Back home, I hardly ever see you drink more than one beer."

"That's because I know exactly how stupid I can get when I've drunk too much. This, my friend, comes from experience. When one has learned this lesson from experience, one does not allow himself to get thoroughly drunk."

"I think I've only ever actually been drunk once," Noah said, "when you guys threw the bachelor party. I have no intention of trying it again in the near future."

"Which makes you the smartest of us all," Sarah said, coming up behind him. "I've been drunk a few times, and trust me, it's not worth it."

Noah aimed his face upward and she bent down for a kiss, then poured her own coffee and took a chair at the table. "I've got to get started on this pretty shortly," Noah said. "I've got to go through all the motions as if it were real, so we might as well get started now." He took out his phone and dialed Morgan's number.

"Hello," Morgan said, and Noah could hear the pent-up anger still in his voice.

"It's Rex," he said. "I thought you'd like to know I found the guy who really killed David Pritchett."

Morgan hesitated for a split second, then caught on and played along. "You did? Well, that's excellent. Are you gonna take him on down to the sheriff?"

"Yeah, Aubrey and I will handle it. The poor fellow really wants to confess."

Morgan almost choked. "Confess? Seriously?"

"Yep. He and I had a long talk last night, and he realizes what he's done and that he has to own up to it. He doesn't want your poor innocent son in trouble for something he did. Isn't that good?"

Morgan burst out laughing. "As soon as you get done, you get your butt out here. I'm starting to wonder how I ever got by without you, Rex. You come see me as soon as you're finished, okay?"

"Sure will," Noah said, "and with any luck, I'll have Ralph with me. I'm not certain about that, yet, but I'm going to try."

He ended the call and put the phone in his pocket, then looked at Marco. "You about ready?"

"Oh, *mon ami*," Marco said, "I be born ready! We go now, yes?"

"We go now." Noah stood and kissed Sarah once more, then walked out the back door with Marco following. When they got to the shed, Forney was standing against the wall, yawning and obviously looking forward to the opportunity to get some sleep of his own. When Noah entered, he snapped to attention and kicked Lindell, who was curled up asleep on the floor beside him.

"How did it go overnight?" Noah asked.

"He passed out around midnight," Forney said. "He woke up again around three or so, opened another bottle and drained it in about half an hour, then passed out again. He kept going on about how he never killed anybody before, so I just kept telling him it was all going to be okay once the sheriff understood what happened."

Noah grinned at him. "Perfect," he said. "Let's see if we can get him at least partly awake."

He and Marco each took one of Wesley's arms and dragged him up off the pallet. Marco had to slap him a few times to get a response, but finally his eyes opened and turned blearily toward Noah.

"I didn't mean to kill him," he said. "I didn't never killed nobody before."

"I know," Noah said, feigning sympathy. "Let's go see the sheriff, and we'll get this all straightened out, okay?"

Wesley nodded, almost managing not to let his head fall to one side or the other. "Yeah, let's go see the sheriff. 'Splain everything..." His head fell forward until his chin hit his chest.

Marco waved a hand under his nose as a response to the smell of urine— Wesley had pissed himself at least once during the night—then looked at Noah. "Mebbe we bes' jus' carry dis ol' boy, eh, Rex?"

"I guess we might as well," Noah said. "I don't think he's in any shape to do any kind of walking."

Wesley tried. His feet and legs moved in a poor approximation of walking, trying to keep the bottom half of his body somewhat close to the top half as it was carried along toward the Charger. When they got to the car, Noah opened the passenger door and flipped the seat forward, and then he and Marco managed to pick Wesley up and stuff him into the back seat.

"I didn' mean to kill him," Wesley mumbled. "I didn' never kill nobody before..."

"What you t'ink he weigh, maybe half as much as me?" Marco asked. "He be one heavy drunk fellow."

"Dead weight," Noah said. "Come on, let's go." He walked around and got behind the wheel as Marco climbed into the passenger side, then started up the car and turned it around to head out. Behind him, Forney and Lindell were climbing into Forney's car, and they followed him out the driveway.

Forney honked and turned off in another direction as they got into town, but Noah drove on until he hit the highway that ran through its center. He took a left at the light and followed the road east until he came to the sheriff's office, then turned in and parked near the front door.

CHAPTER EIGHTEEN

"**W**ait here with our friend," he said to Marco. He got out and walked up to the door. It was unlocked, so he stepped inside and walked up to the reception counter. A female deputy sat there and looked up at him questioningly.

"Can I help you?"

"My name is Rex Madison," Noah said. "I need to see the sheriff."

"Can I say what this is in regard to?"

"Yes," Noah said. "You can tell him I brought him David Pritchett's real killer."

The woman stared at him, appearing to be confused, but she picked up a phone on her desk and pushed a button. "Sheriff? This is Debbie, out front. I've got a Rex Madison out here, and he says he's got Davey Pritchett's real killer with him."

Her eyes went wide, and then she put the phone down and looked up at Noah. "He says he'll be right out," she said. "If you'd like to have a..."

That was as far as she got, because a door to Noah's left opened and Sheriff Dan Redford came through it. He looked at Noah and gave him a suspicious grin. "Hey, Rex," he said. "Debbie said something about Dave Pritchett's real killer?"

Noah nodded. "That's right," he said. "He's been insisting on coming to see you this morning to confess. He's in the back seat of my car, out front."

Redford glanced through the glass on the door and started walking that direction, with Noah falling into step beside him. "How did you happen to find him?" Redford asked.

"I just sent some of the boys to ask around and see if anyone knew who did it," Noah said. "They found a few people who were unwilling to come forward but were happy to tell our boys what they saw. Apparently, this guy Peter Wesley got into some kind of argument with the Pritchett boy behind the school and just went nuts on him."

Redford's eyes were wide, but he continued walking out the door. When they got to the Charger, he leaned down and looked through the windows. "That's Pete, all right. Is he drunk?"

"Wasted," Noah said. "He said he got his check a couple days ago, and he's been drinking ever since. Kept telling us that he's never killed anybody before, and how sorry he is."

Redford shook his head. "Well, let's see if we can get him out of there."

Noah signaled Marco to get out, and the two of them managed to drag Wesley back out of the car. He was a bit more awake by the time they got him on his feet, and when his eyes focused on Redford he burst into tears. "I didn't mean to," he whined. "I didn't never do this before, I don't know what happened. I just wanted to party, that's all. I stole ol' Ralphie's wallet to get some money to party with—I just wanted to party, that's all. Davey didn't want the girls to come, tha's what happened. We just got in a fight and—that's all I know. That's all I know, I swear."

Redford stared at him for a moment, then turned to Noah. "You and I both know this man never hurt anybody," he said softly. "Do you really expect me to release Ralph, just because you got some drunk to take the blame for what he did?"

Noah looked at the sheriff in the eye. "Yes, I do," he said, "because the alternative would mean Jimmy Morgan storming this place with a small army to get his son back. Now, that would obviously mean the end of his little empire, and it probably wouldn't be long before the feds showed up to start tearing this county apart. Jimmy would probably go out in a blaze of glory, a big shootout with the FBI or whoever, but I suspect they'd manage to round up quite a few of his people before they were done. At least some of them will probably take the plea deal they get offered, a short sentence or maybe even just proba-tion in return for their testimony against any local officials who coop-erated with Jimmy. Now, in my experience, most people involved in criminal enterprises never really trust each other, so they tend to keep any kind of notes and evidence that will incriminate somebody else that they can. How much are you willing to bet that none of them have anything they can pin on you?"

Redford's face remained calm, but the way his jaw clenched, Noah could tell that there was turmoil going on behind those eyes. He stood there for a full minute and a half, then carefully reached behind himself and pulled out a set of handcuffs. Without a word, he put them on Peter Wesley and then put an arm around him and walked him inside.

He turned and looked at Noah over his shoulder. "Under the cir-cumstances," he said, "I'm going to release young Mr. Morgan into your care. I trust you'll see that he gets home safely?"

Noah gave him a big smile. "Why, it'll be my pleasure to be of ser-vice to the sheriff's office," he said.

It took an extra fifteen minutes to get Ralph dressed and out of his cell, but the boy looked at Noah with eyes full of affection when he was escorted out to the lobby. Noah warned him with a look not to say a word, then took hold of his arm and walked him out to the car. Marco opened the passenger door, and Ralph climbed willingly into the back seat.

"Oh, man, I can't believe you did it," Ralph said. "This is—man, I owe you one. You just tell me what I can do for you, and I'll..."

"Shut up," Noah growled as he started the car. "Do you have any idea how much damage you've done? What the hell made you think you could kill that boy and get away with it?"

"But..." Ralph's eyes were wide, and the tears were trying to brim over. "I swear, I never meant to kill him. I don't know what happened—I just lost it, I guess."

"Dat's bool shit!" Marco said. "You done made a fool out yourself, and out your daddy, too. If you was my boy, I make you bleed on your ass, dat how hard I whip you!"

"He's right," Noah said. "Your old man's reputation took a big hit over this. Even with somebody else taking the fall, there are going to be plenty of people around here who don't believe he did it. The stories about you being a killer are never going to go away, and people are going to be a lot less trusting of your father from now on. Word about this will spread throughout his territory, and you can bet the feds will be trying to get in on it. It's quite possible they've already got a case coming together, and if that's so, then you just handed them everything they need to put your dad away."

"But—but my pa didn't have anything to do with this," Ralph whined. "They couldn't pin anything on him, could they?"

"Not without finding several people who would be willing to testify against him," Noah said, "and up until now, finding even one such person would have been difficult. Now? From what I understand, this boy David was pretty popular around here. You can bet that anyone who really cared about him will be more than willing to tell anything they know about your dad, and about you. The only way you're going to come out of this is if we can make people believe you were honestly innocent, and the only way we can do that is by completely changing how people see you."

"You gotta be a whole new boy," Marco said. "You don' be no trouble at all, you don' let nobody see you get mad, nothin'. Dat gonna be de only way."

Ralph sat back and looked out the windows, but Noah could see his tears in the rearview mirror. He waited a moment, then waved a hand to get the boy's attention once more.

"Ralph," he said, "tell me something. How did it feel when you realized he was dead?"

"Man, I told you, I never meant to..."

"Can that crap. You think I don't know an act when I see it? You're trying to be all sorry and contrite, but I think you actually enjoyed it. Am I right?"

Ralph stared into his eyes in the rearview mirror, and that's when he realized that Noah was smiling at him. He continued to watch for a few seconds, and then a tentative smile began on his own face.

"It was—it was some kind of intense, man."

Noah had watched his eyes, and he let his smile grow wider. "I heard there's been rumors that you killed before," he said. "It's true, isn't it? This wasn't the first time, was it?"

"Man, screw you," Ralph said, still grinning. "If I say it was true, my pa would beat me half to death."

"Not if I never tell him," Noah said. "Look, kid, one killer to another, I know that look in your eye. You didn't lose control on that boy; you just didn't want to stop beating him. You knew damn good and well if you didn't stop he was going to die, but you kept on going. Don't try to lie your way out of it with me. I know damn well I'm right."

Ralph met his eyes in the mirror again. "Maybe so," he said. "If I'd realized I'd lost my wallet and picked it up, they never could have even tried to pin it on me."

"See, now that's where you're wrong. There were enough people who saw you and the kid go back behind the stadium, and then when he got found dead, that's all they need to make you a suspect. If they really tried, considering your knuckles are split in a couple places, they could probably find DNA evidence on the victim or around where his body was found, evidence that would prove you were there at the time he died. Now, I've just fixed this mess so the sheriff isn't about to dig any further, but the last thing in the world you want to do is ever give him a reason to suspect you of murder again. He's walking a tightrope, right now, trying to keep his place with your dad, but also trying not to have the feds come in here and crawl up his ass. You give him any more problems, he's going to probably hang you himself."

"Fine," Ralph said, and there was no longer any trace of remorse or tears in his voice. "He won't be sheriff forever, though. One day, whoever wears that badge will be answering to me, and I won't need anybody to save my ass then."

"Yeah, but right now it's your father we got to worry about. All of us, including you and me, we've got to depend on him keeping his power so we don't end up losing everything. I guarantee you, I don't want to go back to Beaumont. You screw things up bad enough for that, I'll put a bullet through your head myself."

Ralph smiled into the mirror. "You like to try to scare people," he said, "but I don't really scare that easy. You might want to stay on my good side, Rex. Might not be that much longer before I'm running things, and I might want to keep you as my right-hand man, same way Pa wants to keep you right now. You don't want to mess that up, do you?"

Something in the boy's words caught Noah's attention. He slowed the car down and looked him in the eye in the mirror once more. "You think something's going to happen to your dad?"

Ralph shrugged. "You just never know," he said. "There might be somebody out there like Benny, somebody who might want to kill my old man. Guess who takes over if that happens?"

Noah drove in silence for several seconds, his eyes flicking from the road to the mirror and back again. Each time he looked at Ralph, the boy was staring directly into his eyes. At last, he said, "And what would somebody who tried that stand to gain?"

Ralph's smile spread out across his face. "All depends," he said. "I might just decide to make him my top man."

"What about all the rest? All the other lieutenants? Do you really think they'd take their orders from you?"

"Oh, there's some who would get upset about it," Ralph said. "That's why I'd want somebody like you right there with me. I'd even be willing to cut that somebody in for a nice share, say ten percent?"

Marco was watching Noah, and Noah caught the wink he tossed. He shot back a thumbs-up, his hand down where Ralph could not see it.

"No more BS," he said. "Are you seriously thinking about trying to get rid of your old man? Ten percent—that's an awful lot of money, and it definitely wouldn't break my heart if I was the guy getting it."

"No BS," Ralph said, suddenly sitting forward and leaning in between the front bucket seats. "You think you could do it?"

"I could do it. What I want to know is how I'm supposed to trust you after you sit here ready to betray your own father."

"Because it's not a betrayal," Ralph said. "It's just business. I know I could do a better job of running everything, but Pa's not going to let me take over as long as he's alive. You get rid of him, and then you back me up against everybody else, and I'll give you that ten percent."

Noah slowed to make the turn toward Morgan's house and stared into the mirror at Ralph for a few more seconds. "I'll take care of it," he said. "You just keep your mouth shut for now, got that? I find out you said anything to anybody about this, it won't be your father I blow away. Got that?"

"I got it," Ralph said. "Same to you. Don't you go telling anybody else I made the offer. I've got a few people loyal to me already."

"I won't," Noah said, "and neither will Aubrey. Just understand that wherever I go, he goes."

"Deal," Ralph said. "Besides, I like the way he talks."

Both Noah and Marco chuckled at that and rode the rest of the way without talking. By the time they arrived at Morgan's house, Ralph was looking ashamed and red-faced once again.

The men standing out front stared in disbelief when Ralph climbed out of the back seat of the Charger, but then they smiled at Noah as the three of them walked up the stairs. Ralph opened the door without knocking and motioned for Noah and Marco to follow him in, but Marlene had heard footsteps on the porch and was already headed their way. When she saw Ralph, she let out a squeal and threw her arms around him.

"Oh, my goodness," she said, "my goodness, my goodness. Oh, Ralphie, I can't believe you're home."

"You can thank Rex for that," Jimmy said, coming down the hall in a hurry. "Damn, Rex, you really pulled it off. How did the sheriff take it?"

"He wasn't happy," Noah said, "but I was able to make him see the wisdom of prosecuting Mr. Wesley for the murder. It'll probably get reduced to manslaughter or something, but with Wesley offering an unsolicited confession as soon as he saw the sheriff, there really isn't much else he could do."

"Oh, Rex, he too modest," Marco said. "He tell de sheriff, he say, you don' want no war, you do what I say, yes? Sheriff, he say okay, he don' want no war, den he go get your boy and bring him out." He slapped Noah on the shoulder, making him stumble forward a half step. "Rex, back in de Beaumont, every time somebody tried to give him any trouble, he make dem back down. He tell dem all about how much trouble dey gonna have from ol' Aubrey if anything happen to him, an' dey always back down."

Morgan smiled and shook his head. "Best day yet when you came along," he said to Noah. "Come on, you guys want some breakfast?" He wrapped an arm around his son and took him down the hall toward the dining room.

Noah and Marco followed, making a show of being delighted to sit down and eat. Marlene happily brought them scrambled eggs and sausage patties, and they dug in.

"So, is this all done?" Morgan asked. "Is there anything else we gotta do about it?"

Noah nodded. "Yep, there is," he said. "We've got to start on a public relations campaign. Now that somebody else is being charged with the murder, it's time we work on Ralph's public image. And for that, we're going to need everybody you've got." He shoved a forkful of eggs and sausage into his mouth, then swallowed before he went on. "What's the chance we can get all your top people together so I can explain how this has to go?"

"Hell, that's easy," Morgan said. "You just tell me where and when."

"Needs to be someplace where nobody else will be paying any attention to us," Noah said. "How about that big shop building out at your junkyard? Would that work?"

"Sure, no problem. When do you want me to set it up?"

"The sooner, the better. How about this evening? Think you could get everyone to show up, say, around six thirty or so?"

"Six thirty it is," Morgan said. "Don't worry, I'll make sure everyone is there. Hell, I'll even order in pizza."

Noah nodded. "That'll be perfect," he said. "Just make sure nobody brings family with them. We don't need any of this getting outside of your lieutenants."

CHAPTER NINETEEN

When breakfast was over, Noah and Morgan went to the office, where Noah told him about his success in arranging truckloads of liquor.

"Matt says he can have the first deliveries coming by the beginning of next week," Noah said. "I told him what you're looking for, and he says he can handle it. He wants ten thousand a trailer, but there should be about a quarter million worth of product in each one."

Morgan nodded. "That's about what I thought," he said. "And he can handle thirty trailers a month?"

"Actually," Noah said with a grin, "he said that would be okay in the beginning, but he could probably raise that to fifty a month if you reach a point you can handle it."

"Fifty trailer loads a month? You tell him to bring it on, I can handle it. That's half a million dollars for twelve, maybe fourteen million in product. Oh, hell, yes. You tell him to bring it on."

"I'll let you tell him," Noah said. "He'll be driving the first truck when it comes in next week. He wants to meet you, and I figured you might want to meet him."

Morgan shook his head. "Rex, I was serious when I said I don't know how I ever got by without you. The way you handled this mess with Ralphie, I've never seen anybody could keep their cool and think like you can."

Noah gave him a modest grin and shrugged. "It's not that hard," he said. "You just have to remember that most people aren't all that smart, and those that are usually have something they're afraid to lose. You can outwit the first ones, as long as you're willing to put the fear into the rest."

"And you did, you did. That damn Redford ain't likely to ever want to cross me again, not after this." He leaned back in his chair and looked at Noah. "So, what are you planning to do today?"

"I thought I'd take Aubrey out and kinda show him the lay of the land," Noah said. "If that's okay with you, of course."

Morgan waved him off. "Sure, no problem. If he's gonna be working with you, he needs to know what's going on. I'll go ahead and get this meeting set up for tonight, and you just come on down when it's time. Make sure everybody you talk to knows to show up, and this will be a good time to let them know that I'm making you my number two."

Noah let the grin spread into a smile. "Thank you," he said. "I'll do my best not to let you down." He got to his feet and shook hands with Morgan, then walked out and collected Marco on his way to the front door. They got into the car, and Noah waited until they were on the road before he turned to Marco.

"The meeting is set for six thirty this evening," he said. "I'm going to tell Sarah and Neil to load up and head out now."

He took out his phone and dialed Sarah, who answered on the first ring.

"How's it going, babe?"

"It's going," Noah said. "Remember last night, we were talking about you and your brother taking a trip to see your mom?"

"Yeah," Sarah said slowly. "You think we should go ahead and go?"

"I think now would be a good time, yeah," he said. "I'm going to be busy for a little while, anyway, so you might as well take advantage of the time while you can."

"Okay, baby," Sarah replied. "I'll see you soon, then, right?" He could hear the concern in her voice, even though she was trying to keep it hidden.

"Yep. I'll call you as soon as everything settles, and we can talk about when we'll be together again then."

They exchanged love words, and Noah ended the call. A moment later, he dialed Kate's number and got her voicemail. He left her a message about having a migraine, then ended the call and dropped the phone back into his pocket, but it rang almost immediately.

"Hello?"

"Hey, bro, it's Kate. You called?"

"Yeah," Noah said. "I just wanted to ask you if you know of anything I can take for this migraine. It's really a killer."

There was only a second of hesitation. "Wow, sorry to hear that. Can you go home and sleep it off for a while?"

"No, not right now. I got something to do tonight, around six thirty, and then I can get some rest. I just thought I'd ask."

"Well, I'm glad you called. I just wish I could do something to help."

"No problem, sis. I'll catch you later, okay?"

"Okay," Kate said. "I hope you get to feeling better soon. Bye-bye."

Noah cut off the call and put the phone into his pocket, and this time it stayed quiet.

He drove Marco out to the junkyard and pointed it out as they passed it. "That's where Morgan got started," he said. "I think it's fitting that it's the same place where it's all going to come to an end."

"Poetic justice," Marco said. "Who would've believed you had it in you?"

"Good point. Let's just hope everyone shows up. Doing it there, we probably can avoid any innocent deaths, and I'd prefer to."

Marco looked at him. "Little bit of the old conscience starting to prick at you?"

"No, I just prefer to avoid collateral damage if we can. I don't know for sure where God stands on sanctioned assassination, but I suspect He isn't too pleased when somebody innocent gets caught up in it."

Marco shrugged. "I don't know," he said, "but there are some passages in the Old Testament that say God ordered the Israelites to slaughter entire nations, men, women, and children. You know some of them had to have been innocent, right?"

"Of course," Noah said, "but you've got to remember that those books were written by religious scholars and priests of the day. I'm pretty sure they would want the world to believe that any genocide they committed was only on God's orders, wouldn't you think?"

"Yeah, maybe. Still, you can't always make sure there won't be any innocent bystanders who get hurt."

"True. But until God tells me not to worry about it, I'm going to do my best to avoid it."

Marco chuckled. "Yeah, that's probably the smart way to handle it."

To keep up appearances, Noah took Marco around to all of the local places and introduced him. He used each stop to reinforce the necessity of having the lieutenants attend the meeting that night, refusing to tell them exactly what it was about but making it clear that it was important.

A few of them asked about Ralph. Heather, when he stopped to introduce Marco, told him he was a hero and tried to give him a kiss, but Noah laughed it off. Marco offered, in his Cajun accent, to accept the kiss on Noah's behalf, and Heather laughed as she cooperated.

As they drove away, Marco looked at Noah. "She's one of them, right? One of the lieutenants who will be at the meeting tonight?"

"Yes. The unfortunate thing is that she has children."

Marco shrugged. "She made the choice to become a criminal," he said. "Just feels weird to know I kissed a woman who's about to die. You think that's gonna damage my karma?"

"If I believed in karma," Noah said, "I'd say probably."

Leonard, at the casino, surprised Marco by speaking to him in Cajun English. "Oh, you from de bayou country, yes?" he asked when he heard "Aubrey" speak. "I been up out de bayou more than twenty years, now. You come, pass a good time here! I give you big big pile of chips, you play, win money."

Marco broke out in a delighted smile. "*Mais j'mais,*" he said. "I don' never got to play dese games before. Mebbe you make a trap, eh? You get ol' Aubrey in here, make me lose all my money, yes?"

"But of course," Leonard said, his own smile just as big. "That why I am here, *oui*? To take away all you money, yes?"

They exchanged a few more sarcastic pleasantries, and then Noah reminded Leonard to be at the meeting. Moments later, they were back in the car and headed to get some lunch.

They stopped at an interesting restaurant, one that had an outdoor dining area. While the air was getting cool, there were small heaters scattered around among the tables that seemed to be putting out enough heat to keep the area warm. The two of them took a table and ordered burgers, and were surprised at how quickly they got them. They were even more surprised at how delicious they were. As they left, Marco bemoaned the fact that they would probably never get to eat there again, but Noah reminded him that the food at the Sagebrush Saloon was every bit as good. Marco shrugged and agreed, and they continued their tour.

At just after two, Sarah called to let Noah know that she and Neil were on the road. They had packed up everything they needed to take with them and were headed back toward Kirtland.

"You know," Sarah said, "when they gave us the mission, they thought we were going to be here for months. Do you realize that it's been less than two weeks? You don't want to put this off a while longer, just let us enjoy acting like a halfway normal couple?"

"No," Noah said. "I want to get back to our real lives. I think we're a much more normal couple back in Kirtland than we ever could be out here. At least back there, I don't have to go off and pretend to be a criminal every day."

"Yeah, I guess you're right," Sarah replied. "I love you, Noah. Don't you forget that."

"I love you, too," Noah said. "As soon as we get this done tonight, we'll be hitting the road ourselves. If you stop to get a room, call and let me know where. We might just catch up with you."

The call ended, and Noah stopped for gas a few minutes later. He filled up the Charger, and then he and Marco simply cruised around for the rest of the afternoon.

JIMMY MORGAN HAD CONTACTED all of his top lieutenants, and even some of their underlings. There would be more than a hundred people attending the meeting that evening, and he was almost rubbing his hands in anticipation. He'd never seen anyone who could think through a problem as fast as Rex Madison, and he couldn't wait to see how Rex would handle this meeting. It never occurred to him to wonder why anyone would want all of his top people in one place, and even if it had, he would never have guessed the real reason.

He was Jimmy Morgan. No one would ever seriously try to take him out, he knew that.

He had spent the day in his office, making those calls and several others, getting everything set up to start the liquor distributorship. He needed to have a warehouse ready to go before the first trailer even showed up, and that meant keeping his people on their toes. By five o'clock, everything was arranged. He would be able to sign the papers within a couple of days, and the warehouse would be a reality.

All of that was done, finally, and it was getting close to six o'clock. He made one more call, to the local pizza delivery store, and arranged for three dozen large pizzas to be delivered to the junkyard as soon as possible, then walked out of his office and started toward the front door.

He'd almost made it when Ralph appeared in the hallway. "Pa?"

Morgan was still angry with the boy, but he was so relieved that Ralphie was out of jail that he was biting it off rather than letting it out. "Hey, Ralph," he said. "How you doing?"

Ralph shrugged. "I still feel bad about what happened," he said. "I guess I just don't know my own strength."

Morgan nodded. "I understand," he said. "Back when I was your age, I was pretty stout, myself. More than one guy found out taking me on was a bad idea. I guess you're just a chip off the old block, in some ways."

Ralph shrugged again. "You going to the meeting?"

"Yep," Morgan said. "You want to come? I mean, it's all about you, anyway."

"Can I? I wasn't sure if you wanted me to go along, you know, after everything that happened."

"I think maybe you should. It doesn't hurt a man to face up to his mistakes, and everybody needs to know that you're gonna handle it and move past it. Come on, let's go. Tell your shadows they can follow in their car."

The two of them walked out the door and got into the back seat of Morgan's Lincoln limousine. Walter, his chauffeur, closed the door he was holding open and got behind the wheel. He already knew where they were going, so he simply started the car and put it in gear. Moments later, they were out on the two-lane blacktop and headed toward town, when Morgan's cell phone rang.

"Hello," he said as he answered.

"Jimmy? It's Dave Walters."

"Hey," Morgan said with a smile. "You're gonna make it to our meeting tonight, right? It starts in just a little while, and I'm bringing pizza."

"I'll be there," Walters said, "but you might not want to turn it into a party. There's something going on, and we got a problem."

Morgan's brow furrowed. "What kind of problem, Dave? What's going on?"

"What's going on," Walters said, "is that your new right-hand man's sister is a damned FBI agent."

NOAH HAD GOTTEN HIMSELF into position at just past five thirty, parking the car among some trees on the top of Allred Mountain, which overlooked the junkyard. They had a perfect view of the entrance and parking lot, but the mountain was almost two miles away. Noah and Marco were looking through binoculars they had bought earlier in the day at a sporting goods store.

"It's after six," Marco said. "I see half a dozen cars down there. Do you know any of them?"

Noah shook his head. "No, but I've seen a couple people I recognize. They're all coming in, just like they were told."

"How long you going to give them? You know a few will be late, right?"

"Not as late as I'll be," Noah said. "I figure I'll call Jimmy at about twenty till seven and tell him I'm on the way but running a few minutes late. Five minutes after that, I'll set them off."

"I wonder if they'll hear the blast back in town? How far out are we?"

"About eight miles, I think, but the junkyard sits down in that little valley. Depending on how big the blast cloud is, they may see it, rather than hear it."

"In which case we'll have a matter of minutes to get the hell out of here. You know which way to go?"

"Yes. I've even got it programmed into my GPS, just to be sure. We'll go out across Pension Mountain—that's County Road 550. It'll take us down to Metalton, and we can take the cutoff road from there over to pick up Highway 103 and go north. That goes up through Green Forest, and then we can make it into Missouri. Once we get there, it should be clear sailing."

Marco grinned as he stared through the binoculars. "Sounds good to me, boss."

They watched as more and more cars pulled into the parking lot, including Jimmy Morgan's limo. Noah grunted when he saw Ralph climb out of the car with his father, but then Marco tapped him on the arm.

"Check this out," he said.

Noah turned his binoculars toward the entrance of the yard and saw a pizza delivery car pulling in. A young woman stepped out and started stacking pizzas, then looked relieved when a couple of men came out to help carry them in. She went inside the building for a moment, carrying five of them herself, but came out a few minutes later with a big smile on her face. She got into her car and drove away, and Marco breathed a sigh of relief.

"Morgan must be a good tipper," he said. "You see the smile she was wearing? I bet he gave her a hundred."

"Wouldn't surprise me," Noah said. "He seems to think of himself as some kind of Robin Hood character, even though he doesn't really care that much about the poor. I'm just glad they didn't invite her to stick around."

They watched for a few more minutes, and then Noah decided it was time. He took out his phone and called Morgan.

"Rex? Where are you?"

"I'm about five minutes out," Noah said. "I would've been on time, but Aubrey had to make a stop at a restroom. Do not ever let that man eat hamburgers for lunch—they go through him like oil through a funnel."

Morgan laughed. "I'll remember that. Hurry up and get here, there's not a lot of pizza left."

"I'm hurrying. Everybody there?"

"Yeah, I think so. The place is packed, I can tell you that."

"Sounds good," Noah said. "I'll be there in a matter of minutes."

"Well, come on," Morgan said. "Oh, by the way—your sister decided to join us. She ought to be here any second now."

CHAPTER TWENTY

Noah snapped the binoculars up to his face again and stared down at the junkyard. Seconds later, a car came into view on the winding road that ran in front of it and slowed in order to make the turn into its driveway. It pulled up among the other cars already present and stopped, and a moment later Dave Walters stepped out of the driver's seat. He opened the back door on the driver's side and reached in, coming out a moment later with Kate Madison's arm crushed in his hand.

Her hands were bound behind her back, and he marched her into the building without even looking around. Noah saw that her face was set and stubborn, and he knew that she had resigned herself to the strong probability that she was about to die.

He turned to Marco. "They've got Kate," he said. "I don't know how they found out about her, but they've got her."

Marco looked at him without a word for several seconds, then grinned. "Well, I know how you feel about collateral damage," he said. "How are we going to get her out of this?"

Noah sat quietly for a moment, then opened the door and got out of the car. He walked around to the trunk and opened it, then came back a moment later with the smart guns and set them on the hood. Marco got out and stepped up beside him as he opened the first one.

"I managed to get pictures of most of the top people," Noah said, "and I've already downloaded them to my phone, a total of about thirty-six pictures. Each of these guns only hold fifteen rounds, so I'm going to send a dozen pictures to each one. You'll have to slip into the junkyard and put them around the building, while I give the people

226

inside a reason to come running out. With any luck, these will take out a lot of Morgan's guns."

Marco nodded. "You want me to go cross-country?"

Noah shook his head. "No. That would take too long, and things might get out of hand. Once I get them loaded with targets, we'll drive down. I'll stop just out of side of the yard and let you out, then I'll give you about fifteen minutes to get set up. That building only has two doors, the one that leads into its office and the big one they take vehicles in and out through. Try to set these up so that they have line of sight on both doors. The way I've divided the pictures, we should have two guns firing at each person who comes out."

"Okay, fifteen minutes. Then what?"

"Then I drive in and draw them out. Try to stay out of the line of fire, but be ready to back me up if I need you."

Marco grinned. "Oh, yeah, boss," he said, his Cajun accent in full attack mode. "I be dere. I garontee!"

It took only a couple of minutes get all the guns set up, and then they tossed the boxes onto the ground while Marco held all six of the devices and got back into the car. He didn't bother with the seat belt as Noah started up and backed around onto the old country road.

There were enough curves to make it impossible to really give the Charger its head, but Noah made it down the mountain in only four minutes. He put the car in neutral and let the big engine idle as it rolled the last quarter mile, then stopped and let Marco out just a few hundred yards short of the entrance to the junkyard. Marco, for all his bulk and muscle, moved with the grace of a gazelle. He vanished into the woods alongside the road, and Noah began counting the seconds.

Suddenly, Noah took out his phone and quickly found the contact for Allison. He hit it with his thumb, and a moment later she answered.

"Camelot? Report."

"I've had an idea," Noah said. Quickly he explained what he had in mind, and Allison gave him the okay without even asking a question.

When he reached nine hundred, he reached down alongside the seat and pushed a button, then dropped the car into gear again and pushed his foot into the accelerator pedal. The Charger leapt forward and got up to forty miles per hour by the time it got to the entrance, and Noah fishtailed the car into the parking lot. He got it straightened out so that it was aimed directly at the shop building and then stopped.

On the windshield, the computer had put up the FLIR display, showing the infrared image of the shop building and what was happening inside it. There were several large bright spots that Noah knew would mean groups of people, but he saw one very small group that caught his attention. Someone in the middle of it was sitting on something low, and he knew that had to be Kate. Morgan would want her in as vulnerable a position as possible, he knew, and Morgan's idea of keeping you vulnerable was to be towering over you.

Noah reached down and pushed the first button and the video display came to life in the dashboard. He tapped the screen in the area where one of the groups was gathered, then squeezed the trigger button on the steering wheel. He held it tight as he tapped the screen several times over that same area, then looked at the FLIR display again.

The machine guns of bullets had penetrated the corrugated steel siding like it was paper, and the group was scattering. There were several bright flashes as some of those inside tried to return fire, but they didn't seem to know where to aim. Noah was about to fire into the group again when the office door burst open and a half-dozen people came running out, guns in hand. They spotted the Charger and began firing in his direction, but then suddenly they began dropping.

Pop, pop, pop! The smart guns were taking their shots, one or two at a time. The loud popping continued until all that one of those who had come outside was down. The lone survivor dived under a car, his gun lost in his scramble to hide and his hands over his head.

Noah fired another six-second burst into the building, and this time more than a dozen came running out. Several of them were holding assault rifles, and Noah saw sparks as the bullets bounced off the car and the carbonite windshield. He spun the steering wheel and hit the gas pedal for a second, turning the car to bring this group into his line of fire, then tapped the screen and squeezed the trigger. The machine gun spat and several fell, and Noah tapped again and again and again. Those that weren't down were running, but the smart guns were doing their job. *Pop, pop, pop, pop...* The last two survivors ran back into the building, trying to get away from the unseen sniper that was picking them off one by one.

Movement off to the right caught Noah's eyes, and he started to aim the machine gun but saw that it was Marco, moving stealthily toward the door. Noah gunned the car again and spun the wheel to line it up on the big overhead door. He reached down and selected the high-explosive rounds, tapped the screen over the door, and squeezed the trigger once.

The door exploded, and several people behind it went tumbling across the concrete floor. Noah floored the car and raced through the wreckage, spinning to his right as he got inside the building. He had guessed correctly, as he saw Jimmy Morgan and Dave Walters holding Kate as they backed away from the car, each of them pointing a gun at her head.

Noah popped the transmission into neutral and revved the engine once before letting it drop back to an idle. Several people fired at the car, and Noah was almost surprised to see that Heather was among them. He sat in the car as bullets ricocheted all around the building, and then he heard Morgan screaming for the shooting to stop.

The firing came to an end, but there were still more than twenty armed criminals in the building with him. Stepping out of the car, he knew, would be suicidal, but he didn't know how he could save Kate by remaining inside. He put the car back in drive and eased his foot off the brake, and the car began moving forward very slowly.

"Rex," Morgan yelled. "All I wanted you to do was explain, Rex. Dave found out your sister is with the FBI, and I just wanted to know who you are." He looked down at Kate, who was holding her head up high. "She says you don't know who she works for, but I find that a little hard to believe. I mean, come on, wouldn't you?"

Noah stopped the car and sat there, thinking about how to get control of the situation. He had Morgan, Walters, and Kate straight ahead of him, a dozen armed men and women to his left and several more spreading out around the car at the back and on the right. He glanced to his right and saw Scott Forney crabbing sideways with a pistol held out in front of him, and then Forney stepped out into the void where the overhead door had been.

There was a single *pop*, and a 9 mm bullet blew most of Forney's brain out through a gaping hole in the left side of his skull. He dropped like a stone, and several others screamed, but two of them tried to run outside. *Pop, pop*, and they dropped into the gravel of the parking lot.

One of them was Leanne, Noah noticed, and then he turned his attention back to Morgan and Kate, just in time to see Walters rushing at him, the pistol in his hand firing as he did so. Three bullets ricocheted off the carbonite windshield, and Noah dropped his foot onto the accelerator. The rear tires screamed as the car jumped forward, and Walters realized too late what was happening. He tried to stop and turn to the side, but the torque applied to the rear axle had raised the front end of the car, and he went down as it struck him. The car rolled over him, and Noah spun it around.

The remaining lieutenants were gathered into two groups and staring at Walters's body on the concrete floor. The Charger was pointed at an angle toward the open overhead door, but Noah reached over and poked his finger on the center of the video display as he floored the gas pedal again and squeezed the trigger button. The car spun to the right, the machine gun firing the entire time and dropping all but two of the lieutenants. Those two turned and ran, screaming as they fled the building, and rushed right into the crosshairs of the smart guns.

Pop, pop.

Noah continued the doughnut he had spun on the concrete floor until the car was facing toward where he had last seen Morgan and Kate. They were gone; Morgan had dragged Kate through a doorway into another section of the building, and Noah heard an engine start. The sound rushed around the back of the building, and seconds later a new Camaro roared past the open overhead door on its way to the gate and then fishtailed as it turned right onto the blacktop.

Marco appeared in the lot, aiming a gun at the fleeing Camaro, but it was already gone. Noah floored the car and roared out the door, slid to a stop beside him, and waited for Marco to get in.

"That was Morgan," Marco yelled as he got in. "He had the woman with him, and I think I saw the kid in the back seat."

Noah had already put the car into motion and was using all of his driving skills to chase down the Camaro. The curves made it difficult, but the Charger was built to hold the road, and Noah skidded around one curve after another, turning in to the skids and riding it through until he could get the car straight again.

The Camaro was less than a quarter mile ahead, but that was a good lead on a road like this. Smaller and lighter, the Camaro was handling the curves better than the Charger, but Noah wasn't about to back off. He kept his foot down and fought the car when it tried to slide off the road, barely managing to keep it between the ditches.

Pension Mountain Road is several miles long, winding around and up and down, reminding Noah of a roller coaster. Still he kept going, doing everything he could to keep the tail end of the Camaro in sight, and it paid off. After several minutes, he saw brake lights flash up ahead as the car came to the end of the country blacktop where it met Highway 21. He saw it turn left and begin to accelerate, and then he was at the intersection and cutting the wheel to make the car slide sideways as he took the turn at nearly fifty miles per hour.

The highway was where the Charger could be king, and Noah watched the speedometer climb. Signs told him that the next curve required a speed of forty-five miles per hour, but Noah took it at seventy, and when he came out of the curve he saw that he had gained on the Camaro. For almost fourteen miles, Noah slowly drew closer to the smaller car, and then he gained more quickly as they came into Berryville, but Morgan wasn't about to make a stand. He slid around the broad turn lane onto Highway 62, heading toward Green Forest, and Noah managed to stay within fifty feet as he came out of the turn, himself.

And then Noah understood. As they came around the bend leading out of Berryville, he saw the roadblock up ahead. Several sheriff's cars were lined up across the road, and deputies were leaning across them holding rifles and shotguns. Morgan's Camaro slowed and eased over onto the shoulder and was allowed to pass, but then the deputies opened fire on the Charger.

"Hang on," Noah yelled, and then he floored the accelerator again. The deputies kept firing, but their buckshot and bullets were simply ricocheting away, until they realized that the big car was not going to stop. Noah reached down beside the seat and pressed a button, then tapped the screen on one of the squad cars blocking the road. He squeezed the trigger button on the steering wheel twice, launching two of the explosive rounds and blowing the car in half. Shrapnel and chunks of metal took out several deputies and damaged the other cars, and then Noah rammed two of the squad cars where they had been backed up together. Both of them spun away as the Charger crashed on through.

Both front fenders were shattered and pieces were flapping in the wind, but the Charger kept going. In the Camaro ahead, Morgan realized what had happened and shoved his own foot down. The LT4 engine in the Chevy, cranking almost eight hundred horsepower, was moving the smaller car down the road at nearly one hundred sixty miles per hour as they passed the sheriff's office on the left.

Noah's big Hemi was stronger, but the bigger car was heavier. Even with all of the carbon fiber and Kevlar in the body, the Camaro's lighter weight was helping it to stay ahead.

"Make sure you've got a grip on something," Noah said. "I've got to bring them to a stop, and the only way I can do that is to get ahead of them."

"How the hell you gonna do that?" Marco asked, but then he watched as Noah reached down beside the seat and pressed the last button.

A scream began under the hood, and the hidden supercharger kicked in. Noah and Marco were thrust back in their seats as the speedometer shot from one sixty to over one ninety in less than five seconds. Noah held on to the wheel with everything he had, as the Charger shot around the left side of the Camaro and got in front of it.

Noah let off the gas, signaling the supercharger to cut off, and the car began to slow imperceptibly. He eased down on the brake pedal, but his speed was so great that it almost seemed to have no effect. Within seconds, he and Marco could smell the burning brake pads, but then they began to do their job and the speedometer started falling.

In the rearview mirror, the Camaro was already nearly half a mile behind them, so Noah rode the brakes hard. "Get your window down," he yelled at Marco. "Try to shoot out his radiator or hit something in the engine. Don't aim for Morgan—if that car crashes at that speed, nobody's going to survive it."

Marco was already hanging out the window by the time Noah finished speaking, both of his guns aimed straight back behind them. When the Charger had slowed to the point that the Camaro was barreling in on them, he opened fire, blasting away at the front of the Chevrolet.

Steam began rolling out from under the Camaro's hood, and the car began losing speed only a few seconds later. "I don't know what I hit," Marco yelled, "but it must've been important."

Both cars dropped to under fifty miles per hour, and then Morgan slammed on his brakes and tried to spin the Camaro around the other way. He ended up making a wide, skidding U-turn, but when he floored the accelerator again, the engine barely seemed to be running. It was roaring, but there was a loud banging sound coming from it as well, and by the time Noah managed to turn the Charger around, the Camaro's powerful engine gave up the ghost. There was a tremendously loud bang, and the car began coasting to a stop.

Noah roared up around it and spun out so that he was facing back toward the Camaro. He and Marco were instantly out of the car, both of them aiming directly at Morgan as he sat behind the wheel.

Noah fired once, piercing the Camaro's windshield and Jimmy Morgan's forehead at the same time. The crime boss's head snapped back and then fell forward onto the steering wheel. The Camaro's horn began to blare.

Marco kept his gun trained on Ralph Morgan, in the back seat, as the boy sat and stared at the gory mess that had been his father. Noah walked around to the passenger side and yanked open the door, then reached in and helped Kate get out and onto her feet. He holstered his pistol and used his Swiss Army knife to cut the zip ties holding her hands behind her back, and then Kate spun around and threw her arms around his neck as she sobbed against his chest.

"Hey, Rex," Marco yelled, back in character. "What you want me do wid dis boy? I put de bullet in his head, no?"

Noah shook his head. "No," he said. "I've got plans for little Ralphie."

He carefully extracted himself from Kate's arms and leaned down to look into the back seat of the Camaro. "Ralph," he said. "Come on out of there. You're going with me."

Ralph carefully climbed out and went to the Charger when Noah pointed. Marco got into the back seat with him, as Noah and Kate climbed into the front.

"I don't think we need to go back to Berryville just yet," Noah said. "Let's get out of sight for a while and wait for reinforcements to show up." He started the car and drove the short distance to the entrance of a gravel road, then turned onto it and moved as quickly as he could into the cover of trees a quarter of a mile away. The road continued through them, and Noah kept going until it curved around to the left and finally intersected with Highway 103. He went straight across and continued down another gravel road for several minutes, finally pulling in behind an old church building and shutting the car down.

He turned to Kate. "Okay, any idea how they caught on to you?"

Kate gave him a weary smile. "Oh, yeah," she said. "That asshole Walters was happy to tell me that he had a snitch working inside the Fayetteville FBI office. Somehow, even though it wasn't supposed to happen, that office was given access to the restricted file on the Morgan Mafia, and it specifically named me as the undercover observer. Didn't take him long to figure out that you probably weren't really my brother. He tried to beat it out of me, find out who you are, but I'm happy to say I managed not to give you up."

Noah took her chin in his hand and turned her face from side to side, looking at the numerous bruises she was wearing. "Not that we are likely to be in this situation again," he said, "but it wouldn't have mattered if you had. Even if they knew my name, I don't even officially exist, so they wouldn't have gained anything from knowing it. As for E & E, they probably would've thought you were lying, anyway. Most people can't believe the US would bother with assassination, and those who can would expect it to be the CIA. Besides, they were all going to be dead before long, anyway. It really wouldn't have mattered if you had told them anything about me."

Kate looked at him, and it took him a moment to realize that she was angry. "Really? It wouldn't have mattered? Well, let me tell you something, Mr. Big Shot Assassin." She took a deep breath and then shouted, "*It would have mattered to me!*"

Noah nodded. "I understand," he said. "I apologize."

He took out his phone and handed it to Kate. "I think you need to call this in," he said. "We need the feds in here as soon as possible. Morgan's body has been found by now, so Redford and everybody else will be scrambling to try to find out just how bad the situation is. Your people need to come in and start making arrests right away."

Kate looked at him for a moment, then grinned as she dialed a number. A moment later, the grin vanished as she went to work. "This is SSA Kate Madison," she said. "Patch me through to the deputy director."

It took her a few minutes to explain that the "Special Operation" requested by the Department of Justice had finally been implemented. The deputy director of the FBI congratulated her on the successful conclusion of her undercover mission and promised to have a waiting special task force, a group of fifty agents who had been stashed in various small towns just across the line in Missouri, immediately start rounding up the cooperating officials she had been able to identify, while the Arkansas State Police Investigators would be handling civilian criminal investigations.

She disconnected and handed the phone back to Noah. "A team of special agents will hit Berryville in about twenty minutes," she said. "They want me to give them a couple of hours, then meet them at the sheriff's office. Think we can get there without being blown away?"

"Yes," Noah said. He turned and looked into the back seat at Ralph Morgan, who was sitting quietly with his eyes focused on his own knees. "Ralph," he said, "this is where you get to make a choice. I'm going to tell you something, and it's your one and only chance to live through this. You do want to live, don't you?"

The boy nodded, but would not look up at him.

"Okay, here it is. I'm not Rex Madison, which I'm sure you figured out by now. My name is Noah Wolf, and I am a professional assassin in the employ of the United States government. I was recruited because I'm very good at what I do, but we've got a few others like me who were recruited simply because they enjoy killing. Since I know you happen to be one of those people, and since I was sent here with orders to eliminate your father and his entire operation, I took it upon myself to suggest to my superiors that you might be a good candidate for our organization."

Ralph finally looked up at him. "You want me to be an assassin?"

"I think you might have potential," Noah said. "If you can learn a little bit of self-discipline and how to follow orders, you might be good to keep around. If you want this chance to stay alive, all you have to do is say so. If you don't, then I'll kill you right here and now. It's your call, but you have to make a choice immediately."

Ralph was staring into his eyes, but then he turned and looked at Marco. Marco gave him a big smile. "Hey, kid," he said. "Take it from me, being alive beats the hell out of being dead. All you gotta do is say yes, and we take you back with us to be trained. If you're any good, you might end up running a team the way Noah does, someday."

Ralph looked back at Noah. "Running a team? What does that mean?"

"I have a team that helps me do my job. Marco, there, is one of them. If you honestly have talent for this type of killing, it's possible you could have a team of your own one day."

Ralph looked down at his knees again for a moment, then raised his eyes back up to Noah's. "Okay," he said. "I'll do it."

"Lucky little bastard," Kate mumbled.

Noah took out his phone and opened the war game app, then tapped the screen to bring up the password form. He entered "absolution" and carefully deselected the knives Neil had made, which were still in the trunk of the car in his bag, and then he dropped his thumb on the button marked "GO."

Several miles away, a medium-sized mushroom cloud rose into the air. Four smaller ones in different parts of the area marked Morgan lieutenants who had failed to come to the meeting.

CHAPTER TWENTY-ONE

Two hours and ten minutes later, the battered Charger pulled up in front of the Carroll County Sheriff's Office. Noah shut the car down, and he, Kate, Marco, and Ralph all climbed out. Marco took charge of Ralph and hustled him over to a bench, keeping a hand on his shoulder as they sat down.

A man in a suit stepped out the front door and looked at Kate and Noah. Kate smiled and held out her hand.

"Good to see you, Jared," she said. She glanced at Noah, then turned back to to the man she had spoken to. "SSA Jared Carter, this is Noah Wolf. Noah, Jared heads up the task force that's been behind my observation mission all this time."

Carter looked at Noah and extended a hand, and Noah shook with him. "Good to meet you," he said. "I wish we hadn't had to resort to calling you in, but it's good to know the option is available when it's needed."

"Just doing my job," Noah said.

"And going above and beyond the call of duty," Kate said. "I don't know if you've been briefed on it, but someone in the Fayetteville office actually gave me up to Morgan today. Noah had to change plans in a hurry to get me out alive, and I'm very grateful that he did."

Carter's eyebrows rose. "No, I hadn't been told," he said. "Any idea who it was who sold you out?"

"I'm afraid not. One of Morgan's men apparently knew whoever it was, and somehow they got hold of documentation that named me as the observer. How are things going here?"

"Well, we've got the sheriff and almost all of his people in custody. The state police are supposed to arrive any minute now, and the governor has been gracious enough to assign some troopers to fill in as deputies, and the coroner, who was never implicated in any of Morgan's activities, will serve until a new sheriff is appointed to fill the vacancy until the next election. Most of the city police are either in custody or on the run, including their chief, as well as the county prosecutor and four judges." He sighed. "It's gonna be a long night. We don't even know where some of these people are."

"Most of them are probably gone," Kate said. "Noah had to crash through a sheriff's roadblock that let Morgan pass, so I'm surprised you even managed to get any of them."

Carter looked at Noah, his face registering surprise. "Is that what happened? We found five of their squad cars nearly totaled just up the road a little ways. Look like one of them had been hit by a missile."

"You're not that far off," Noah said. "It's more like a grenade launcher, but it gets the job done."

"I'll say it does. Whatever it was, it killed three of the deputies and wounded seven others badly enough they weren't going to be back in action anytime soon. The only one there who wasn't hurt was the sheriff, and he was apparently in a rage that none of the others was able to pursue."

Noah looked him in the eye. "They shouldn't have gotten in my way."

Carter started to say something, but Kate put a hand on his arm. "Jared, trust me," she said. "Just let it go."

Carter looked at her for a long moment, then turned his eyes over to where Ralph and Marco were sitting on the bench. "Is that Morgan's kid?"

"Yes," Noah said, "but I'm taking him into personal custody. He'll be dealt with by my organization. You have any questions about that, contact the State Department."

Carter stared at Ralph for a moment, then looked back at Noah and Kate. "We been hearing something about how that kid killed another boy, but there's a man in jail who's been charged with the murder. You guys know anything about that?"

"Mr. Wesley is innocent of the murder," Noah said, "though you might want to look into him for contributing to the delinquency of minors. Apparently he's been providing drugs and alcohol to teenagers in return for sex with the girls. He was charged with murder by the sheriff, who didn't want to get into a fight with Morgan over his son."

"But you're just going to take that kid and let him get away with this? If he killed somebody, he should..."

"Agent Carter," Noah said calmly, "where do you think my organization gets its recruits?"

"What, aren't you guys all ex-military, ex-special forces, something like that?"

"No. Most of us were recruited out of prison, because we already had murders on our records. I was on death row awaiting execution when they came for me. Ralph Morgan is a killer, and he's young enough that we can train him. As much as most of the world may hate killers, there comes a time when a killer is what's needed. My organization lost several of its best sometime back, and I think young Ralph might eventually fill one of those empty slots. The day may come when DOJ puts in a request like this one and it's Ralph Morgan who is sent out to take care of it."

Carter looked flustered. "Well, how the hell am I supposed to write that up in the paperwork?"

"You want my advice? I'd suggest that young Mr. Morgan, there, died in the big explosion out at his father's junkyard."

Carter blinked and shook his head. "The explosion at the junkyard? Did you have something to do that?"

"My orders were to eliminate Morgan and all of his lieutenants," Noah said. "How I chose to accomplish that mission was left up to me."

"Jared, I'm telling you," Kate said, "you really want let this go. Noah did his job, and I'm alive because of him. Let it go."

Carter blew air out in frustration, shaking his head. "Okay, fine," he said. "This ain't my first rodeo. If I raise a stink, I'm quite sure somebody from the State Department will come down and tell us to shut up, anyway." He focused on Kate. "You ready to help me sort through all this mess?"

"Give me a couple of minutes," she said, "and I'll come on in. I just need to say goodbye before Noah leaves."

Carter looked at her, turned his eyes to Noah for a moment, then threw his hands in the air and turned around. He walked into the sheriff's office, yanking the door open so hard that it rattled the glass.

Kate looked up at Noah. "Well, it was nice to have my brother back for a little while. You're so much like him, Noah, you really have no idea. There were moments when it almost felt real."

"I'm glad," Noah said. "You're a good person, Kate. I'm sorry you had to go through this, tonight, but I'm glad I was able to get you back."

Kate burst out laughing. "You think you're glad? I'm absolutely overjoyed." She got herself under control, and her eyes softened. "Listen, you tell Angie, or whatever her real name is, that I enjoyed meeting her. I don't know if it's allowed, but if you guys ever want to come visit me, you'll be welcome."

"I'll tell her," Noah said. "And don't be surprised if we take you up on that invitation sometime. We don't have many friends outside the organization, might be nice to be able to say we have at least one."

"You do. You definitely do." She reached up and hugged him around the neck, kissed him quickly on his cheek, and then turned and walked into the building.

Noah turned and motioned for Marco and Ralph to get back into the car, but then he took a good look at the front end of the Charger. The fenders were damaged, and the headlights on the passenger side were gone, as was the high beam on the driver's side. He knelt down and took a good look and saw that both of the guns were still in place, but there was no way he could drive the car back to Kirtland in that condition.

Marco and Ralph came to stand behind him. "Poor old girl's seen better days, boss," Marco said. "What do we do about this?"

Noah stood up again. "Let's go get your truck," he said. "I know there's someplace around here I can rent a trailer. I'm not leaving this car behind, no way." They climbed inside and Noah started up, then drove with his one lonely headlight back out to the farmhouse.

Unfortunately, there was nowhere to rent a car-hauling trailer at almost 10:30 at night. They went into the house, and Noah found some leftover chicken in the refrigerator. He set it on the table and offered some to Marco and Ralph. He wasn't surprised when both of them dug in.

He took out his phone and called Sarah.

"Noah?" Sarah asked as she answered the call. "Everything okay?"

"Yes," Noah said. "The mission is complete, the feds are in town taking over, but the Charger was damaged and I can't get a trailer until tomorrow morning. Marco's pickup truck is still here, so we'll go get one tomorrow and load the Charger up on it, then be home by tomorrow night."

"Wait a minute," Sarah said. "What happened to the Charger?"

"Well, we had an unexpected glitch in the plan," Noah replied. "Today, for some reason, someone in the Fayetteville FBI office found out about Kate and told one of Morgan's people that she was FBI. Just as I was ready to blow the whole bunch of them into the atmosphere, Kate got dragged into the building. I had to do something, so I had Marco sneak in and set up the smart guns, then I used the car to launch an attack. Morgan managed to grab Kate and Ralph and get away in a fast car of his own, and I had to chase him down. Morgan called the sheriff, and he tried to set up a roadblock to stop me, but I crashed through it and it sort of wiped out the headlights. I want to bring the car back so Rodney can get it fixed up again."

Sarah was quiet for several seconds. "But you said everything was okay," she said. "When I first answered the phone, I asked you if everything was okay and you said yes. Noah, none of that was okay."

"But everything is okay," Noah said. "We got Kate back safe, Morgan is dead, his organization is finished, the feds are in charge, and I'm bringing Ralph back so that he can be trained for E & E."

"You're doing what? Noah, what will Allison say? He's a kid!"

"He's a killer, babe. Now, I could have killed him, but I think the kid may have potential for the organization. If I'm right, there could be missions that call for someone that young, and he'd be an asset. If I'm wrong, he'll flunk out and someone will terminate him."

Across the table, Ralph's eyes had grown very wide.

"But, Allison..."

"I already checked with her, and she okayed this. All I'm going to do is bring him back and turn him over to her and Doc Parker. They can decide whether he's worth saving or should be put down like a mad dog."

Noah heard her force her breathing to slow down. "So, what are you doing for tonight? Are you at the farmhouse?"

"Yes. We're going to stay here tonight, then I'll send Marco to get a trailer in the morning while I keep an eye on Ralph. As soon as we get the car loaded up, we'll be on the road. After this mission, I just want to get home."

"Amen to that," Marco yelled so Sarah could hear. "He told you we crashed through the roadblock, but he didn't tell you about this massive bruise I got from the seat belt. It hurts. Tell Renée I need her to take care of me when I get home."

Despite herself, Sarah chuckled. "Tell him I will," she said. "Neil and I stopped somewhere in the middle of Kansas and got a room about an hour ago. I was getting worried, and he said my driving was scaring him, anyway, so I decided to stop for the night." She yawned. "And on top of that, I'm still tired from when we drove to Kirtland and back the other day. We're going to get some sleep and then head on home tomorrow morning."

"Okay, babe. I'll let you get some rest, and I'm going to do likewise, right after I make sure Ralph can't get away. I'll see you tomorrow night, sometime. I love you, Sarah."

"Oh," Sarah said. "You said it to me first, this time. I love you, too, baby, and I want you to call me in the morning when you get up, okay?"

"Okay. Good night." He waited for her to answer, then disconnected the call and immediately dialed Allison. He told her quickly about everything that had happened, and she responded that he should report for debriefing at nine o'clock the morning after he got back home. Noah hung up the phone and dropped it into his pocket.

Ralph was staring at him. "What?" Noah asked.

"Were you, like, serious? They might actually kill me?"

"If you don't make it through your training, or if they think you won't work out for any reason, yes."

The boy looked down at his plate for a moment, then looked back up at Noah. "Will you be the one training me?"

Noah shook his head. "No, they've got an actual school set up. Training normally takes about a year, unless your instructors think you're ready sooner than that. The big thing for you will probably be the physical training. It's tough, and I'm not sure you'll be up to it."

Ralph glared at him. "You kidding me? I played football all through high school—I don't think a little exercise is going to hurt me."

"Football," Noah said, "is like fighting your way through cotton candy compared to what Mr. Jackson will put you through. Have you ever heard of parkour?"

"Yeah, that's those guys who do stunts on YouTube. Jumping around and running up walls, that kind of stuff. They do that?"

"Yes, and if you can't keep up, they only let you keep trying for so long. If you don't make it..." Noah drew a thumb across his throat.

Ralph swallowed hard, but then he started eating again. "Well," he said, "at least I ain't dead yet."

When they finished eating, Noah took Ralph into the bedroom he had shared with Sarah. "Here's the choice you've got now," he said. "You can sleep in the bathtub, and I'll block the door so you can't get out, or you can sleep on the floor beside the bed. If you try to get up, I'll know, and if you try to get away, I'll kill you. Any questions?"

Ralph stared at him for a moment, then looked at the floor. "This'll work," he said. Noah opened the closet and pulled down a couple of blankets and handed them to him, then took one of the pillows off the bed and passed that to him, as well. While Ralph made himself a pallet on the floor, Noah closed the door and lay down on the bed, tucking his gun under the pillow.

"Hey," Ralph said. "You won't shoot me for snoring, will you?"

"I don't know," Noah said. "It depends on how loud you are."

He was asleep only a minute later.

Noah woke up at seven and immediately looked over to where Ralph had made his pallet. The boy was sound asleep, so Noah called out to him. "Ralph," he said. "Ralph, it's time to get up."

Ralph sat up quickly, looking around as if he was confused, but then his eyes found Noah and he let out a sigh. "Oh, man," he said. "I thought it was all a dream."

"The time for dreams is over," Noah said. "It's time to get up. Use the bathroom if you need to, then I will."

Ralph got up and made his way into the bathroom, and came out just a couple of minutes later. Noah took care of his own morning necessities and then led the boy down to the kitchen. Sarah had left the coffee sitting on the counter, so he made a pot. Marco came out as it was finishing, and the three of them sat there and drank a cup together.

"You can go get the trailer," Noah said to Marco. "I'll wait here with Ralph until you get back, and then we can hit the road."

"No problem," Marco replied. "I saw a rental place down by Walmart. Won't take me half an hour." He got up and walked out the door, and the pickup truck rolled away a minute later.

Ralph looked up at Noah. "Do you think I've really got a chance to make it? In your outfit, I mean?"

"If I didn't, I wouldn't have suggested it. I had more than enough chances to kill you, Ralph, and I need you to understand that the fact I'm getting this chance for you has nothing to do with compassion. For me, it's simple logic; you're a killer, and you enjoy it. Some of the others like me also enjoy the killing, so the only question is whether you can learn to control that urge and only use it when you're on a mission. If you can, then yes, you've got a good chance to make it. If not, then you'll just be eliminated. You won't see it coming, you won't be told, you'll just be dead."

Ralph nodded slowly. "I wonder what it's like, when you're dead. I wonder if you even know it."

Noah shrugged. "Do you believe in God?"

Ralph bit his bottom lip. "I don't know," he said. "Marlene used to take me to church, but I stopped going a few years ago." He suddenly looked up at Noah. "Damn. What's gonna happen to Marlene?"

"Probably nothing. As far as I could tell, she was not actively involved in any of your father's illegal activities. It's possible she might be charged with something minor, because she never came forward and reported what he was doing, but I doubt it sincerely. Your father would've killed her in a heartbeat if he thought she was going to testify against him, so I don't think anyone would blame her for keeping her mouth shut. From what I know, most of the people around here knew enough about what he was doing to testify, but none of them were ever willing. If they charged Marlene with anything, they'd almost have to prosecute the whole county."

"Yeah, probably. I was really just thinking about how she'll get by, now. With my pa gone, she's out of a job."

"I suspect she'll be all right," Noah said. "She's not your problem, anymore."

"Yeah, I guess not. Anyway, you asked if I believe in God. I guess I do, but I don't really know how to feel about it."

"Then my advice to you would be to find a way to make peace with Him. I do believe in God, and I believe that we go on after this life is over. I'm just not sure whether He's going to want anything to do with me by the time I get there."

Ralph looked at him for a long moment but didn't say anything more.

Marco took longer than he had expected, coming back an hour later with a trailer hooked to the back of the truck. Noah and Ralph went outside, and Noah started up the car and drove it onto the trailer. Then he and Marco strapped it down and hooked up the safety chains that would keep it from coming off the trailer if the straps were to snap. Once they were satisfied, Marco climbed behind the wheel, and Noah told Ralph to sit in the middle. Noah climbed in beside him and put on his seat belt, and they were back on the road only a few minutes later.

The trip was long, but they finally rolled into Kirtland a little after six p.m. Noah had called Allison when they were getting close, and she told him to drop Ralph off at Doc Parker's place. Noah wasn't surprised to see another man waiting there when they arrived.

"Hey, Noah," the man said. Noah recognized him as one of the instructors he had met during his own training. "I understand you brought in a new recruit."

"Yes," Noah said as he and Ralph got out of the truck. "This is Ralph Morgan. He's only nineteen, but he's already killed more than once, and I thought it might be a good idea to find out if he's made of the right stuff."

"Allison gave me a quick briefing on him. Ralph, I'm Jerry. We're going to go see Doc Parker; he's sort of the man who decides where we put you. Once he's done with you, I'll take you to our motel and set you up with a room." He looked at Noah. "He didn't bring any clothes or anything?"

"No, this was sort of a spur-of-the-moment situation."

Jerry nodded. "That's no problem," he said. "We can provide whatever he needs."

Ralph looked at Noah, but Jerry had already taken hold of his arm. He turned and followed the man into Parker's office, and Noah got back into the truck. Marco put it back in gear and headed for Noah's house.

Sarah, Renée, Neil, and Jenny were sitting at Noah's picnic table when they arrived, and Sarah ran to the truck. She threw herself at Noah as he got out, laughing and planting kisses all over his face.

Neil walked over and looked at the Charger, shaking his head. "Man," he said, "I thought this car was supposed to be indestructible."

"Not exactly," Noah said. "I can tell you it was definitely bullet-proof, though. Probably a hundred of them bounced right off."

Renée was a little more subdued than Sarah, slipping her arms around Marco and kissing him gently. "I'm glad you're back," she said. "And I'm glad you were gone as long as you were supposed to be. I've missed you."

"I think we may have started something," Sarah said to Noah as they watched Marco and Renée. "I just hope they can handle it.

Sometimes, I wonder if we can." She turned and looked up at him. "And then I remember how much I love you, and I stop worrying about it."

Since everyone was there, Noah decided they might as well all come inside. He and Marco were hungry, so Sarah pulled pizzas out of the freezer and heated up the oven. A half hour later, they all sat down around the kitchen table to eat and simply be together.

The incredible double mission was over, and both had been brought to successful conclusions. Noah sat at the table and looked around at his friends, wondering what the next mission might be. Whatever it was, he had no doubt that he and Team Camelot would be ready.

SPECIAL OFFER

Building a relationship with my readers is the ultimate goal with writing. At least, it should be. Without you guys, us writers would just be making up stories for ourselves...which would be weird. That's why I like to connect with my readers in a way many big name authors don't.

I occasionally send newsletters with details on new releases, special offers and other bits of news relating to Sam Prichard, Noah Wolf, and the other varies series and stand alone novels that I write.

And if you sign up to the mailing list today, I'll send you this free content:

- A free copy of the first Sam Prichard novella, FALLBACK (plus the audiobook version)

- A free copy of the first Noah Wolf novella, THE WAY OF THE WOLF (plus the audiobook version)

- Exclusive content and pricing to my mailing list – you can't get this anywhere else. Every book launch I set a discounted price for my mailing list for a couple days. This is exclusive to my list *only,* and something that isn't publicized anywhere else.

You can get the novella's, the audiobook's, and the exclusive discounted pricing **for free,** by at: www.davidarcherbooks.com/vip

NOTE FROM THE AUTHOR

I f you enjoyed this adventure, would you please consider taking a moment and leaving your thoughts for others who might also enjoy this book?

It takes only a handful of seconds to leave a review, but can literally make or break a self published career. Please don't feel any obligation to do so, but if you had fun, or perhaps enjoyed yourself at all, then I'd sincerely appreciate it!

Thanks so much,

David Archer

Made in the USA
Las Vegas, NV
24 June 2022